Secret BLOSSOM

SKYLINE MANSION BOOK THREE

NOLA LI BARR

Edited by Corina Douglas
Cover design by The Red Leaf Book Design / www.redleafbookdesign.com

ISBN 978-1-7327814-7-4 (ebook)
ISBN 978-1-7327814-8-1 (paperback)

www.nolalibarr.com

The Lin Family

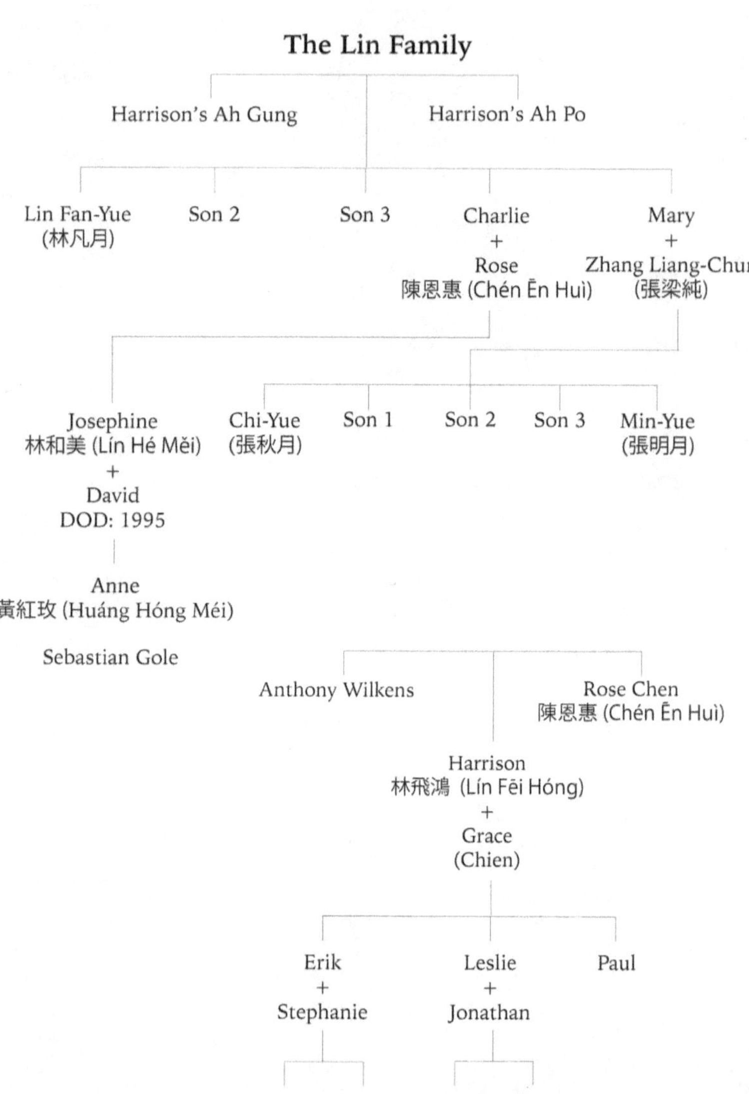

The Wilkens Family

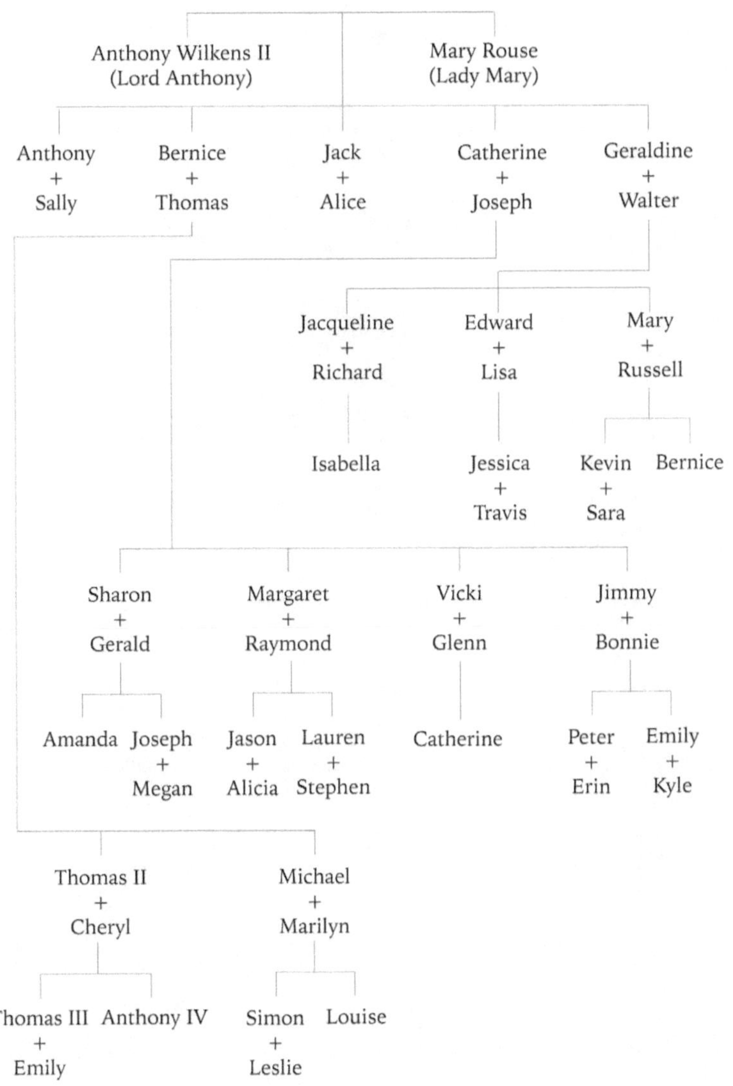

ABOUT THIS BOOK

After failing to find her uncle in Taiwan, Anne is back at Skyline Mansion and wants life to be quiet for a change. But when Harrison suddenly makes an appearance, only to disappear a few days later, her life is once again turned upside down.

When Anne receives Harrison's journal with a note requesting her to read it before she decides to search for him again, Anne takes the mission to heart. She once again forsakes her family and friends as she delves into her uncle's past, unravelling a history of more secrets, pain, and loss.

At the same time, another Wilkens family member has reached out to her. The girl is charming, but she wants something, and Anne suspects her true intentions, especially when she learns that she is best friends with her arch nemesis—the same woman who still has eyes on Anne's inheritance.

CHAPTER 1

HARRISON

"Is it time to clean up some of this mess, Dad?"

I looked up to see my son, Erik, standing in the doorway. "Are you here to help?"

"No, Mom wants you to come home. Caitlin has been asking for you all day, and it's almost dinner time."

"Ah, dinner already? Time flies these days," I mumbled as I looked around the space I was trying to tidy. When did this place get so piled up with junk? It was supposed to be a small postcard store, somewhere I could hide my artwork in the back since Grace was tired of the paint and canvases all over the house.

"What should I tell her?" Erik pressed.

I smiled wryly. Even my boys knew that I preferred to stay here and keep painting. "Just give me five minutes. I need to clean up my work area."

"Okay, I'll wait in the car."

As Erik left the store, I 'tidied up' by going to my art studio, sitting down in my chair, and just staring at all my works in progress. My career-changing piece—or my *cu di gras,* as Bettie, the curator at Taiwan Living Art's Gallery liked to call it—was sitting front and center. It was a much bigger canvas than my other pieces, and because I'd been so secretive about it, others have jumped to the conclusion that it's my biggest work yet. I don't know why everyone says this as no one has seen it, but it's more personal to me, yes, and maybe, just maybe, I've put a bit more love into this one.

My mama's face looks back at me. I tell Grace that I don't want to learn more about my mama, but I think she can see right through me.

After finding out that Mary wasn't my mother, and then spending time with my real father, Anthony, I hadn't wanted anything to do with my family ever again. I'd subsequently left Taiwan with Grace and never gone back.

Grace had never complained but I knew she missed her home. She has been by my side ever since I could remember. I would do anything for her—except visit Taiwan, or Oregon for that matter. Every time I thought about my birth mama standing in the Astoria bakery with her husband and child, my heart hurt. There was no point digging into the past, no point at all . . . because I would just get hurt again.

Besides, I have Grace, I have my children, and now I have my grandkids. What more could I ask for? I'd held strong to this reminder when I'd told this Anne person that I was dead. She had recently emailed me asking if we could meet and I hoped she wouldn't contact me again. And yet, something continued to pull at me, and I couldn't help coming back here to look at my painting again . . . at my birth mother.

What if Anne was telling the truth? What if this young woman was my niece? What if she had something important to tell me and my stubbornness kept me from whatever that message was? Grace has always said I'm stubborn and proud to a fault, that I could have lived so much more if I wasn't.

At the beep of a horn, I'm reminded of Erik, sitting outside in his car, waiting for me. I placed a cloth over the painting of my mama and locked up.

One day I'll clean up the postcards at the front of the store. One day.

CHAPTER 2

ANNE—THREE WEEKS LATER AND TWO STATES NORTH

As a country, Taiwan is not one to be missed. You can cross it from tip to tip in less than seven hours if you're driving, but this journey can be as fast as ninety minutes if you take the high-speed rail. The variety of people, culture, and food are never ending. Taoyuen Airport is an hour away from Taipei. A bus or taxi ride will get you from the airport to Taipei in an hour. I prefer the bus because you get a cushy seat and you're one of many travelers. It's also cheaper, and you can get lost in the scenery without having to talk to anyone.

Taipei is a mini NYC. There are people, cars, yellow taxis, buses, and subways everywhere. The only difference between Taipei and NYC is that there are hundreds of mopeds. At first, it's disorienting to cross the road when a mass of mopeds are turning in your direction, but over time you will come to realize that if you keep moving they will go around you, and that it is when you hesitate that an accident is more likely to happen. It is like Dory says in *Finding Nemo,* "Just keep swimming, just keep swimming."

OH MY GOODNESS, NOW I'M REFERENCING DISNEY MOVIES? THIS wasn't going to work. *International Travels* wanted the first revision of my article on Taiwan within the next two days, and all I could focus on was my uncle. I swear I saw Harrison in the office at the gallery, but maybe it was just an office worker . . . ? But the man didn't look Taiwanese, and he didn't have jet-black hair. And he was tall—too tall to be a Taiwanese person. Then again, I did see a few tall Taiwanese people while there. Okay, maybe more than a few as I'm tall for a Taiwanese person. *Ugh, I'm getting way off track again.*

"Anne?"

I looked up to find my best friend standing in the middle of my bedroom. "Oh, hi, Victoria."

"Oh, hi? You're still reminiscing over the guy you saw in the office, aren't you?"

"Yes, and so what if I am? Don't you and Paul have a date to go on?"

"Don't change the subject. I'm not against you. You just don't know who that guy was. For all we know, he worked there and probably went into the office to grab a pen and left."

"Yeah . . ." But I couldn't tell her that the feeling he was who I thought he was wouldn't go away.

"Have you unpacked from the trip yet?" Sebastian asked as he came and joined us in the bedroom. His dark brown hair was wet, and a few short strands fell across his forehead, making me smile. He had complained about the heat in Taiwan, saying his thick hair was absorbing too much heat. He'd almost went to a hairdresser and shaved all his hair off, but I persuaded him otherwise, thank goodness.

"Earth to Anne?" he said now, standing right in front of me. I could smell his cologne and wished Victoria wasn't here in this moment, but I also knew there was no way she was going to leave. I could sense she had something on her mind.

"Yes, what did you ask me?" I asked Sebastian with a sweet smile.

A hearty laugh came out of his mouth, making my lips widen. "I asked if you have unpacked from the trip to Taiwan —which I can see would be a no."

"Almost." I looked around the room. My stuff was strewn all over the bed, dresser, and floor. Lady, my cocker spaniel, started barking right then.

Sebastian raised a brow. "It seems Lady agrees it's a mess."

I made a face at him. "I'll get to it when I get to it."

"Are *you* unpacked?" Victoria asked, pointing at Sebastian.

"Of course. I did it all on the first day."

"Sebastian likes things orderly," I said. "It's one of the reasons he's such a good lawyer."

Victoria's eyes grew big at my acknowledgement. "Wow! I'm with Anne. Things will go where they need to when it's time to put them away. For example, I am in search of my flat iron and I think I put it in one of your bags, Anne."

"That's my cue to leave then," Sebastian said, raising his hands. "Anne, I'll let you know when I'm on my way home." He came and gave me a kiss that made Victoria turn away and suddenly busy herself searching for her flat iron.

I remained standing there, following the sound of Sebastian's footfalls all the way out the front door before I turned to look back at Victoria. She was now looking flustered that she couldn't find the flat iron. "You can just borrow mine, you know," I suggested.

"Yes, I know, I know." Victoria turned and looked at me with her head slanted to one side. "But you know something?"

"What?"

"I never understood why you needed a flat iron. You have perfectly straight hair. You wake up in the morning and don't have to do anything to it."

"That's a misconceived perception," I said, walking to one of my bags to retrieve the coveted item. "I have waves under all this straight hair, you see. I have to brush it and flatten it if I want it to look nice."

"If you say so," she said dubiously. She took the flat iron from me. "Thank you. I will not be returning this until I find mine, so you'll have to deal with your so-called waves unless you come to my room to use it."

"Oh no, I can only deal with one messy room at a time."

We both started laughing, breaking the lingering tension in the room. I knew this conversation was never about the flat iron. Sobering, I said to Victoria, "Just spit it out already. I know you want to ask me something."

Her smile slipped and she asked quietly, "So . . . have you thought more about what Isabella said?"

"I knew you were going to ask that!" I burst out.

"Well, I agree with Sebastian. I think it's your only hope of finding your uncle. We need a professional."

"I know."

She looked relieved at my response. "If it makes you feel any better, I asked around about this Nick guy and heard that he's a pretty good detective. So, don't take it from Isabella, but from me that I want you to hire him. We spent weeks looking for him in Taiwan and all to no avail. I really think you need closure in order to move on."

"You make good points," I mumbled.

She didn't smile. "I make the right points and you know it."

From the look on her face, I knew I wasn't getting out of this one. "Fine, I'll give him a call."

Victoria promptly held out her hand. "Here, use my phone."

I raised an eyebrow. "I have a perfectly good phone."

"Of which you have no idea where it is and will hence postpone this call to another day."

I sighed. "Okay, fine."

I took her phone and dialed Nick's number. It wasn't like I hadn't thought about Isabella's offer to hire the detective over and over again. She had sent me his number and I had looked at it every day to the point that I had it memorized by heart. Victoria was right, I didn't want to be taking any favors from Isabella, but there didn't seem to be a way out of this.

The phone was picked up on the other end.

"Hello?" a low voice said, sounding kind of sleepy. I looked at Victoria, who was listening quietly as I had the phone on speaker. Was this the right person? Maybe I should have gone looking for his number before dialing.

"Hi, is this Nick?"

"It is. Who is this?"

"This is Anne. I got your number from—"

"Anne! I've been expecting your call. Isabella has said so much about you." I heard a distinct splash and some expletives and wondered again if this was the right choice. "Sorry about that," Nick continued. "I was just sleeping next to the pool when you rang, and my niece thought it would be funny to splash me." I heard giggling in the background. "Hold on a second, Anne. Let me move into the house."

Victoria and I exchanged glances.

A moment later he came back on. "Sorry about that. Yes, Isabella had mentioned that you were looking for your uncle."

"Yes, that was—"

"I could come by today if you are free," he cut in quickly. "We could discuss your case."

I felt I had no choice but to agree. "Sure . . ."

"Great! You're at Skyline Mansion, right?"

"That's right. Do you know how to get here?"

"I've been there loads. Done a lot of work for the family. One note, though, can you make sure it's just you and me when we meet in person? I like to keep my identity hidden from as many people as I can. My job depends on me being discreet given the society we're in is very small."

"I'm going to be there too," Victoria interjected before I could stop her.

There was silence on the other end of the phone for a second before Nick said, "Who is that?"

"It's Victoria; she's my best friend."

"Um . . ."

Victoria jumped in before he could say more. "I don't know anyone in your society except Anne, and for her sake I won't be telling anyone who you are. I cross my heart and hope to die. Stick a—"

"All right, all right, all right. She's okay." Nick seemed to be letting out a lot of air in a drawn-out sigh. "I need to go. I'll see you this afternoon about twoish." And with that, he hung up.

Victoria looked at me. "Well, if anything, he's not going to be boring—nothing like those television shows we used to watch."

"No kidding. I have no idea what just happened."

Sure enough, Nick came 'about' twoish, which was really closer to fourish. He was suave, if that was the right word, dressed in a relaxed suit that I imagined someone in the eighties would wear. His hair was bleached blond and long on the top, with black rimmed sunglasses perched on the crown of his head.

He actually swaggered into the library and made himself comfortable on one of the sofas. I had only said "hello" and "please come in."

Much to my surprise, Lady jumped into his lap and made herself comfortable.

"Is there anything I can get you?" I asked, hoping he didn't need a thing because after what I'd just seen, I still didn't really want him here.

"Oh yes. Can Cook make her infamous drink? The one with rum in it and an umbrella on top?"

"Sure." Victoria and I shared a look before I headed to the kitchen to talk to Cook. Most of the staff hadn't returned to the mansion yet since I'd given them the month off. I'd thought I'd be in Taiwan longer, but having my search for my uncle come to a dead end had caused me to lose all motivation in extending our trip.

As I left the room, I could hear Victoria trying to have a conversation with Nick. I took a deep breath and reminded myself that this was the right thing to do.

When I walked into the kitchen, I also remembered that Cook had taken a few days off—not for a vacation, but because her son had need of her, and her daughter, Jasmine, had insisted. Jasmine was replacing her in the kitchen and she was going to be head cook one day—if her mom ever retired. I found Jasmine with her head bent over a pot on the stove. It smelled divine.

"Jasmine, whatever you're cooking I'll eat the whole thing," I said in greeting.

She sent me a smile. "It's vegetable barley soup. I'm trying to make it taste like meat without putting any in it."

"Let me know when I can try some."

She beamed. "I will." Jasmine was always experimenting

and so far, I had liked everything she had made. "But what can I help you with?" she asked. "You must have come down here for a reason."

"We have a visitor." No one needed to know I was hiring a detective. "He's been here before and said Cook had a signature drink that had rum in it and it comes with an umbrella."

"Oh yes, the Floater. Everyone loves that drink. I don't know why, it's so simple. I'll make one up for you right away."

"Thanks, Jasmine."

I went back upstairs to find Victoria and Nick having a vibrant conversation. She had her auburn hair tied back and her elbows on her knees as she leaned forward with a smile on her face. As soon as I entered, her attention whipped to me and I got the full blast of a happy Victoria.

"Anne, did you know Nick lived in San Antonio at the same time I did? He just moved back to Portland a couple of years ago," Victoria said, quite animated.

"We were just talking about their use of "y'all" all the time." At this, Nick and Victoria burst out laughing.

"Okay . . ." Not knowing what else to say to that, I turned to Nick and said, "I saw Jasmine and she's going to be bringing your drink up very soon."

"Speak of the devil," Nick said just as Jasmine came in and set the drink down. Without a word, she left the room. Nick added, "This is my favorite drink. I don't know why, but it always relaxes me."

We watched as Nick took a good helping of the concoction and then as he relaxed into the sofa.

I got straight to the point. "Nick, as you know, I'd like to hire you to find my uncle. He's a man that has not wanted to be found for decades and is therefore adept at hiding. What makes you think that you can find him?"

His answer was short and abrupt. "You have money."

"Excuse you?" Victoria said. Any signs of pleasantry from earlier had dissipated.

"Anne has a lot of money," he explained. "And money talks. Add that with my connections and I'll have no problem finding your uncle. I just need you to tell me all you know so far, and I can get started today."

Victoria looked skeptical. "You said you worked for the Wilkens family a lot. What cases have you worked on?" Clearly, his first answer about money had put her on edge.

"Oh yes, well, there's been a few kids from the family who have tried to run away. One of them was almost successful. He was hard to find, but I found him. He was living on a vineyard in Italy with his girlfriend's family." He leaned forward and looked me in the eye. "I know people, Anne. There's nowhere your uncle can go that I can't find him."

"And we should just take your word for it?" Victoria pressed.

"Isabella recommended me, didn't she?" Nick returned. "Would she ever tarnish her name by recommending someone she didn't trust?"

"That's true," I said.

"But Isabella has also tricked Anne before," Victoria said bluntly.

I knew Victoria was not going to back down without me stepping in, so I put a hand on her arm and made sure she was looking at me before saying, "Victoria, it's okay. I think we should hire him."

"Great!" Nick said instantly. "I've got my notebook and pen. Shoot."

So, for the next hour, I told him all I knew about Harrison, and that the last known place he'd lived was in the States.

After jotting down all his notes, Nick stood. "Well, this is a great start. As soon as I find out where he is, I'll let you know. Thank you."

We walked out of the library and showed him to the door, then watched as he drove away.

"Definitely not boring," Victoria said.

CHAPTER 3

ISABELLA

"Did you get anything new out of her?" I asked.

"No, it was all information we already knew," Nick responded.

"Well, I hope you didn't give her Harrison's address."

"Of course not. I told her I would let her know when I found it. She doesn't need to know I already have it."

"Great. Why don't you go and pay Harrison a visit then?"

"Already heading to the airport."

"Good, I'll give Grandma Geraldine an update."

CHAPTER 4

ANNE

"W HERE SHOULD I GO NEXT?" I ASKED SEBASTIAN the next day while we were lounging in the sitting room.

"Why don't you relax at home for a bit before deciding where to go," Sebastian suggested.

"I second that," Victoria piped up, looking half-asleep. "And don't ask any more questions. Just be quiet."

We were all exhausted. The time change was wracking havoc on our ability to talk comprehensively.

"I can't just sit at home and do nothing," I argued.

"Yes, you can," Sebastian and Victoria said at the same time.

"Now be quiet, we're trying to sleep," Sebastian added.

"Aye Aye!" Victoria said in agreement, pointing a finger at me with her eyes closed. It was more of a finger in the air pointing at nothing, but I got the meaning and decided to sleep some too. For some reason, the return journey home was always the worst with jet lag setting in fast, whereas on the way to whatever country I was going to, jet lag was never a problem. Maybe it was because I had more adrenaline and was pumped to be going someplace new. On that, I needed to figure out my next place to go.

There was a small noise and then someone spoke. "Miss, there is a visitor here to see you in the library. I told him you weren't home but he insisted on staying and waiting for you."

I looked up to see Ben, standing halfway in the room, trying his best to be discreet. "Really?" I stretched and wanted to stay put for just five more minutes, but Ben was still standing there. I missed Andy; he would have known to give me a little bit of time before arising. "Ben, call me Anne, please."

"Yes Miss—I mean, Anne. The visitor is in the library if you would like to see him now."

"Give me five minutes please."

"Oh, of course," Ben said, blushing a bright red.

"It's okay, I just need to wake up a bit."

"Yes, of course. I'll let him know."

Ben turned and left the room. Shortly after, we heard a soft, gentle, low voice in the hallway ask, "Is there any way I can get some water?"

"Who is that?" Victoria said. "It doesn't sound like anyone we know."

"I have no idea but I should get up and check." I rolled off the sofa and made myself stand up. Time to be host. Maybe it was a solicitor that wanted money. If so, I could shoo him out the door quickly and come back here to sleep some more.

I walked out into the hallway to see an old man in trousers and a button-down shirt. His back was a bit humped, and his head was bald on top. Wisps of gray hair graced the sides and back of his head and thin wire glasses completed his look.

"Sir, I'm Anne. Can I help you?" When he turned around,

I gasped and almost knocked into the table against the wall. "You're . . . You're . . ."

"Harrison Lin."

I gaped at him. "What . . . what are you doing here?"

"I came to see you."

Grasping at every string of reality I could while trying to get my thoughts together, I managed to say, "You're the man I saw at the gallery. It was you!"

"It was. I came to see you but once I got there, I lost my courage."

"The others thought I had seen things. They thought it wasn't you—but I knew it!"

"What is all the commotion about?" Sebastian asked. He and Victoria had run out of the sitting room at the sound of my shouting, but both stopped in their tracks when they saw Harrison.

I made a big wave of my arm and said, "Sebastian and Victoria, I would like you to meet the one and only, Harrison Lin."

"What the . . .?" Victoria trailed off.

"I told you that he's the one I saw at the gallery. I wasn't crazy!" I said triumphantly.

"He looks just like Anthony," Victoria said, and then clamped her hand over her mouth realizing what she had just said.

"I do look like Anthony; there is no denying that I am his son," Harrison agreed. "His family made it quite clear how much they disliked that fact when I visited here."

We were all silent for a moment, soaking this in, and I understood that this was Harrison's second time inside this mansion. I wondered what he was feeling.

Victoria nudged me from behind, which brought me out of my thoughts and I realized that I should formally invite him in. "Why don't we all go into the library where it's cozier and catch up?" I suggested. "I'll have some tea brought up for us."

Before we could move, Harrison said sharply, "Just Anne for now, please."

I looked at Victoria and Sebastian in silent inquiry.

Sebastian said, "Sure, we'll wait in the sitting room." He and Victoria started to head back in.

I held up a hand to my uncle and said, "I'll be right there, Harrison. I just need to grab something from the sitting room," and hurried after them.

I walked into the room and at first, I just stared at Sebastian and Victoria with wide eyes. I then did some jogging in place, then sat down and breathed for a bit, before getting up again and pacing the room. The whole time, Sebastian's blue eyes followed me. Needing him, I walked toward him. His arms enveloped me, and I snuggled in close and whispered, "I want my old life back."

"No, you don't."

"Yes, I do."

"But I'm not in your old life."

"Well, I want *part* of my old life back," I whined.

At this, Sebastian started laughing. "Just go and see what he wants. He could be here to grant you another mansion."

I pushed him away and caught his silly grin. I then gave him a big kiss and walked to the door—where I suddenly stopped.

I could hear Sebastian starting to move toward me. "Come on, Anne, you can do it," he said. "We'll be right here if you need us."

I jerked my head in a sharp nod before taking a deep breath and heading to the library.

I saw Ben standing close to the library doors, looking sheepish. "Ben, can I help you with something?"

"I was going to ask you the same thing." His request

came out as more of an automatic response rather than a genuine statement. We stared at each other for what seemed like a minute.

I decided to put him out of his misery. "Just don't eavesdrop right behind the door. I don't want him to hear you guys breathing."

Ben turned bright red, and I could hear snickering coming from behind the kitchen door. "No, ma'am, of course not."

With that, I walked into the library.

"Who are you?" Harrison asked before I had gotten both feet into the room. He said this without malice, but I felt like I was being schooled by a headmaster after doing something wrong. I didn't have time to decide how I felt about the question before he started talking again. "I don't know how you found me, but whoever you are, you had no right sending me that email."

That comment made me jerk out of my stupor to ask, "Then why are you here?"

He let out a sigh and flopped in one of the armchairs by the fireplace. The fire was taking the chill off the room, but it couldn't remove the discomfort between us. I walked slowly toward him and settled into the other armchair next to his, not daring to make a sound. What was it leaders said? The first one who broke the silence lost? Sure, that sounded good. I wasn't going to be the first one who broke the silence.

"Who are you?" he asked again, but this time it came out in a voice like a little lost boy.

My heart broke at the emotion that little question conveyed, and I realized I needed him as much as he needed me. "If you're who I think you are, I'm your niece."

At this, he lifted his head from his hands and looked at me. A single tear ran down his left cheek. "If it's money you want—"

"No! That is the last thing I want." I waved a hand at the

room. "I just inherited this place and everything that came with it last year. I do not want or need any more money."

He looked at me, seemingly perplexed. "I've never met anyone who says no to money." He still looked sad and uncomfortable, but I could see he'd now relaxed into the chair and his curiosity was piqued.

"It's a long story."

"I have time if you would like to share."

"Well, I don't know for sure if you are who you claim to be," I returned.

He looked down at his legs, rubbing his hands along his thighs before looking back up at me. "My name is Harrison Lin. I grew up in Taiwan with my mama, Mary, my baba, Liang-Chun, and their kids. I am also the son of Anthony Wilkens and Rose Chen. I got to know Anthony a little bit, but I never met Rose." I had to strain to hear the last part. At my silence, he asked, "Would you like me to keep going?"

"Yes please, anyone could have found that information."

He put his hand in his pocket and rummaged through what seemed to be quite a lot of stuff. He pulled out something in his hand, which was noticeably shaking. "Here."

I reached my hand out to take what was hidden in his clenched fist. His hand opened over mine and a small piece of paper dropped into my palm. It was no bigger than a matchbox, but it distinctly portrayed the faces of a young Mary, who looked to be in her early twenties, and a little boy who looked of mixed race. Being a sepia-colored photograph, I couldn't tell the color of the boy's eyes or hair, but it was clear that he had lighter hair than Mary's, and big, round American eyes with long lashes. I looked up at Harrison. Those same eyes were looking back at me, distinctive and unquestionably the same.

"You are Harrison," I breathed.

"I am."

We stared at each other for some time, both lost in our thoughts. The only sound was the crackling of the fire, which provided an earie glow around the room, and yet seemed very appropriate for the setting. My uncle was sitting across from me and all I could think was, *He's really here! Actually right in front of me, and I have no idea what to do!*

"You seem as lost as me," Harrison finally said, breaking the silence.

"Yes . . . How did you find me?"

"I asked Bettie. She gave me your address."

"Oh right . . . Bettie. So, you were the man I saw in her office?"

"I was."

More silence, only broken by the sound of my stomach gurgling.

Harrison continued, "You must be hungry. A lady who said to call her Jasmine said she had a pot of lamb soup in the kitchen."

"That's a great idea."

I showed him to the kitchen and who should we see there but Sebastian and Victoria, both of them with a mouthful of carrot cake.

"We'll leave; we were just finishing," Victoria said, and they both started getting up from the table.

"No, stay. The more people the better." I stopped and looked at Harrison. "At least, I think so. I can't think very straight right now."

"Okay . . ." Victoria said dubiously.

Sebastian and Victoria sat back down very slowly. They had questions written all over their faces. I sat down to show them that everything was okay; Harrison wasn't going to bite.

"I see you two started without me," I said, indicating the cake.

"We were hungry, and Jasmine said the food was getting cold," Sebastian said.

I turned to look at the stove where a small fire was keeping the pot nice and warm. "I'm sure she did," I said with a smile. I got up and ladled two big bowls of soup and passed one to Harrison. We gobbled it down without a word between us. After the soup, I went and got two slices of carrot cake—this was one cake I never said no to!

Harrison suddenly stuck his hand out to Sebastian. "I'm Harrison. Apparently, I am Anne's long-lost half uncle."

"Right, I'm Sebastian, Anne's boyfriend."

Once they'd shaken, Harrison turned to Victoria. She held out her hand and said, "I'm Victoria, Anne's best friend."

"It's nice to meet you two."

"Nice to meet you too," they both said.

"Harrison was just telling me that Bettie gave him my address and that's how he knew where to find me," I chimed in.

"You two must have a lot to talk about. We can make ourselves scarce," Victoria suggested.

"No, I think you should stay." Now that they were both here, I didn't want them to leave. I needed some physical support, even if it was just their presence.

"Okay, but you two better get talking because I'm going to get bored very quickly if you both keep hemming and hawing," Victoria said.

Harrison took that as his cue to start asking questions. "Anne, how did you find me? During all these years no one has been able to come close to locating me. And if they did try, I never knew about it."

"Well, it's a long story."

"I have time. My wife is tired of me questioning my past all these years. She sees this as a chance to acquire some answers and I'm not allowed home until I do so. My wife also threatened that if I didn't find any answers then I could still come home, but only if I stopped moping around."

"I see, and would your wife happen to be Grace Chien?"

"Yes! How did you know?"

I saw distrust seep into his eyes. It was scary how quickly his emotions changed. "From Mary," I explained.

"You've met Mary?" he asked, almost in a whisper.

"Yes, but it's a long story. Do you have a place to stay?"

He nodded. "I have a hotel downtown."

"That won't do. You should stay here. I have so many rooms and I have no idea what I'm going to do with all of them. They shouldn't remain empty."

"That would be much better than a hotel," he agreed. "Then we could share our stories with each other without any hinderance."

Hmm . . . maybe I hadn't thought this through. He would be here every day, and I knew nothing about him. What if he was a psychopath? What if he wasn't who he said he was, and had learned everything he knew in order to steal my money?

I could feel my chest getting tight. Before I did something embarrassing, like hyperventilate, I got up and rang for Ben. When he came in, I introduced him to Harrison, and asked if he could show him to one of the rooms upstairs.

When they left, Victoria put a hand on my arm. "You doing okay?" she asked.

"Yeah. It's just too much all at once."

Sebastian jumped to his feet. "I'll be right back. Jasmine made a tub of coffee ice cream that is just sitting in the freezer."

"That sounds divine," I said. Ice cream always made things better.

CHAPTER 5

T HE NEXT MORNING, I WOKE UP TO THE SUN
shining and Sebastian's arms around me. And was that birds I heard? I turned and nestled into Sebastian's arms; he responded by holding me tighter.

"Can we stay like this forever?" I asked.

"We can until breakfast. I'm starving."

"You're so romantic."

"I know," Sebastian said, trying to hold a straight face. I watched as he tried to keep his lips in a line, how he forced his cheeks to stay neutral, and how his eyelashes fluttered with every twitch. Then his mouth gave way into a broad smile and next thing I knew, we were giggling under the covers and he was tickling me all over.

"Stop! Stop!" I said in between laughs. "I can't take it anymore."

"Come on, let's go have breakfast now. I'm sure Harrison is already in the kitchen telling Cook everything. You don't want her to find out all the juicy bits of information before you do."

"Cook's not here," I returned.

Sebastian shook his head. "She is; she came back last night."

I sat up in bed so fast that Sebastian laughed even more.

"That's not funny!" I exclaimed. "He better not be telling her anything!"

I was then out of the bed in a flash, Sebastian grabbing at thin air as he reached for me.

Lounge pants and an oversized shirt were the first things I grabbed out of my dresser. Then out the room I went, but not before turning back to give Sebastian a kiss.

Sure enough, Harrison was sitting at the table eating a big bowl of porridge with newspaper in hand. Cook really was back and I saw her standing off to the side with a frustrated look on her face. That made me smile—Harrison wasn't a talker.

"Good morning," I said.

"Anne! I've missed you," Cook said, coming over to me and enveloping me in a big hug.

"I've missed you too," I said, giving her an equally big hug back. I really had missed her, and not just her food either. Cook had been here for so long that she was my biggest source of information on anything about the house, the Wilkens's family, and life in general. She was my mom when Mom wasn't around.

"I see you brought a friend," she whispered to me.

"More like a long lost relative," I whispered back. *Why were we whispering?*

"Really?" she asked in her normal voice, pushing me an arm's length away and giving me that 'what are you not telling me' look.

"He hasn't told you anything, has he?" I asked her quietly.

"No, nothing at all." I saw her frustration seep in again. Before it could cement even further, I pulled her over to the table where my uncle sat.

"Cook, this is Harrison, a long lost uncle of mine and Mom's half brother."

"You could have told me as much, Harrison! Why all the secrecy?"

Cook never let things be and I loved that about her. Harrison, however, wouldn't look at her. He kept spinning his spoon in his bowl and not saying a thing. Right when I was about to ask him what his deal was, he said, "It's a long story, and I was curious if you'd remember me."

"You were a boy then," Cook huffed. "And we have the time." Her hands had migrated to her hips and her eyes had a look of determination. She would wait out his stubbornness if it was the last thing she did.

But Harrison was not so easily swayed. "I would prefer to tell Anne only."

"Hmph," Cook replied. Then I thought I heard her mumble to herself, "I'm always in on secrets."

It made me smile again. If she didn't get the secret out of me sooner rather than later, I'd be surprised.

In an effort to change the subject, I asked my uncle, "What are you eating there?"

"Just gruel," Harrison replied with a smile. *He was impossible!*

"Gruel?" Cook said, turning a shade of red I didn't want to see the end result of. "I don't cook gruel!"

"I was just joking," Harrison said, that small smile playing around his lips as he remained looking down at his bowl.

"Cook, we know you don't cook gruel," I said swiftly.

Then I suggested, "Why don't I take Harrison somewhere else so we can talk?"

"Yes, do that," was all she said.

I could feel her eyes on us the whole time we climbed the stairs and exited the room.

"Is she always like that?" Harrison asked as soon as we were out of hearing.

"No, she's actually a very nice person. Cook's just not used to people not telling her everything about themselves and calling her food gruel."

"So, I already have two strikes then."

"You did push her," I said, giving him a smile, but he looked dejected.

He sighed. "That's me. I can't help it. It's how I act when I'm nervous."

"Hey, it's going to be okay. Cook's a good person."

"Right." He seemed to shake himself and asked next, "So, where should we go?"

"How about the library? I've always found that room to be comforting."

"Okay."

"Would you like something to drink? Tea, coffee?"

"Tea would be great," he said while looking around aimlessly.

I went back to the kitchen and asked Cook if Lavender could bring up some tea for us. When I got back to the library, Harrison was seated in one of the armchairs facing the fireplace. The crackle of the fire was the loudest noise in the room. My thumbs started spinning circles around each other, not out of habit, but because they had nothing else to do. We sat there in silence, deep in our thoughts, and mine being: *When was I going to stop learning more secrets about my family?*

We were interrupted by Lavender bringing in the tea. "Here you go, ma'am."

"Lavender, call me Anne."

"Yes, ma'am. I mean, Anne."

She almost ran out of the library, and I wondered how I was going to get through to her that I wasn't someone to be afraid of.

"She seemed pretty scared of you," Harrison said, uttering the first words that would start our journey.

"She's intimidated by me."

"I'm intimidated by you too. Here you are, rich as can be, and head of this whole household. You're the boss."

"I guess you're right. I'd be intimidated of myself too." I sighed. This was not the life I wanted. Catching Harrison's eye, I asked, "Where would you like to start?"

He reclined into his chair and began with, "What do you do?"

"That's where you want to start?" I questioned him.

"It's better to start with something we're comfortable with."

This guy was an enigma. One second, he was to the point and very matter of fact; the next, he could elude a subject, seemingly forever.

"Okay then. What do I do? Well, I travel and then I blog about my travel. I know it doesn't sound like much, but I love traveling. I write about the stuff people could enjoy doing at the destination, the food, the people, the environment, and what I have learned from the locals. It excites me and has kept me moving around the world."

"I used to travel a lot too," Harrison said.

"Really? Where to?"

"Everywhere. I lived in London for a while. I also moved around Europe and settled in America."

"Where in the US?"

"In a big city."

I waited for him to say more but nothing further came. He really liked to keep his cards close to his chest. It was a bit infuriating, but I didn't want to scare him off, so I moved on with, "What made you stop traveling?"

"I'd had enough of wandering. The love of my life wanted a family, so we started one. After that, it wasn't so easy to travel. We still did it, but not to the extent we had before kids. I've been in the US for over thirty years now."

I reflected on the fact that with some things, Harrison could share without a problem, but in others, he couldn't.

"It also got too expensive to travel with a family," he continued. "But I guess that wouldn't be a problem for you because you can afford it." He looked pointedly around the library.

His comment irked me. "No, I only just got this place this year. My inheritance was a total surprise, and it's not the life I wanted."

"A surprise? You make it sound like it wasn't a very good surprise."

"No, it wasn't. My inheritance came with a lot of baggage and way too much money for me to wrap my head around."

"Most people would be happy with that."

"Yeah, Victoria keeps telling me I should just embrace it."

"Well, friends aren't always right. Can you tell me more about how you got to own this place?"

I told him about the letter, the will reading, the gala, about all the people I'd met in the house, and more detail than I thought was necessary, but somehow, I couldn't stop myself from sharing it all with him. Harrison sat there, looking at me the whole time. It was a bit unnerving.

"How did you grow up before all this?" was all he asked after I finished my story.

"With my mom in Astoria. We had a normal life, nothing special. How about you?"

"Me? Well, I grew up in Taiwan, mostly. It was good and bad." He lapsed into silence, but before I could ask him another question, he said, "You said you met Mary. Did you meet her in Taiwan?"

"Yes, we just got back from there actually."

"How is she doing?"

"She misses you and is filled with guilt about you. I know she'd be super happy if you went to visit her."

"I'm not ready," he said with so much finality that I didn't dare object. After a small silence, he asked, "You said you're my niece?"

"Yes." I was good at giving short answers too.

I could see tears forming in his eyes. He was trying so hard to hold them back and I wished he would just let go.

"My mama was your grandmother," he said.

"Yes."

"And I am your mom's half brother." He didn't seem to want me to respond, so we sat there in silence again until he asked, "Why did you start searching for me?"

"I found my Ah Po's journals—your mom's journals."

"You did?" At this, he seemed to perk up, and I watched as his eyes got big. He seemed to be holding his breath.

Before he fainted from over-excitement and forgot to breathe, I decided to intervene. "Would you like to see them?"

"Yes." He was already up and walking toward the door before the word left his mouth.

I waited for him to realize that he didn't know where he was going. At the door, he paused and let me go ahead.

He followed me to my closet, and I opened the trunk while he looked over my shoulder. First, I pulled out the qipao. He held it and just cried for about ten minutes. Not big fat tears, but silent droplets that rolled down his cheeks.

Then, I gestured to the journals. I let Harrison extract them from the trunk. At first, I thought he was just going to look at them, but then one of his hands rubbed over the top cover. He thumbed through a few pages of the first journal, eliciting an old book smell. I saw his hand was shaking as he brought the journal closer toward him.

"I saw her once, you know," he said. "I saw her with her husband and child."

I thought about the letter from Josephine, talking about the boy who stood across the street, staring at his mom and her family.

He continued, "That child is your mama, I suppose?"

"She is."

He went silent for a bit and I let him just sit there and take this moment in. After a while, he said, "I didn't understand why she let me go. I never did. There's people all over the world who look like me now—mixed, they call them. Do you know what it's like to stand out? To not belong anywhere?"

His thoughts were jumping all over the place. It seemed like this was the first time he'd ever spoken his feelings out loud.

He continued, "I met my baba once. Did you know that?" Before I could answer, he added, "He wasn't what I expected. But then again, what was I supposed to expect?"

Silence permeated the air again, and I didn't dare breathe. *Keep going, please.*

As if he'd heard my silent request, he continued, "I was the whitest person anyone had ever met, but regardless, I always thought of myself as Taiwanese. My white baba was the first white person I had ever met, and I hated him. I was just becoming a teenager when I saw him, questioning my past and wondering why I didn't look like others. I was teased at school. Did Mary tell you that?"

He whispered the last question so softly that I had to lean forward to hear it. My movement startled him, and I knew he wouldn't continue. I sighed and waited for the question I knew was coming. It didn't take long.

"Can I borrow this journal to read today?"

"Yes of course," I said swiftly, pushing down my anxiety.

"I will go now. I'm sorry to be so sad."

"I get it. You're finally getting answers. It's a lot to absorb."

"Yeah . . ."

With journal in hand, he got up and walked out without another word. I sat in the closet for I don't know how long. The next thing I knew, Sebastian was sitting next to me, stroking my hair and letting me cry into his chest.

CHAPTER 6

I DIDN'T SEE HARRISON FOR THE REST OF THE DAY. Victoria had gone to stay with her parents, so it was just Sebastian and me.

In order to keep me distracted, Sebastian took me on a road trip to Tillamook. I had to admit, I was pretty numb the whole time. My mind kept going back to Harrison and what he was feeling as he read Ah Po's journal. I hoped he was taking care of it. Part of me wanted to take it back, but I kept reminding myself that Ah Po was his mom, and it was the only physical connection he had to her.

"What flavor do you want?" Sebastian asked.

"What?" I tried to focus on my boyfriend, my brow wrinkling at his question.

"She's asking you what flavor you want," Sebastian said, looking at me worriedly.

"Right. I'll have coffee, please."

I took the scoop of coffee ice cream and followed Sebastian to one of the tables in the sun.

"You've been so quiet this whole trip, Anne."

"I know. I just really want to be there with Harrison while he reads Ah Po's journal."

Sebastian raised a brow. "You know he needs space, right?"

"I know that, but it doesn't make the feeling that I should be there go away. I shouldn't have left him alone. What if he has questions? What if he destroys the journals?"

"Okay, now you're being over dramatic. No one's going to destroy the journals."

"You don't know that."

"You don't either. Harrison might be a bit odd, but I don't think he's the type to destroy other people's property."

"Wouldn't the journals be his property too, though?"

"Your Ah Po gave the journals willingly to Anthony, who then gave them to you. So, no. They belong to you."

"Well, mister big shot lawyer, you would know best."

"That's the first joke you've made in a while. I really want you to enjoy today, Anne." Sebastian reached out to hold my hand. "And your ice cream is melting."

"Oh no." I licked all around the cone till every drop was gone.

We walked along the coastline enjoying the fresh air. I loved the Oregon coast. You didn't have to drive far from Portland to be near nature while still enjoying the city life. Just this morning, we had been in Portland, and here we were on the coast, enjoying a walk on the beach.

Sebastian did a great job distracting me the next day too. We visited the Rose Garden, which in itself was a journey to get to.

"Did you know me and Mom got lost the first time she brought me here?"

Sebastian started laughing. "Really? How old were you?"

"It's not that funny. I was about ten. We got scared because the road just ended. We were in an open pasture with trees about a mile high all around us. There was nothing close by. Paper maps are usually so reliable that it was scary to find out that the map had brought us to the middle of nowhere. Mom didn't come to the city often and she tried to keep up a strong front, but I knew we were lost.

"She knew the garden was near the zoo, so we back-tracked and eventually found it. By that point, Mom did not want to drive anymore, so we got out of the car to walk, but the garden still eluded us. We asked a lady where it was. She was at a crafts fair that was across the parking lot from the zoo. She drew us a hand-drawn map, but we still couldn't find it. That was okay by me because Mom decided that ice cream would be a better choice over the zoo."

"I'm guessing you didn't complain," Sebastian said, giving me a playful nudge.

"What ten-year-old says no to ice cream, especially after driving and walking around what felt like most of Portland for a rose garden?"

"You and your mom should write a book about your many travels one day," Sebastian said, still laughing. "Did you two ever make it back to see the roses?"

"We did, and this time Mom made sure to memorize every road to the Rose Garden. We still got a bit turned around, but we found it in the end."

"Thank goodness! I'm glad the garden stopped being elusive." Sebastian was still laughing, and looking back, I suppose it was a humorous story, but I still gave him a playful punch on the arm.

"You've never stopped sending me roses," I said while we walked through the garden admiring all the different breeds.

"I love sending them every week. It's a reminder that I

love you. I know I'm not always around, so I hope that they provide you with a little bit of me while I'm gone."

I turned to look at him, and despite Victoria's concern that Sebastian worked too long, I still knew he was definitely the man for me. We stayed like that for a bit, hand in hand, enjoying the serenity of the garden.

"You think they hold weddings here?" Sebastian asked, gesturing to a beautiful arch on a big platform nearby.

"They definitely do. It's beautiful here."

"Why don't we have the wedding here, then?" Sebastian suggested. "It holds a special memory for you."

For a moment I was speechless, then I thought about his request seriously. "Well, when you put it that way, I don't want the wedding here as it already has a special memory. Plus, you never actually proposed to me."

"You mean me mentioning that I wanted to spend the rest of my life with you and quitting my job wasn't enough?"

I turned to give him a stern look, but it was mischievousness that I saw lurking in his eyes. He pulled me close and gave me a long lingering kiss. I melted right into him. As he pulled away, he added, "I'll make it up to you when you least expect it."

"Okay," I said with what little breath I had left.

We wandered around some more until Sebastian suggested we head to the zoo. He knew I loved zoos, and I had a special spot in my heart for the Portland Zoo as it was the first zoo I had ever visited. It had just been me and Mom while she introduced me to animals besides cats and dogs. I loved watching the giraffes and the elephants with their long necks and trunks. The monkeys were another favorite, so similar to us and yet so different. I could watch them all day.

"What are you thinking?" Sebastian asked.

He'd had his arm around my shoulders the whole time we'd walked around, not saying a word. I could feel his fingers trailing circles on my back. I loved how we could just 'be' together; there was no need to be talking every single second. Sebastian had once said that he talked enough at work that he loved spending time with me for some peace and quiet. That comment always made me wonder how he and Isabella could have been together for so long, but I chalked it up to them being in different stages of their lives.

"Have you ever thought about how animals can just welcome a new member into their family?" I asked him. "I mean, sometimes there's a fight for dominance, but if there's a new baby or one that needs to be protected, they just take them in, no questions asked and with no expectations."

"What are you getting at, Anne?"

"I'd like to be like them."

"You want to be an animal?"

"A monkey in particular."

"Well, you're the closest to one you'll ever get to be," Sebastian said with a straight face.

"Maybe someone is inventing a machine right this second that can transform us into another animal. You know, like in Harry Potter."

"That was magic, sweetheart."

"Well, we have scientists."

"Okay," Sebastian said, raising both of his hands. "This conversation has officially gone in a totally different direction. Are we still talking about your uncle?"

"Yes." I laughed. "I've been wondering lately what family means. How can some be so connected and then others be so far apart?"

"Well, I don't keep in touch with my family."

"I was perfectly happy with just Mom. Now I'm contending with a bunch of others who have been hiding from everyone."

"Look on the bright side—you've got me," Sebastian said, looking at me with a raised eyebrow.

"I do, don't I." I entwined my fingers with his, feeling a stupid grin plaster across my face. Who needed to worry about anything else in the world as long as Sebastian was by my side?

"I've been meaning to ask you a question: What do you think about you and Harrison having some alone time?" Sebastian asked.

"I would love that. I could get to know him better before I introduce him to Mom."

"Well, I have to go on a business trip tomorrow, so there's an opportunity to do just that."

"That will work out perfectly. I can answer any questions he has, and we can have dinner together. Maybe Cook can make something special for him?"

"For maybe a month."

"What do you think his favorite food is?" Then I clicked with what Sebastian had just said. "Did you just say a month?" I asked.

"Yeah. I'm still sorting through some issues for the Wilkens family, and I have to talk to Bernice and Catherine in person."

"Why a month, though? You could just call them, couldn't you?"

"There are some things that are better not done over the phone."

"You know your own work best, I suppose," I said. But for the rest of the walk we were silent, each of us lost in our own thoughts—mine being why Sebastian had to go away for a whole month and not just a few days.

We drove back to Portland. The foliage seemed to be drooping—or maybe it was my heavy feelings of sadness projecting onto the scenery. I felt a sense of dread creep up my spine. I tried to shake it off, telling myself it was nothing, that I was just hypersensitive because Harrison was here. I didn't know what he was all about, and Sebastian would be gone for a while. Yes, that was all it was.

When we got home, Harrison was sitting on the front lawn reading the journal. I was very relieved to see that it was still intact.

He was so engrossed in the journal that he didn't notice us walk up to him.

Sebastian broke the silence. "It's quite interesting, isn't it?"

"Huh?" Harrison looked up at us with vacant eyes, dried tears caking the perimeter of his eyelids. I saw recognition sink in and a faint smile appeared on his mouth.

The dried tears tore at my heart and I remembered that this was the most he'd ever learned about his mom, and it all came from her own handwriting.

I asked, "How are you doing processing all the information in there? I know it was hard for me to digest when I first read it."

"It is slow for me because it is my own mama, and it's hard for me to wrap my mind around her, but I am also happy that I am finally learning a little about her."

"We're glad to hear that," Sebastian said. He started to pull me toward the house. "We'll leave you to it."

"No, I'll come with you." Harrison pushed himself up into a standing position. "Cook told me that she was making lamb with green onion, sticky rice, butterflied shrimp with garlic, and a fried duck. I hope it's done because I'm hungry."

I laughed. Our family loved food and we traveled on our stomachs. Good thing Cook was an awesome chef.

The three of us entered the house and headed straight for the kitchen. There was a very nice dining area down the hall, but there was something about eating in the kitchen right next to the stove and the person who cooked it that made it feel more like home.

Sure enough, every item Harrison had described was there on the table ready for our consumption. We dug in as soon as we sat down. After about ten minutes of inhaling the food, I looked up to find Cook smiling at us. It always made her happy to see people devouring her food like there was no tomorrow—it made her proud.

"Your food is very good," Harrison said.

"It's the best," she said crisply.

Cook walked away with a smile on her face. She was going to win Harrison over if it was the last thing she did.

"Harrison, did you have any questions about what you've read?" I asked. With some food in us maybe he would open up more.

"I am not sure what I am feeling right now. It is a lot of information to swallow. I did notice the carvings on the walls and on the ceiling in your room, and have since seen these same carvings all over the house. Is this normal in a rich person's house? They were not there when I visited the first time."

"No," Sebastian and I said at the same time.

"Anthony loved Ah Po, and this was his way of showing his love. He got obsessive about it if you couldn't tell," I said.

"I see . . ." Harrison seemed to be lost in his thoughts again, which was starting to worry me. I thought I was reclusive, but he brought the term to a whole new level. He made me nervous.

"Do you know how to carve wood?" I asked, trying to bring him out of his shell.

"Yes, but I didn't do a lot of it—not like this."

"Well, I don't think most people would have done carvings at this scale," Sebastian said. "I think Anthony became obsessed with the carvings."

This seemed to affect Harrison more than either of us thought possible. His eyes widened and he started to stand up. I watched as he brought his bowl to the sink with half of his food still in it. Thank goodness Cook had gone out for a minute.

"Harrison, are you okay? Is there something we can do for you?" I asked.

"No. No. I'm going to go back to my room. I'd like to read some more of my mother's journal."

Sebastian stood up. "Hey, I'm sorry if I offended you. I'm sure Anthony wasn't crazy. He just . . ."

Sebastian was starting to ramble and thank goodness he saw my stare before he could continue. I saw Harrison was already by the door.

"Harrison, we're here for you if you want to ask us anything," I said quickly. "I've read through all the journals. I love reading, and Mom would love to meet you." *Where did that come from?* I hadn't even told Mom he was here. I should probably do that. "Maybe if you wrote down your thoughts on paper and gave them to me to read—would that be easier?" I asked him. Now I was the one rambling.

Sebastian and I both held our breaths while we waited to see what Harrison would do. I didn't want to scare him, but I wanted him to know we were there for him. I craved this relationship more than I thought I would. It had always been Mom and me for what felt like forever. Now there was an uncle, and I didn't want him to disappear.

But it wasn't meant to be. Harrison pushed through the kitchen door and left. I sent Sebastian a pained look.

"You can catch up with him later. I would just give him some space," he said, bringing me in for a warm hug.

"Do you think I'm pushing too much?" I asked. "I just want a relationship with him. I didn't know I would want this so badly. It's always been Mom and me, and it's been fine to this point."

"It's always nice to have more family," Sebastian replied softly. "When I started working for Anthony, my life changed. And not just with the financial side of things, but because it felt like he really cared about me. It's nice to have family, and that family could be anyone—not just a blood relative. So, no, it's not weird that you would want to connect with your uncle."

"Yeah, well, could you not mention the word crazy or Anthony in front of him again?"

"That hit a nerve, didn't it?" Sebastian said, running his hand through his hair, a deep sigh escaping his mouth.

I nodded. "Have you noticed that he's very withdrawn? I worry that he's hiding something that we don't know about."

Sebastian hugged me even tighter. "I'm sure it'll all turn out fine," he said reassuringly. "A good night's rest will be good for all of us. We'll see how he's doing tomorrow."

CHAPTER 7

THE NEXT MORNING STARTED THE SAME WITH ME not wanting to get out of bed. Sebastian was splayed out next to me. I wiped his hair from his eyes. My touch stirred him awake and his arm come around me, pulling me close. We lay like that till I heard the staff in the hallway going about their daily tasks.

My thoughts returned to what I had thought of during the night. I had woken up at three in the morning, scared that if Harrison read more of the journals his demeanor could get worse—that he would become so entrenched that we wouldn't be able to get him out of his room. At first, I thought to ask Mom if she would like to come and meet Harrison, but then I realized that even in my tired middle-of-the-night state, that bringing someone else he didn't know into the equation was probably a bad idea. A new idea had crept in, though, and I couldn't wait to ask him about it.

I wanted to see if Harrison would like to invite his wife to join us here. He knew how much room I had here in the mansion. It wouldn't be a problem to welcome Grace, someone he trusted. And from what I could tell from reading the journals, Grace had been his rock when they were growing up and was most likely just as supportive now. She would be a huge help while he read the journals and came to grips with his past.

I was so excited that I untangled myself from Sebastian and ran to put on my clothes. My first thought was to head to Harrison's room to see if he was awake, but I ran into Ben on the way there.

"Ben, do you know if Harrison is awake yet? If so, could you tell him that I am looking for him, or could you direct me to where he is? I have to ask him something."

"He's already left, ma'am."

"Oh, he went out for breakfast? But Cook would have made him something."

"No, he left, as in he went home." Ben was looking at me with an expression of pity.

I felt my heart rate increase. That was not the response I was expecting. I'd known that something was bothering Harrison, knew that he'd been receding into himself, but going home? That was not what I'd been expecting. I couldn't believe he'd left—just like that and without saying a word!

"He left a note for you," Ben said, breaking the awkward silence. "I put it in my office. Let me go get it."

I followed him to his office in a half-state of consciousness. My brain couldn't compute why Harrison would just leave. But then again, he'd appeared on my doorstep just as fast, completely out of the blue. The man was infuriating. I couldn't keep up with him. Why couldn't he just have the same social cues as the rest of us? One minute he was curious; in the next, he'd disappeared.

"Here it is," Ben said, passing me a note. "I saw him this morning while he was loading up his bags. He said to give it to you after he was gone, but he left so early that I don't know why he was worried. He must not know that you sleep in on weekends."

"Thanks, Ben," I said absentmindedly.

There was the prettiest handwriting on the cream envelope. Harrison must have carried this stationary around with him as I didn't own anything this nice. I rubbed my hands across the lettering. *Anne Huang.* So, he knew my last name. I wondered what else he knew and what he could be hiding.

There was something bumpy in the envelope. I turned it around and lifted the flap, pulling out a folded up note that had been written on cotton stationary and a pink object. For a moment, I just stared at it. *It couldn't be!* Had it really been with him all this time?

A pink, glass plum blossom lay in my hand.

My first thought was to phone Mary and tell her what I held in my hand. She would be so happy to know he'd kept it, but then I thought better of it. She wouldn't care about the glass plum blossom when Harrison himself wasn't here. I held the beloved gift Mary had given Harrison when he was a little boy. I had lost the man who this flower belonged to. *Where had he gone?*

I took the letter to the library where a fire was already burning. Ben had left me in his office while I had stood there like a statue. I was appreciative that he had thought ahead and knew I would head into the library. It was well-known that this room was my haven, my comfort zone. To be surrounded by books was one of my dreams, and I loved that this one had come true.

I unfolded the letter and started to read it.

Anne,

I apologize for leaving. You have been nothing but kind since I arrived, even though I turned up unannounced. I'm starting to realize how much you don't know about our family, too, and I feel bad for coming into your life like this. When I received your email, I looked you up before coming and saw in a newspaper article that you had inherited the Wilkens fortune. I thought you were a gold digger and that you were reaching out to see what else you could gain from the Wilkens's fortune.

Sebastian's comment that Sir Anthony was obsessive to have carved the whole house in plum blossoms struck me deep down, and I've begun to wonder if I might be walking in my baba's footsteps, especially as Grace says I have an artistic madness in me.

The last day I was here, I realized you were worried about me. I am not the best at managing my emotions and the entries in the journals have taken a toll on my mindset. I don't know what to think about my mama and baba. I'm also not sure what a relationship with you and your mother would look like. I called my wife tonight and she said that it was time for me to come home. I have taken the journals home with me. I very much wanted to read all of them here, but I just could not do that in this mansion. There are too many bad memories following me around.

I promise I will take very good care of the journals. No harm will come to them and they will be returned to you soon. In exchange, I leave you this plum blossom. It was given to me by Mary when I was very young and it is one of my most prized possessions, so please know that it means as much to me as these journals do to you.

I hope you can forgive me. I promise I will send the journals back as soon as I am done reading them.

Harrison Lin

I paced in the library, cycling between feeling sorry for myself and being angry at Harrison. What was I supposed to do? Just let him take the journals and trust him to give them back to me in the same condition as they left? Or trust him to send them back at all?

"You're going to make a path in the rug if you keep walking in circles like that," Sebastian said, coming into the library.

"And so what if I do?" I huffed back. I stared up at him and I could tell that he sensed something was wrong because he stopped dead in his tracks, raising his hands up as if to protect himself. Well, he better, because I had so much anger that needed to come out and he was in my line of sight.

"Just saying, not criticizing," he said quickly. "What's wrong?"

I should really explain why before I just start yelling. I tried taking deep breaths. There was always a reasonable explanation, right? "You caught me by surprise," I finally said.

"Want to tell me what's going on? One minute you were next to me and in the next, I'm finding you down here pacing like a lion in a cage."

"Harrison left—he just up and left! And he took Ah Po's journals with him. He took them, Sebastian! He didn't even ask me! I would have let him borrow them too," I said, halting my crazed pacing and feeling tears roll down my cheeks.

Sebastian's eyes widened. "He left? And he took Rose's journals with him?"

"Look for yourself," I said sharply, holding out Harrison's letter.

I watched as Sebastian read the letter once, then twice, and then as his eyes glazed over as everything slowly sunk in.

"This is a bunch of bull!" he exclaimed. "Who would just take the journals? Let's go check the trunk. Maybe it's a bluff for something else."

"How much more straightforward could Harrison be?" I cried.

Sebastian didn't answer me, instead taking my arm and

leading me out of the library. We went up the stairs and past my bedroom.

I paused, pulling Sebastian back toward my room. "Where are you going? The journals are in the trunk in my closet."

"No, they're not. I moved the trunk with Ben's help to Harrison's room yesterday . . ." Then, as if he'd realized what he'd just said, Sebastian stopped walking and turned to look at me. "There's no way it's related, Anne. I didn't know he would take the journals. He had asked me if it'd be possible to have the trunk moved to his room, because he felt bad about going in and out of yours all the time. His request made sense at the time."

I was seething. How could I not have known that? "Why didn't you tell me or at least ask first?"

He shrugged. "It was a reasonable request. I didn't think you'd want him in your room when you're not there."

"You didn't think?" I repeated, feeling the tears starting to stream down my cheeks. My one connection to Ah Po was gone, and I had no idea if I'd ever see the journals again.

"Now, Anne, don't turn my words around on me."

I could see Sebastian was starting to get upset but I couldn't calm down anymore.

He tried again. "Anne, I'm sorry he left. Harrison definitely did not mention that he was leaving, or that he would take the journals. I'm sorry," Sebastian said again, coming over to me.

But I didn't want him to touch me. I backed away a step. This wasn't right. How could someone come in, say they were my uncle, and then take away something that special without asking first?

Sebastian paused in front of me. "Let me ask you something, Anne."

"What?" I snapped.

"Would you have let Harrison borrow them if he had asked you first?"

I wanted to tell Sebastian I would have. I know I would have. But the more the silence dragged out and the words didn't come, the more I started to doubt myself. Those were special, private journals that were given to me specifically. If Anthony had the money and time to keep tabs on me, he was bound to have kept tabs on his own son, right? Why wouldn't the journals have gone to Harrison instead?

Maybe I wouldn't have let him borrow them unless he stayed here to read them, but my rational brain had come and gone. I wasn't proud of the next words out of my mouth, but I couldn't stop myself—my anger had reached a new high.

"No, I probably wouldn't have, but you shouldn't have taken the journals from my room without asking me first. They're my one connection to my Ah Po."

"I thought I was doing you a favor by protecting your privacy."

I didn't even care that the staff could hear us yelling at each other in the middle of the hallway. I couldn't think straight anymore. I had lost something too precious.

Sebastian's voice dropped low and he started talking very slowly, as if it was taking all his strength to remain in control. "Yes, I should have asked you. I'm sorry I didn't. And if you choose to believe me, I do understand how important those journals are to you, Anne. If you remember, I was there when you first started reading them. But Anne—"

"I don't think you understand," I cut in. I didn't want him to keep talking. He was trying to rationalize what had happened and all I wanted to do was figure out a way to get the journals back. But Sebastian cut me off before I could continue.

"They're not your journals," he said. Sebastian was trying

to take deep breaths, but I could tell that he was on edge too. "I've wanted to say this for a while now. You're way too attached to those journals, Anne. Your Ah Po wrote them when she was a teenager. They sat in this house for decades, gathering dust. You were tricked into finding them and now you're obsessed. Harrison has as much right to them as you do. It's his own mother, Anne."

"Now you're defending him!" I cried. "And what about all the inheritance nonsense from Isabella? About me not being the proper owner? You always stood up for me, saying I was the legal owner because the will said so. Therefore, everything in this house belongs to me—including the journals."

Sebastian's expression went from anger to sadness in a split second. I wanted to take back what I'd said. I really did, but the words were out and even I could hear how obsessive they sounded.

Sebastian said slowly, "This isn't you—being petty. Where's the Anne who cares about others and doesn't put a lot of meaning into physical things?" He sighed, then added, "I'm going to go pack and let you brew on this."

And with that, he left me in the hallway by myself, with my thoughts and a whole basketful of embarrassment that began to seep in now that I didn't have anyone to yell at anymore.

CHAPTER 8

THE NEXT FEW DAYS WERE UNEVENTFUL. I SAID goodbye to Sebastian, who was still miffed at me for being petty. I couldn't blame him for that. Victoria's parents took her on an impromptu trip to New York City, and Mom was still elbow deep in preparing for her art show.

I, on the other hand, lounged around, bored as ever. My travel article was creeping along at a snail's pace. At this rate, I wouldn't be surprised if my sponsor dropped me. The pity party I was throwing for myself knew no bounds.

My thoughts often wandered to Mary, and I imagined her sitting at home, wringing her fingers and wondering where Harrison was all these years.

My head was spinning in circles and I had no idea what to do. So, I called the one person who was already doing some-thing to help my cause. As the phone rang, I wondered if he had found anything new.

"Nick here. How can I help you?"

"Nick, this is Anne."

"Anne dear, how good to hear from you! I was just going to call you later today, but now is good!"

He sure shouted a lot. In contrast, I said somberly, "I wanted to see if you had found anything new on my uncle."

"I sure have—I found out his address."

"You did? That was fast."

"I'm good at what I do."

I could hear the pride in his voice and I imagined that he was giving himself a pat on the back. "Well, where is he?"

"He lives in Oakland. I have to warn you, though, that it's not a very posh neighborhood. There was no place to park, homeless people were around every corner, there were many cars on the street, and the house has seen better days."

"Wait, you've been there?"

"Well, yes, I had to go and verify his address before I told you. What did you think? That I just take the word of whomever gives me an address and I just pass it along to the client without checking if the information is legit?"

"I guess . . ."

"I don't guess, I know. I take offense to what you assumed. Look, I have to go, I'll text you the address shortly."

He hung up before I could register what had just happened. Nick could definitely do his job. That was fast work, yes, but that conversation was just weird.

"Anne, I'm sorry to bother you."

At those words, I turned to see Ben standing at the door hesitantly. I waved my hand at him. "Come in. Come in."

"You have a package that has just arrived," he said, handing me a parchment-wrapped box about the size of an A1 paper. It was about five inches tall but not very heavy, and when I shook it, there was no sound.

I tore the package open to reveal a beautiful wooden box that looked like it had seen better days. It had a few paint chips and a missing box foot, but it was decorated with beautiful carvings and was mostly still lacquered. Underneath the box was a journal. It had a blue cover and was thread bound. The paper was thin and gridded and Chinese covered every inch of every sheet. Drawings were thrown in here and there. A note, nestled just in front of the first page, fluttered to the ground, and I bent to pick it up. It looked like it had been recently penned. I focused on the words.

Anne,

After much persuasion on Grace's part, I'm loaning you my journal. It covers the period when I ran away, and I hope this will answer some of the questions you might have.

My mama's journals are fascinating. You've read Mary's journals, and now I hope you can partake in some of mine. It's an interesting way to learn about your family history. I think it is a privilege to learn things through words when the people themselves are too shy to come out and say what they would like to say. There have been too many years of silence on the subject that it makes our history impossible to discuss without bringing up a lot of old feelings. I implore you to read this journal first to determine if you want to get to know me further. I say this because I am not the type of person most people want to meet. I express myself better through paintings, therefore, the journal is not very long as I don't have a lot of words, and it was written from the ramblings of a thirteen-year-old boy.

Please know that I am taking good care of Mama's journals. Do not worry.

I know I was not the best house guest after imposing myself on you by surprise. Again, I am sorry I left in such haste.

Enjoy,

Harrison

PS. The box is for the glass plum blossom. It's the original box it came in. I thought you would like to keep it safe.

. . .

"That was nice of him to give you those."

"Huh?" I looked up to see Ben was watching me.

His face was slowly turning a bright red. "I'm sorry Miss. I couldn't help myself. I'll leave now."

"Oh, Ben, it's okay. I'm taken by surprise too. And it's nice that I'm not the only one who saw this letter."

"Yes." Right then the phone rang, and Ben hightailed it out of the room before I could say another word. He came back not five minutes later and handed me a slip of paper with a series of numbers on it that I didn't recognize.

"You have a message from a woman called Lauren," he said. "She said she's related to Isabella. This is her number. I told her you were busy and that you'd call her back later."

"A relative? Not another person who wants the house?" *Whoops, did I say that out loud?*

"I don't know," Ben replied, and then he blushed.

"Okay, thanks Ben."

He seemed to hesitate. "Is there anything you would like me to do at this time?"

"No, take the day off if you'd like."

He inclined his head. "Thank you, Miss. I mean, Anne."

I couldn't help laughing. "We're all still getting used to this, aren't we? And thanks, Ben."

I looked at the number in my hand again before finally digging out my cell phone and dialing it. What's the worst that could happen? *Well, it could be Isabella masquerading as a cousin so that she could come at me from another angle.* I shook my head at the thought. I'd inherited all of this legally; I needed to stop being so paranoid.

Besides, I had big plans for the funds I'd inherited. It was an opportunity to support one of the places I loved the most —the Portland Zoo. We'd been on important calls lately as I wanted to build a foundation so that they would always have enough money to keep the zoo running.

Mom was my second focus. She wouldn't let me pay for anything, so I planned to secretly buy some of her paintings at her upcoming art show and surprise her by displaying them in the mansion. I hadn't really thought this one through. There was a high possibility that she would be mad at me, but I figured I still had time to come up with a plausible reason. The last time I'd talked to Mom, she was still busy painting and hadn't set a date for the show yet.

The phone was still ringing, and I was secretly hoping someone would pick up because I didn't know if I would have the nerve to call again or even leave a message. After what had happened with Harrison, I didn't need another family reunion for a while.

"Hello?" a voice said. It definitely was not Isabella; this voice was sweet and innocent.

"Hi. Is . . ." I looked at the name under the phone number and added, "Lauren there?"

"This is her. Oh! Are you Anne?"

"Yes."

"I'm so excited to meet you! I hoped you would call back. You're so on top of things—I think I only just left my number not more than ten minutes ago. I hope you don't find this intrusive. I know how Isabella can be, and I can only imagine what image you have of our family, but we're not all like her. She really is a nice person deep down. I wish she would show more people that side of her, though. She's so supportive when anyone in the family needs help. I don't know what I would do without her sometimes.

"We've known each other our whole lives. Our grandmothers are sisters, you see—Anthony's sisters, the one you inherited everything from. Personally, I think it's great to have you in the family. I never did like the house, and I don't know what I would do with all that money. It would just scare me. More money, more problems, right? I believe that wholeheartedly because I think we should all be more frugal.

"My mother is the best. She inherited a bunch of money from Anthony, and she's divided it up amongst all her children, evenly too. There's so much trust in our family. It's how we were raised—to live on what we have. I truly believe that, you know. But that's why I say what I say about Isabella. She's so sweet, she really is, but it's the way she was raised. Her grandmother is so conniving. Now, don't go telling anyone I said that, but between you and me, I feel bad for Isabella because she is such a caring person.

"Sebastian was all wrong for her. I have no idea why she hung out with him for so long, but she tells me that he's with you now. I bet you two are great together. I personally think she should be with Nick, but oops, I've said too much. That's me—I love to talk! Sorry, I can't help it. I think I get that from my grandmother. People say I'm just like her. I love her, you know? It makes me so happy to hear that I'm just like her."

This was more information about the family than I had ever heard before. Minus the fact that I had no idea who this person was, I was soaking up all the information she was telling me—which was quite a lot. I had never met a person who could talk so much at once before. And did she just say Nick? I wondered if it was the same Nick that I'd hired to find Harrison's address. Come to think of it, Isabella did recommend him to me. I wondered if they'd ever dated. But then, no, I was overthinking this, it might not be the same person.

I focused on what Lauren was saying, thinking that she made the family sound so normal.

"I'm so sorry, there I go again," Lauren was saying now in a rush. "Rambling on when I haven't properly introduced myself. As you know, my name is Lauren, and my mother is

Margaret. She's the second oldest of five kids, and her mother is Catherine Wilkens, one of Anthony's sisters."

I thought back to the hearing of Anthony's will, and the memory of Catherine made me smile. She had been colorful and full of life and very down-to-earth. Her family had seemed the same. How she could be related to Geraldine's family proved how families were made up of all kinds of people. Her granddaughter sounded just like her and that made me so relieved, as so far, I didn't feel as though I was going to be attacked or blindsided by Lauren or Catherine.

"Would you be free to have a drink with me sometime?" Lauren suddenly asked. "Anne, are you still there?"

"Yeah. I mean yes, I'm still here."

"Can we grab a drink sometime?" Lauren said again. "I'd like to ask you something, but I think it more appropriate to ask in person. Plus, I'd like to meet you."

"That would be nice. I'd love that." . . . *Would I, though?*

"Great! Would tomorrow do? I happen to be in Portland, and I know of a wonderful brunch spot in the Pearl District. It's divine, you'll love it. How's eleven o'clock? I'm not an early riser. Would that work for you?"

"Yes," I said before she could keep going.

"Great! I'll send you the name then and I'll see you tomorrow. Ciao!" And with that, she hung up.

I felt like I had just been hurled back into high school and was required to navigate the land of gossip. *What had I just agreed to?*

CHAPTER 9

ISABELLA

"Why did you give her the address?" I shouted at Nick. "What kind of doofus gives away our secret before we need to?"

"I didn't think we needed to keep it a secret anymore. I already visited Harrison's family and they weren't receptive to my questions. I got a vase thrown at me!"

"Don't worry, there are other means to get them to change their mind. You talked to his wife, Grace, right?"

"Yes, and her son was there too. He has quite an arm."

"It's Harrison we need to talk to, remember. He's the only one who can legally sign over his ownership of the property in Taiwan. He's also the only one that can persuade Anne to let go of her claim too."

"Right. I just got the address for his shop so I'll go back and pay him a visit."

"Good. Just don't give that address to Anne. She can find out where it is in her own sweet time."

CHAPTER 10

ANNE

How had I never been to this place? The line to the boulangerie was out the door, and every single table inside and outside was full. The French bakery, St. Honore, sat on the corner of Thurman Street and Twenty-third Place. I moved aside as a sea of people left and an equally large group of new customers took their place. There was every kind of pastry in front of me, calling for me to try all of them.

I saw a lot of customers carrying the same bags that were lined up along the front of the counter and I wondered what was in them. Then I saw my favorite bakery item—an almond croissant. I couldn't go wrong there, and besides, I hadn't had one in a long time. Lauren also hadn't arrived yet, so I had time to people watch and convince myself that I didn't need anything else to eat.

In the end, though, I bought the almond croissant, a croque monsieur, and a bag of what I learned to be croquets, which were so good that I was already halfway through the bag when an auburn-haired woman in form-fitting jeans and a silk, sleeveless top entered the room and started looking around. She looked to be about my age. Her eyes caught mine and I knew instantly that this was Lauren. I waved to her and a huge smile spread across her face. She had a radiance to her that parted the sea of people in front of her.

"Hi, Anne! So lovely to meet you. I've been so curious about you! It's amazing the type of people who come into your life, isn't it? I never thought I would be friends with a commoner. But you aren't anymore, are you? Wow—I love your shirt! Did you make that yourself? I heard your grandmother was the Wilkens's seamstress."

Big doe eyes looked back at me and I couldn't be mad at her. She radiated happiness and didn't appear to have any side meaning to her words. She made me feel happy and I didn't take offense as I replied, "No, I'm not a commoner anymore, and no, I didn't make this shirt. I bought it from Banana."

"Oh, I'm so sorry. Stephen keeps telling me that I can't use certain words when talking with people outside of my circle. He's opened me up to so much more than the life I knew. I love him so much. I can't wait for the two of you to meet! You'll love him. Oh, but I digress. Can I have some of that croque monsieur? I'm starving, and I'm too excited to go back in line now that I've met you."

"Are you sure? The line seems to be moving pretty fast."

"I'm sure," she said, nodding eagerly.

I watched as she devoured my entire croque monsieur, and I moved my almond croissant closer toward me in case she had eyes on that too.

"Oh, but where was I?" she asked as she dabbed at her mouth with a napkin. "I've been so rude. I'm keeping you in suspense."

"It's fine, I'm okay. Why don't you finish?" It was fascinating to watch her. She was like a well-bred peacock who graced you with their presence and you found yourself unable to look away.

"I'm good now, and thank you, I was so hungry. So, I wanted to meet you because I want to ask your permission about something. Isabella gave me this idea by the way. I love her and I look up to her. We grew up together, you see. I didn't live far from her, but I digress again—I do that, you know."

Yes, I had noticed.

"I wanted to ask you if I could hold my bachelorette party at the Hawaii house," she continued. "Of course, you would be invited. I couldn't imagine you not being there anyway. Please say yes. It would give you an excuse to go and see the property. It is such a nice place—the perfect location. You'll love it. And my maid of honor has grand ideas for everyone. Oh, please say yes."

How could I say no? She was the sweetest, nicest, most vibrant person I had ever met. Not even close to what Isabella was. How could the two of them be friends or even related? Then again, I loved Jack, and he was related to Lauren too. *I wonder how he is?*

After receiving my agreement, for the next thirty minutes, Lauren talked about the invitations she was going to get made. She had a friend, who was designing the invitation. Then, she would bring the design to the best printing press in Portland, a shop called Ander's Printing where they did letter pressing. These invitations were going to be top-of-the-line. By the end of the conversation, I was wondering if this was all a dream. Even talking art with Mom was nowhere as vibrant.

A thought came into my mind that art must run in the family. Anthony had been into carving and drawing; Isabella, interior decorating; and Lauren loved every detail that went into party planning. By the end of brunch, I really liked Lauren, and I felt guilty that I had thought she would be calculating like Isabella.

It was time to call Mom. I had held off long enough. I stared at my phone while it rang on speaker and thought about what I would say.

She picked up right when I thought her voicemail would kick in. "Anne, I can't really talk right now. I'm in the middle of the final coat of paint on this six by six. It's gorgeous. I can't wait for you to see it, but I have to get it done; Derek's coming by tonight to see my progress."

I just threw it out there. "Mom, Harrison stopped by."

"And I hope he'll— Wait, what did you say?"

"Harrison stopped by to say hi."

For a moment, there was silence. Then she said, "Just out of the blue?"

"Yes."

"Can I talk to him?"

"Not really. He left after staying a couple of days here. He's a bit odd; very quiet and reserved. He told me that Grace wanted him to come here and get some answers about his family because she was tired of him moping around. We started getting to know each other on the first day he was here, but then something spooked him and he left the next morning. And he also took Ah Po's journals, Mom!"

"Well, they are his mom's journals."

"Mom! They belong to me! He never asked if he could borrow them."

"Well, that is rude but I'm sure there's a reasonable explanation. Did he leave a phone number or address?"

"No, it's infuriating. I hired the private detective Isabella referred me to."

"Good for you. I know you and Isabella don't get along, but now's not the time to dwell on that. Did the private detective find anything?"

"He found an address in Oakland and said it was in a not very nice neighborhood. I was thinking of visiting, but I just had something else come up that's very strange."

"What's that?"

"Shoot, I forgot—you have your painting to finish."

"Anne Huang! You better spill or I'm going to have to come over there to ask you in person, and you know I'll be even madder then."

"Okay, okay," I rushed out. "The other news is that Isabella recommended that Lauren, her cousin, should hold her bachelorette party at the house in Hawaii. Apparently it used to be the place where the Wilkens family had big get-togethers, so she has a lot of fond memories there. She's invited me to go, too, and is even asking me for my opinion on things."

"That's fantastic!"

"You don't think it's weird that Isabella is being nice all of a sudden? Offering the services of her detective and then putting her cousin in touch with me?"

"That is one way to see it, but you could also just see it as her turning over a new leaf."

"I highly doubt that."

"How was this Lauren person? Was she like Isabella?"

"No, she was the complete opposite!"

"See, there you go. I'm sure she's a perfectly good person. When is the party?"

"It's this weekend."

"Ah, I see what the real problem is here. You can't go to the party *and* visit Harrison to persuade him to give you back the journals."

I sighed. "You understand me so well."

"Why don't we do this then," my mom suggested. "I'm in need of a vacation and I would like to get to know my half brother. Why don't I go visit him?"

"Yeah? You'd be okay going? I know you've got all these paintings to finish . . ."

"It'll be fine. With this last one I'm doing, Derek will be ecstatic. Plus, he's probably going to tell me that the show had to get pushed out again."

"What do you mean it had to get pushed out again?"

"Oh, well, the owners of the gallery keep receiving work from other important artists, so they keep pushing the date of my show out."

"Mom, that's not fair!" I exclaimed.

"It's really not important right now, Anne. Really. Look, I have to go. Derek will be here soon, and I need to finish this painting. Talk to you soon. I love you, Anne."

"Love you too, Mom."

CHAPTER 11

"What if she's playing a trick?" I asked Sebastian. "As my lawyer, I need an answer."

I'd called him at the crack of dawn as I'd been unable to sleep last night with all the thoughts running through my head.

"As your lawyer and as your boyfriend, I think you are overthinking things and that you should let your boyfriend go back to bed. I worked until five in the morning and you literally woke me up an hour after I went to bed."

"Oh, I'm so sorry. Yes, go back to sleep."

He sighed, then said softly, "Anne, I really don't think you have anything to worry about. I've met Lauren before, and she really is the person you met yesterday: nice, bubbly, talkative, and she means well—every quality you just described to me. I think this will be great for you. You'll meet other family members besides Isabella and her family. There really are a lot of nice people in the Wilkens family."

"You're right. I just needed you to say it out loud."

"Well, case closed. I'm going back to bed. Goodnight, I love you."

"I love you too."

"And by the way, if you help Lauren with the bachelorette party and travel to Hawaii, this might get your mind off Harrison while also scratching your itch for travel."

"You have a point there."

I hung up the phone and slipped back under the covers and tried to sleep, but my brain wouldn't shut down. I was nervous about this trip to Hawaii. How many people would be going? Would they all be from the family? It was for her wedding, so there was bound to be friends there. Were they all rich? I was going to stand out like a sore thumb. I bet all of them would be white too. Just the thought of being there was making me anxious. These thoughts kept running through my head over and over again that in the end, I did the unthinkable.

I went out to the garden, found the gardener, and told him I needed something to do with my hands, something that was physical enough that would take my mind off things for a while. I could see he wanted to laugh, but he could tell I was serious and the next thing I knew, I was digging up old plants, mixing fertilizer into the soil, and planting new seeds for the garden. He had me weeding, which I had never done before, and trimming the bushes. I worked on those plants from early morning through to lunchtime. By that point, I was sweating, had drank about a gallon of water, and I felt great. *So, this is how people feel when they exercise . . . . Hmm, I could keep doing this.*

"I never thought I'd see this!" a voice crowed.

I jerked my head up at the familiar voice. "Victoria!" I ran over and enclosed her in a tight hug. "How was your trip?"

"My parents are good and they've seen I'm alive. They've met Paul, too, and they love him so I'm super happy. Now, on to you. What is this about a party in Hawaii? I'm invited, right?"

My mouth dropped open. "You know about it already?"

"Sebastian called me this morning and said I should probably pay you a visit. So, here I am."

My heart warmed. "You two are so good to me."

"You better believe it. Now, I deserve some cake. Let's go raid the kitchen."

Despite myself, I smiled. "But you just got here! Why don't you help me prune some bushes?"

"You're kidding, right?"

I looked at her, then looked at the pruning tool in my hand, then back at her, and we both started laughing. "Let me just finish this bush then, and I promise we can go in and see what there is to eat next."

"Miss, I can take it from here," said the gardener, suddenly stepping up beside me. I paused when I saw his face. His expression looked like one of pain. I stepped back and looked at the pruning I had done. The bushes were going down at a slight angle about five feet away. I had been so focused on each section I was working on that I hadn't paid attention to the shape of the whole bush.

"Sorry! Yes, it's probably best you have these back. Here you go," I said, handing him back the pruners.

"It's not for everyone, Miss."

"It's Anne. You can call me Anne."

"I prefer Miss," he said very matter-of-factly.

"Okay." *I didn't like it, but I wasn't going to start an argument. What if he quit? Then all my bushes would be crooked.*

"I can see your brain working against you," Victoria said, hooking an arm through mine and dragging me from the garden before I could do any more damage.

"So, what's up with this party?" Victoria asked with a mouthful of cake. Chocolate cake to be exact, with a scrumptious raspberry filling. I was amazed most of it was making it into her mouth as she couldn't inhale it fast enough.

"I'm not sure as she only asked me yesterday. She's working on the invitations right now."

"What is she like?"

"She's super nice. Lauren is her name and she's very talkative. I can't even remember saying anything. She just went on and on, and apparently she loves Isabella. They grew up together and she looks up to her."

At this, Victoria stopped eating and looked at me with a raised eyebrow.

"I don't know either," I said quickly. "I couldn't make heads or tails of it. But I wasn't going to say anything then. I don't even know the woman."

Victoria put down her fork before saying, "I don't think a close friend—especially a family member of Isabella's—can be trusted."

Some of the worries from the past few months started giving off little sparks of anxiety in my brain. Trust was a big issue between me and Isabella. It was not something to be taken lightly and yet, Lauren seemed genuine. She didn't seem like she had a mean bone in her body. How could someone like her be friends with Isabella?

A voice interrupted my thoughts. "There you are—eating up my cake! Not even asking me if I planned on using it for something else."

"Oh no, Cook, we're sorry," I said contritely while Victoria and I scrambled to put the cake back in its container. "I didn't think to ask. I just thought your cake was always up for grabs."

"That's what you young ones always think, but don't

worry, that cake is for you to eat. I always make sure there's one here for you," Cook said, smiling at her inside joke.

I sat down with a thud. The rush of apprehension mixed with the anxiety of the Hawaii trip made me want to sit there and not do anything for a while. The cake couldn't even entice me anymore.

Victoria always knew how to get me out of my funk, though. "Let's go to a spa," she suggested. "We haven't been to one in a while and I've been craving to go again. Your treat."

A nice massage sounded like the perfect way to relax. "I would love that. Let's go."

Cannery Pier Hotel and Spa was a place where Victoria and I went to after skipping school once. We'd saved up enough money to spend the whole day getting pampered. To this day, it is still our little secret and we have no idea how our parents never found out. The funny thing is that there were plenty of great spas in Portland that were all within five minutes, but instead, we chose to drive the two hours to Astoria. The place held a certain meaning and charm that called us to it.

"We should do this more often," Victoria said, her voice muffled under a wet, warm towel.

"Yeah." Coming here might not have been the best idea. Despite the pampering and the calm atmosphere, I was still tense. My mind was reeling. Every thought that I had left back in Portland currently had free range to crowd every corner of my brain.

Someone came in and started unwrapping the cloth. Maybe getting into the sauna would do me some good—I could sweat out my problems.

We wrapped ourselves in our robes and headed for the saunas that were next to the hot tubs. I hadn't been in a sauna since we sneaked out in high school and I was very much looking forward to it. While we walked, Victoria told me about what we should do when we were in Hawaii. Aside from swimming in the ocean, she wanted to go snorkeling, ziplining, and swimming with the dolphins. I heard about half of what she was saying because someone had come up beside me. At first, I thought the hallway was just getting crowded, but then I realized that this person was actually directing her words at me.

I put a hand to my chest. "I'm sorry, I didn't realize you were talking to me."

"No problem, Miss. I came to tell you that there is someone waiting for you in the lobby. She's been here for the last thirty minutes. I told her you were busy, but she insists on waiting for you. I thought I would just come back and ask if you wanted to see her."

"Who is it?" Victoria asked.

"She said her name is Lauren. I think her boyfriend or husband dropped her off. They said they were in Astoria sight-seeing. Like I said, it's not urgent, but she's been waiting so I thought I would let you know."

"Thank you—" I looked down at her nametag and added, "Barbara. I appreciate you telling me."

While Barbara walked away, I could feel Victoria bristling beside me. "How does she know you are here? And why would she be in Astoria sight-seeing? Do you think she's a Goonie's fan?"

"I have no idea. She didn't give off that vibe. Would you like to meet her?"

"Would I? I thought you'd never ask." And just like that, Victoria headed straight to the dressing room to change. I walked a bit slower behind her, wondering what Lauren could possibly want.

CHAPTER 12

"She's so polished. She reminds me of a nicer Isabella," Victoria whispered into my ear as we peeked behind the door that led to the waiting room.

"That's her pretty much in a nutshell. But wait till you talk to her. She's totally different."

"Are we going to go out and say hi to her? Or are we just going to stand here and spy on her until one of us leaves?" Victoria asked from behind me.

I had frozen in place. I just wanted to turn back and pretend Lauren wasn't here.

"What are you scared of?" Victoria pressed. "You said so yourself that she's nice."

"She's best friends with Isabella, that's why; and my brain is telling me to be cautious because there could be an ulterior motive behind this whole Hawaii thing. I keep picturing Isabella popping up out of nowhere and scaring the bejeezus out of me."

"Valid point. But—"

"But I don't feel that from her, I know," I said, cutting Victoria off. "Lauren seems genuinely fond of Isabella and she thinks the world of her. She also seems like the type of person I would like."

"More than me?"

I turned to look at Victoria with a raised eyebrow. "Really? Are you jealous already?"

"Just curious," she said, shrugging her shoulders. "Go talk to her." Victoria shoved me in the back and I spluttered as I was pushed out into the waiting room.

Lauren's eyes lit up at the sight of me. "Anne! I'm so glad you came to Astoria today! You've made Stephen so happy. I stopped by your house and Ben said you had gone out. He didn't know where you were, so I had him call your chauffeur and he said you had gone to this spa in Astoria. You do know there are far better spas in Portland, right? I'll have to take you some time. You must not know about them, but this place is not half bad. The people here have been very professional and it looks clean. But you've made Stephen—who you'll have to meet by the way—so happy! He has been wanting to bring me here for the longest time because of his obsession with *The Goonies*. Have you seen the movie? Apparently, the movie was filmed here so he's going to take me around to see everything, but I told him I had to come and see you first. Business first and fun later, right? The reason why I've come is because I have something I want to show you and I'd like your approval."

I could feel Victoria's skeptical gaze about the fact that Lauren needed approval from me, but I didn't care. I was thinking how kind that was of her to ask me.

Lauren pulled out a cream-colored envelope from her purse and placed it into my hands. It felt like silk in my fingers. How could something so mundane be so luxurious?

"Open it!" Lauren squealed. "I can't wait for you to see it."

"Is this . . . ?"

"Yes! Sorry, I didn't mean to squeal so loudly but I'm so excited. Anders Printing finished making the invite exactly how I wanted it, and I had them rush a sample."

"But I just talked to you yesterday. They really got it done in a day?"

"Oh, silly! I started this a month ago. Isabella said you wouldn't say no, and I trust her to the fullest. Besides, if you did say no, I would still have had the sample made. I would just need to adjust the venue for the final. Better to be prepared, don't you think? Well, open it. I really want you to see it."

"Yeah, open it. I want to see it too," Victoria said, coming up behind me.

I jumped. "You scared me," I said to Victoria. She had initially stood off to the side, but her curiosity had obviously gotten the better of her.

"I couldn't stand back any longer," she said. "I want to see! Come on now, open it."

Lauren looked intrigued at Victoria's presence. "I'm Lauren," she said, sticking out her hand to Victoria.

"I'm Victoria, Anne's best friend."

"Oh, it's so good to finally meet you! Isabella has said so much about you. What a treat that you're both here. It was such a good decision to come to Astoria—I got to see both of you!" She clapped her hands together in excitement. "Come on, I want to take both of you to lunch. My treat. You two pick where given you know this town better than me. Where is the best place to eat around here? Oh, but wait, I'm getting sidetracked. I love to eat, you see. You'll learn that about me soon enough. I could talk about food all day long, but I should stop talking about food and you should open the envelope. I'm so excited about it!" She started jumping up and down.

But I hesitated, looking around. "Isn't Stephen here with you?"

"Oh, he dropped me off and went to see one of his friends. He said he'll pick me up when I'm ready so there's no hurry."

I looked over at Victoria, who had a raised eyebrow and half of a smile on her face. Yup, that was about the impression that I'd thought Lauren would make on her.

"What has Isabella said about me?" Victoria asked.

"You know, I think I should open this invitation," I said suddenly. Now was not the time to go into anything Isabella related. Luckily, Victoria was happy to shelve her question and both girls calmed down and watched me pull out the invitation. It was breathtaking.

"It's a letterpress," Lauren explained. "I really wanted something old." She laced her fingers together in anticipation.

"Wow," Victoria and I both said at the same time. "It's very pretty."

I was impressed by the entire invitation and had never received anything so expensive-looking before. It was on thick cotton-like paper with indentions that were part of the design and lettering, and I now understood what she meant by a letter-pressed invitation. Come to think of it, I remembered Mom dabbling in this kind of thing when I was younger. It had flowers in some light colors and the appropriate introductory note on the front.

After a moment, I realized that there was still something in the envelope. It felt quite heavy. I tipped the item out of the envelope and looked in awe at what landed in my hand. It was a glass lapel pin about an inch in diameter.

"Do you like it?" Lauren was so close to me now that I had to take half a step back so that she wasn't breathing on me.

"What is it?" I asked.

"It's a plum blossom, silly."

"I know. I mean . . ."

"Why is it in the invitation?"

"Yes," I said, raising my eyes to look up at her. Her face glowed with happiness, and I couldn't help but think she really would be the prettiest bride I'd ever seen.

"Grandma Catherine loved her brother, Anthony," she said, a somberness clouding her features. "She adored him. She would always tell us stories of when they were small and the messes they'd get into. He always looked out for her even though they couldn't be more different."

She swallowed, then looked at me directly. "You're not blind, Anne. You would have seen that my grandmother is colorful and flamboyant. She didn't care what others thought. On the other hand, Anthony was what my mother likes to call chiseled and practical. He was the oldest of them all and I guess he had the most responsibility. When Anthony passed, my grandmother was heartbroken. It was like she had lost one of her best friends.

"Grandma Catherine turned seventy-eight last year. She and Anthony were planning a big birthday party for her at the house in Hawaii. Everyone was invited. All her siblings, their kids, the grandkids, and her friends. Don't ask me how everyone was going to fit, but it's a big house and they've held big parties there before so I have no doubt that they would have fit everyone. But, well, with Anthony's passing the birthday party never happened."

She must have seen our eyes grow big at the mention that everyone was invited. I was getting more and more curious about this house that I owned.

"I've invited my grandmother to my bachelorette party, you know. Isabella thinks I'm crazy. She's never been too fond of Grandmother, but then again, I've never been too fond of hers."

At this, she started laughing like this was some sort of inside joke between her and Isabella. This whole family dynamic was so odd. I had no idea what to make of it.

"Anyways," Lauren continued, "I wanted something that everyone could keep to commemorate Great Uncle Anthony since his passing. I also wanted to give something to Grandmother that would remind her of him. I heard the house in Hawaii is covered in carvings of plum blossoms, much like the house you're living in now. I can't wait to see it; I've always loved art."

Some of her chirpiness had come back at the mention of the party and I was glad to see it. I hadn't realized that it would hurt me to see someone who was so happy all the time suddenly become somber. I wanted to fix her sadness but I had no idea how.

"Well, I think it's a really nice gesture. Why the plum blossom, though, besides that it was something Anthony liked? I'm sure there were other things that were a common link between the two of them."

"Oh, it's the one thing that Grandma Catherine always wore on the collar of her jacket. She adored it. Isabella told me once that she wore it to make Great Aunt Geraldine mad, but I never did get the whole story behind why. I tried asking Grandma Catherine, but she just laughed and didn't say anything else. I think it's just a story they made up because there's no way Grandma Catherine would do anything nasty like that to upset her family. Although Great Aunt Geraldine does scare me! My mother said it might have had something to do with their seamstress." At this, Lauren's eyes seemed to grow wider right in front of me. "Oh, your grandmother! She was the seamstress, wasn't she? Would you know why this was significant?"

"I have no idea," I blurted out. What was I supposed to say? That the flower was a token of the love held between Anthony and my grandmother? And that the reason why her great aunt Geraldine hated her grandmother wearing the lapel pin was because she thought their love was an abomination?

From what I had learned of Catherine, and the one time I had seen her last year, she was a much more free-spirited person than her sister, Geraldine, and I could totally see her wearing that brooch in order to make Geraldine mad. I couldn't say that to Lauren, though, and burst her happy bubble.

"Well, in any case, I think she'll love it," Lauren exclaimed. "It'll be a bachelorette—slash—birthday party for my grandmother."

"You must really love your grandmother to invite her to a party that's supposed to be all about you," Victoria chimed in from behind me.

"I love her so much!" Lauren squealed. "She took care of me for a long time when I was small. Mother was working on her PhD and had started traveling a lot, and Dad . . . well, Dad worked a lot, too, so Grandma Catherine was my mother till I was about ten. She basically raised me." Her voice had dropped to a whisper and she seemed to be lost in a memory about the past.

"I think the invitation is beautiful and very thoughtful, and I'm looking forward to the party," I said truthfully.

That seemed to snap her out of her thoughts. "I'm so glad you like it!" she exclaimed. "I'll let Anders Printing know that everything's been approved so they can run off the stack, and then I can get them sent out soon. Right, now that's sorted, I'm starving! Why don't we all go to lunch? My treat, remember, but where should we go?"

"Bowpicker!" Victoria and I said at the same time. It

wasn't a restaurant that we had eaten at growing up, but it was one that we always went to now when we came home. I loved it because the food was cooked and served out of a real-life boat.

"Well then, show me the way."

"Um . . . we should go get changed first," I suggested.

Lauren blinked as she took in our robes. She smiled. "Oh, of course. I'll wait here." And with that, our spa day was done.

CHAPTER 13

"I like her," Victoria whispered to me as we walked to Bowpicker together.

It was a good thirty-minute walk, but Lauren didn't seem to mind. She was chatting away on the phone with someone, ooing and aahing about everything as we walked by. She seemed fascinated by the trinkets in the stores, the boats on the piers, and pretty much the whole town in general. Every once in a while the conversation would get heated, but when we glanced over, her demeanor would go back to being cheery.

"You see what I mean now about being conflicted?" I said to Victoria.

"Yes, I do."

"What am I going to do?"

"You're going to help her with the party just like you helped set up the gala last year. Then you're going to attend the party and make her your next best friend."

"You say that like it's the easiest thing for me to do."

"It is! You'll offer and she'll probably say that she already has it all taken care of."

"But what if she doesn't? I don't want to do any of it."

"Come on, party pooper, get some excitement in you! She's actually nice! You should see this as an opportunity to meet some more of the family. People who could tell you more about Anthony's past, and therefore, your grandmother's history."

"Don't be so reasonable."

"Well, I know you, and that is the only way to get through to you."

I gave her a slight punch and walked faster, but she caught up easily enough and enveloped me in a big hug. "Come on, Anne, give this a chance. You know Sebastian would want this for you."

"Okay. Fine," I said a bit too loudly because it got Lauren's attention.

"Oh! I have to go," she was saying on the phone. "Yes, I'll talk to you later. Yes, I got it. I said I got it!" She hung up and turned her attention to us. "What are you guys talking about?"

"Oh, nothing really, just what we should order for lunch."

"Mmmm, I can't wait. I've only had fish and chips once, and that was when Father took us to London on a business trip. The chef had made some fish and chips as appetizers at the company party, and I loved it. I've never had a chance to eat them again so I'm really looking forward to it."

"Well, you don't have to wait long because we're here," Victoria said, waving one hand toward the boat that was sitting in front of us.

To say Lauren was shocked would be saying too little, but to give her credit, she recovered fast. "It's so cute! Do we order at the window?"

"Yeah, do you want me to order for you?" I asked her.

"Yes, that would be great. Just get me whatever you're getting."

I ordered for the three of us while Victoria showed Lauren that we would be sitting on plastic benches underneath the neighboring tree. I could see that Lauren was uncomfortable, but she was the epitome of lady-like manners. Part of me felt sorry for her. We loved Bowpicker and came here a lot, but I should have picked a nice sit-down restaurant to take Lauren to as it was her first time to Astoria. And maybe Victoria was right—I shouldn't assume Lauren was like Isabella just because they were related. Lauren was such a happy person. She made everyone around her comfortable. I decided to let my guard down and not rush through lunch.

Thank goodness the food came fast, though, because we were ravenous. The three of us dug in without another word between us.

"That was the best food I've had in a while," Lauren said, wiping her mouth after devouring all four pieces of fish and the fries.

Wow, Lauren had gobbled up her basket like she'd just come out of a famine!

"Best food?" Victoria queried, still working on her last piece of fish. I was too.

"I eat well, don't get me wrong, but I've been on probably eight different diets since last year. I found the perfect wedding dress and it's gorgeous. Problem is, they only had it in one size too small for me. I needed to cut back anyways, so I asked Isabella, and she suggested these diet plans. Some worked, but some just put the pounds right back on. Right now, I'm on the "eat as little as possible" plan. I still have to fit into my dress, but I couldn't resist the fish and chips. They smelled divine and you two said they were the best. I couldn't stop myself. I didn't realize how hungry I was. I'll just have to work off the extra pounds later."

I raised an eyebrow at Victoria, but she wasn't looking at me. Her fish was halfway to her mouth as she stared at

Lauren. I kicked her under the table and she collected herself after giving me a look.

"I'm glad you enjoyed yourself. We could walk to the Oregon Film Museum after this if you want to meet Stephen there. It's one of the spots where they filmed *The Goonies*," I suggested.

"Oh, there's no need for that. Stephen can just pick me up here. I know he wants to be the one to show me the sights. And anyway, that call that I was on earlier was Isabella. She was telling me that she's set up a fitting for my bridal party tonight, so I need to get back to Portland sooner than I thought. The girls booked an evening at a bridal shop to surprise me, and they're going to be bringing champagne and hors-d'oeuvres. I'm so sorry to have to leave you guys, but I'm super excited. Oh—wait! Why don't you two join us? It's six o'clock at Blossom Boutique."

I gave a start at the name of the shop. It had to be a coincidence, nothing more. "I have plans already but thank you for the invite."

"You have plans?" Victoria asked me.

She knew I didn't have plans, but I wasn't going to go and hang out with a bunch of Lauren's friends and family when they were picking out their bridal dresses, especially when Isabella was going to be there too. It was too intimate and scary at the same time.

"Yes, I have plans," I said, giving Victoria a knowing stare. Thank goodness she backed off, but I was surprised by what she said next.

"Lauren, I'd be glad to join you. It sounds like a lot of fun."

Now it was my turn to look at her incredulously. Was she seriously going to ditch me to go to Lauren's bridal party?

"Oh, I'm so happy!" Lauren gushed. "Anne, I wish you could join us, but I totally understand. This was very last minute; I wouldn't expect you to be able to make it. Victoria, you're going to love my friends and family. You've already met Isabella, but there's my mother, Margaret, and my grandmother, Catherine. Oh, you might have met her already, but a couple of my cousins and friends will be there too. I'm so excited. More the merrier, I always say."

On our way back to the car, Victoria accosted me. "I really think you should join me tonight. I think it'll be fun, and you'll meet other members of the Wilkens family."

"No thanks," I said with finality.

"Well, party pooper, I will let you know about all the fun you're missing."

By this time, we were back at the car. But before heading to Portland, we went to see my mom for a bit, because she would not be happy if she found out that I had driven to Astoria and hadn't stopped to visit her. She, of course, was happy to see both of us and asked us to stay. I was super tempted, but Victoria reminded me of the event she had to attend, so we left just in time for me to drop her off at Blossom Boutique. I watched as she walked in and was greeted by Lauren and some other women. Then, as those people parted, my breath caught in my throat when I caught a glimpse of Isabella, laughing. She was impeccably put together, as usual. My hands tightened around the steering wheel, and I told myself to calm down because I didn't want to be driving like a maniac all the way home. A motion caught my attention, and I saw Victoria waving and blowing kisses at me through the window.

This was the place for Victoria—social gatherings with people who were just as vibrant as she was. I'm glad she went, but I couldn't deny I felt a little bit jealous.

Home was quiet. After a day of impromptu adventures with Victoria and a run-in with Lauren, home was . . . too quiet. I found myself wandering around the corridors, looking at the family photos and wondering if I would ever add my own to the walls, or if this house would be passed down to anyone else or whether it would stop with me. Sebastian had mentioned he wanted kids and if that future ever came about, then this legacy could be passed on.

I tried calling him to see how he was, but his ringtone went straight to voicemail. I felt guilty for yelling at Sebastian about moving the journals when it really wasn't his fault. I'd talked to him a couple of times since he'd left, but he was busy most of the time or sleeping. The roses he sent once a week were all that held me together while he was gone. I'd told myself I didn't want to be the type of girlfriend that clung to her boyfriend every second and continuously called him till he picked up. But here I was—feeling that desire right now.

Appalled at my feelings of insecurity, I wondered why I was feeling so down. Then, something started to spark inside me. Why was I sitting around while everyone else was off doing something? Maybe Victoria was right when she staged that intervention before Taiwan—I was getting complacent. I pulled myself up and went to my room. I had a habit of placing color coded sticky notes all over my room, surely I had a related task I could finish right now?

Once in my room, I saw all the notes I had written during my stay in Taiwan. There was also some notes on my blog that I still wanted to write. Then I saw Harrison's journal sitting on my nightstand. Looking at it reminded me that I still hadn't learned more about my uncle; reading his journal would enable me to focus on someone besides myself. I was becoming too self-absorbed and I didn't like it.

I grabbed the journal and went downstairs for a cup of hot

tea before curling up in the library. That eerie feeling of being all by myself slowly dissipated as I read Harrison's journal amongst all the books.

50年12月5日 (Tuesday, December 5, 1961)

Mr. Wang, and Mei-Jing—or Grace as she wants to be called now—are making me write in this journal. Grace got mad at me when she found out that I'd run away to the countryside without telling her. I've never seen her so mad at me before, but she still doesn't understand that I'm not going home. I can't. I've had enough of the lies. Mary isn't my mama, and no one will tell me who my real mama is. All I hear Mary and Liang-Chun say is how mad they are at Anthony for meeting with me. I don't understand. Anthony seemed nice and he looked so much like me. I didn't know he was my baba as he didn't introduce himself as my baba. He only said that he was a longtime friend of my mama's and asked if I wanted to learn more . . .

Agh! I don't want to be writing in here. I don't write—I paint! What does Grace think this will accomplish?

50年12月11日 (Monday, December 11, 1961)

Grace came by today and told me I should give Mary and Liang-Chun a break. She said Mary is very upset and asking anyone and everyone if they've seen any sign of me. Grace told me that she'll ignore me from now on if I don't tell Mary that I'm sorry for running away and causing so much heartache. But what does Grace know? And why should I be the one who must apologize?! She's never had to live through the bullying, the questioning looks, or feeling like an outcast. How could she yell at me? Grace would do the same as me if she found out that her parents weren't actually her parents—especially if her real parents showed up one day and said "Surprise!" She definitely would. I don't care what she says; I am not whiny or feeling sorry for myself. Why am I even writing in this?

50年12月14日 (Thursday, December 14, 1961)

Mr. Wang wouldn't let me prep his paint today because I didn't write in this journal. So, I'm writing in it now. Are you happy now, Mr. Wang? I'm writing. Writing. Writing. Writing. There. Lots of words.

50年12月15日 (Friday, December 15, 1961)

I got in trouble for my journal entry yesterday. What is the big deal? Today I've been tasked with writing about something happy, something that I did with Mary. Why is he making me think of Mary? She's a liar. They all are, pretending they loved me, pretending everything was fine and I would never ask questions. As if I didn't notice that I looked different from everyone else.

I told Mary once that I looked too different, and she said when she lived in America that there were people of all different skin color there. They called it a "melting pot," and even then, she stood out during the time she lived there. Mary remembered what it felt like to be an outcast and to want to blend in, but she said she still made good friends there, still lived. She also didn't shy away from living her life and going to school.

That's where I should be—in America. Where there's people of all different colors. My green eyes would not be special there, they wouldn't be a prophecy for anything. I'm tired of older people saying there's something about me that I need to be careful about. That I shouldn't be too loud. That I should be patient with everyone around me. Don't get in arguments, it'll be bad for me, it'll bring a bad omen, and so on, and so on.

What about all the other kids? Why do they get to be

loud and argue with adults? Why am I treated differently? I don't want to be special! I don't want to stand out! I want to be just like everyone else. Why can't my hair be black? Why can't my eyes be black? Why can't my skin be a little bit more yellow? Why couldn't my Taiwanese features be more distinct? I need to find an eraser so I can erase the features I don't like and then redraw myself how I want to look. Wouldn't that be something? Redesign myself to blend in so that no one will make fun of me anymore. They wouldn't even notice me. Wouldn't that be great?

Sorry, journal, but I had to step away because Mr. Wang asked me to help him stretch some canvases. He asked to see my journal and was happy to see that I had written something worthwhile today. I will never admit it to him, but this writing session today might have done some good. It was nice to be able to write out my feelings in here instead of feeling them spin inside me. I'll never admit it to Grace either . . . Okay, maybe Grace, but she still isn't talking to me. I can't help wondering when she is going to come back and see me. How long will she leave me alone with myself? She knows that's not good for me. I need her.

50年12月22日 (Friday, December 22, 1961)

How long does Grace think she can keep doing this? She still isn't talking to me, even though I've written letters and dropped them off at her house. I don't know if she's getting them. Her parents have always liked me, one of the few people who do, but maybe they don't anymore? No one shuns their family, especially ones that have taken care of you for so long. Have I lost Grace as a result of my actions?

I just remembered my birthday was last month. I turned fourteen. No one celebrated my birthday because I didn't tell Po Po about it and Grace didn't know I was in Yilan until I came back to Taipei. She always brings me mochi on my birthday. It's my favorite snack, but she couldn't this year. She was so mad at me when I returned, and I can see why now. If she disappeared without any warning, I would be mad too. I understand now. Please come back Grace.

I don't know how she's been. What is she up to? She always told me what she was doing. I don't know how she gets to go out so much. Her parents are so free with her. Mary always made me come home at a certain time, and I couldn't go out with people unless Mary knew who I was with.

Grace seems to make a new friend every time she goes out. I don't know how she does it. I like to stay to myself. I think the only reason I've talked to others is because of her.

I wonder what she is doing.

50年12月24日 (Sunday, December 24, 1961)

If that's what she wants, then fine! Who needs her? I can survive just fine by myself. I haven't had fresh cooked meat with vegetables in a week, but who needs that? Only Grace needs that. She's spoiled with her perfect family, her perfect mama, her perfect baba, her perfect siblings, and her perfect life with no one making fun of her because of how she looks. Yeah! Who needs her?

50年12月25日 (Monday, December 25, 1961)

I've decided I'm going to move to the United States. California seems the best place to go right now. When I go shopping for food, I hear people talking about the opportunities that are supposed to be available in America, how life is more open and there is so much land. How rich the white people live. It reminds me of a conversation that I had with Mary once. I'd pointed to a lot of the movie posters we saw while walking through town; I'd said America must be made up of beautiful people. Mary could not stop laughing, and it took until dinner time for her to finally tell me why she thought my comment was so funny. She said in all her time living in America, she rarely came across a person who was as pretty as the ones we see on the movie posters and that I shouldn't believe what I see. She said that those people were only a select few of the population in America, and most were just everyday people like us here in Taiwan.

I didn't believe her and I still don't, especially after she lied to me about being my mama.

Life here in Taiwan doesn't suit me. I'm tired of living here and having people stare at me, asking me questions and treating me differently because I don't look Taiwanese—because I look foreign. They think I don't understand Mandarin. They talk to me slowly; some even try to find someone who speaks English to translate. Then, they get all surprised and upset when I respond in perfect Mandarin and they think I've been mocking them. I just can't win. Everywhere I go, I'm faced with a wall in front of my face.

Grace is still not talking to me. I saw her walking to school and tried to catch up to her, but she only walked faster. I thought she didn't see me, but when she got to the door, she turned and gave me a hard stare. I withered inside because I think she is done with me. Yes, there is nothing on this island to hold me here. America, here I come!

50年12月26日 (Tuesday, December 26, 1961)

Mr. Wang gave me a long lecture about going to America. He said there were tests I had to pass in order to leave Taiwan, much less to get into America. I told him I was a grown boy, and that I could do it. He just laughed at me! He laughed at me! I told him I already went to America. He said that was because my rich baba took me over there; he paid for the ticket and claimed me as his own and that was why I was able to go. He reminded me that I threw that all away when I ran away from my family. He reminded me that I wanted him to keep my presence here a secret, that no one was to know that I was working with him and hiding out here.

What am I to do? I am not going back to Mary, I am not going back to Anthony, and I am never setting foot in that big house again where people stared at me worse than they stare at me here—where they treated me as less than human.

50年12月28日 (Thursday, December 28, 1961)

So, I'm not moving to the United States just yet as I've realized that living by myself is not easy. I've also been thinking of Grace. I miss her.

Mr. Wang has let me help him with his shop, and has promised not to let my family know where I am. I am aware of the path I have chosen. I am only fourteen but I don't want to go back.

Mr. Wang has me mixing paints, cleaning brushes, building frames, stretching canvases, sweeping the floor, and buying food for the two of us. I don't think he would eat without me and I often wonder how he lived by himself before I came here.

I'm starting to like writing in here. Mr. Wang says I should write my story. He says it'll not only help me process my past but also my creativity. Maybe I could even draw and paint some of my story? So, I guess I'll start here. There's no reason anyone has to read this. He also said that if I'm thinking of moving to the United States, I should practice my English. I've learned English since I was a little kid. Mary made sure of that, and school educated me some, too, but I guess I should start practicing by writing in English more, and I'll try to do some here in this journal.

50年12月29日 (Friday, December 29, 1961)

Okay, Mr. Wang wants me to start writing my story so here it is. I'd rather be washing brushes and painting on the side, but he is insisting that I do this because the activity can build wrist strength, preciseness, and patience for my paintings. Anyway, here it is . . . .

My earliest memories are of Mary. I called her mama and I spent a lot of time with her. When she was not at home, I remember spending time with Ah Ma and Ah Ba. They were Mary's parents. Ah Ba would let me sit next to him in the office. He would throw sheets of paper down to me, which I would tear up and make a mess of or draw on. There were no crayons but he let me use the pens and pencils he had on his desk. I never remembered him yelling at me. I later learned this was very strange because Ah Ba liked order, but he seemed to have a soft spot for me, and I was also the last of many kids that had gone through his office. So I guess he was probably used to it.

Ah Ma sang me songs all the time. I loved sitting near her and just listening to her sing. I miss those times. Mary would sing me lullabies, too, from time to time. I remember they would let me stack things on the shelf, but only things that weren't made of glass. I broke a few jars once. Milk went everywhere. Oh! I remember I was told to bring milk to a neighbor a few houses down. I walked halfway there and saw three dogs appear. There were a lot of stray dogs around and once, when one of them had bitten me, I'd had to go to the doctor. That was not fun; it hurt a lot. So, when I saw those stray dogs, I ran.

I ran all the way back to the store with the three dogs chasing me, barking all the way. It was horrible. The worse thing was that Mary's older brother was at the store that day and he couldn't stop laughing at me. I was so embarrassed. Mary walked me to the neighbor's house to deliver the milk. She was nice to me and did not laugh. I miss Mary.

This is so hard. Am I supposed to remember my whole life? Maybe if I walk really quietly back into the studio Mr. Wang won't notice if I sneak up behind him and just watch him paint . . . . It'll be much more fun than writing in this journal. Plus, there are no customers in the front of the shop right now, and I think I've put enough words in the journal today.

50年12月30日 (Saturday, December 30, 1961)

I ended up having to clean the whole kitchen yesterday because I didn't listen to Mr. Wang about writing down my story. What is the big deal? Why is he so insistent? And the kitchen was gross! It hadn't been cleaned in so long. Funny thing, though, is that I actually liked cleaning it. It was so different from Ah Ma or Mary's kitchen where everything was cleaned at the end of every day.

It's not a big kitchen. There's a wooden cabinet with a netted door where Mr. Wang keeps some bowls, plates, chopsticks, and leftover food. I buy fresh groceries some mornings for the day's meal, and we eat everything throughout that day. On other days, I just buy pre-made food off the street. It's easy and more delicious than anything we cook.

The stove was the dirtiest, the counter a close second, and then the floor. There was oil everywhere. I'd wondered if this was how a single boy like me would keep their kitchen, and if this was how Mr. Wang had always lived? Okay, I did start feeling kind of grossed out about the state of it. It was not very sanitary. I scrubbed and scrubbed and my hands got so raw, but the kitchen is the cleanest it's ever been and I'm proud of what I did! Thank you to Mary for teaching me to be persistent or I would have given up after only cleaning the sink. I also feel better about cooking in there . . . . But I suppose I should continue my story.

I remember my childhood being very happy before I

started school. It was a time when I didn't notice how different I looked from everyone else. I loved Mary. I still love Mary . . . and I miss her . . .

Here, the paper was crinkled, and I assumed that Harrison must have stopped writing to cry. I felt the surface of the paper, thinking about the tear stains I had seen on Ah Po's journals. There had been so much crying in this family of mine.

I blame my mama for letting this all happen. She should have kept me with her . . . But I'm digressing from the story before I even begin.

My earliest memory is of stinky tofu. Mary took me to a stand right outside the junior high school. I was probably four. The smell was interesting. She said I'd had it before but I didn't remember. The outside of the tofu was deep-fried to a perfect crunchiness and the inside was soft like silk. It was delicious. She took me to the beach, and we sat on the rocks and ate our two bowls of stinky tofu side by side, just her and me.

That's how my days had been—filled with Mary and just Mary. The two of us were together all the time. She's my earliest memory and she's in all of them since. I miss her so much.

But no, I'm not going back. She tricked me! My real mama could have kept me in the US with her. She didn't have to leave me! I don't belong here, I belong with her— with my real mama.

Mr. Wang just yelled at me to write about my past. How he knows that I'm writing nonsense because I don't want to do this is beyond me. But fine.

On the first day of school, I was oblivious. I was about five, and Mary held my hand while we walked to school and found my classroom. It was filled with kids, and I didn't like it at all. The stares that came from the others made me feel uncomfortable. I remember gripping Mary's hand hard, and that she'd had to pry my fingers off when it came time to leave. The look of concern on her face hadn't made me feel any better either. I remember that day so well. People tell me you can't possibly remember something that well at five, but I do. When you stand out like me, and when you feel as uncomfortable as I do, you remember those things. They follow you.

There was a handwritten note on the side of this entry. It had been written in English, as if Harrison had gone back and reread these entries as an older man. I read the note beside his latest memory.

Looking back, I think my guard went up on that first day of school and I've carried it with me ever since. Many things stemmed from that first day, especially the loneliness and the fear that someone would do me harm because I didn't fit in.

I flipped through the journal to see if there were more notes and sure enough, there was. Some looked recent as the ink was not faded but rather stark against the weathered paper. This got me excited—I was going to see young Harrison and old Harrison all in one journal! My first thought was "what a treat," and the more I dwelled on it, the more I felt sorry for Harrison. He seemed to live his life in the shadows, always chasing his past. That made me wonder what type of woman Grace is to put up with someone like him. I sighed, thinking that I had too many questions. Back to reading.

My assigned seat was in the middle of the classroom, which contained about fifty people. The walls were all cement, with windows to my left. I could hear people in gym class running around outside and laughing with their friends. Laughter—it is an unusual sound. I lost the ability to laugh during those initial years of starting school. It's not because I didn't want to; there just wasn't anything to laugh about. Although, now I think on it, I do remember some laughter in my past and always with Grace . . . . But that memory is painful right now, so back to my first day of school.

I was shaking inside, petrified by the other students' stares. People had always stared at me, but I was never trapped in the same room with so many of them without Mary before. Every time the teacher turned her back, a couple of heads from the front would turn around to stare at me. Not a long stare but a quick swish of their head to see what I was doing. No one noticed it except me. But then, I guess I shouldn't focus on the negative. This entry is about school. The rest of the day and all of that week nothing bad happened, just more of the same. We sat in class, teacher taught us, we did some work, we exercised in gym class by running around the track, and I was alone during all of it. No one came to talk to me and no one asked me to play with them unless they were asked by the teacher to be paired with me for a group project.

However, I do remember being hit on the hand by the teacher for the first time. I remember I was tired of the other students whispering about me behind my back and I turned around and yelled at them. The teacher made me come to the front of the class and whacked me on the hand twice with a ruler. It stung for days but it didn't stop the whispering.

Argh! I'm tired of writing about my early years already. It was all the same stuff over and over again. I learned that people didn't like me because I looked different and that

Grace was my only true friend. No, that's not right, I had one other friend but I don't remember his name anymore as he moved away after two years.

I also remember that Mary had put me in Kung Fu lessons. I'd gotten pretty good at it too. Liang-Chun had taught me, and I'd liked him. He treated me good . . . but now he and Mary are too preoccupied with their other kids.

51年1月1日 (Monday, January 1, 1962)

New Years—the Western New Year. Yippee!

. . . Except there's nothing new here. Grace is still not talking to me, and I still do not want to go back to Mary. I also never want to see my white family again. But I'm still learning to paint and Mr. Wang says I have talent. That's why he let me join him in the first place, but he says I need to work harder. He wants me to do more sketches and to practice more. He says I spend too much time moping around. I do not! I work hard.

. . . But where is Grace?

51年1月2日 (Tuesday, January 2, 1962)

I'm tired of writing about the past so Mr. Wang suggested that I should start copying books. He gave me one, but it's not even an adventure book; it's just a bunch of poems. I don't understand poems, so I'm just going to write about what happened today. Here goes . . . .

I woke up. The place next door opened up pretty early, and when Mr. Wang made me get up at six o'clock so that I could get him breakfast, I headed to the shop. It was always the same breakfast for him: a shao bing with egg and lettuce inside. Nothing more and nothing less. I usually got luo bo gao with sauce, shao bing you tiao, and shui jian bao. Sometimes I'm still hungry, but the usual order eats into the little money that Mr. Wang gives me for breakfast, lunch, and dinner, so I have to be careful not to spend my quota all on breakfast.

We never cook now and I'm okay with that. I've always wanted to eat at restaurants more, and Ah Ma and Ah Ba would only let us eat out once a month. However, when I moved in with Mary, we would eat out every day. Breakfast would always be at a place nearby. It's why I buy more than I can eat sometimes. I can't help it. The food reminds me of when I was happy with Mary and Liang-Chun. Sometimes I don't even want to eat what I buy for breakfast, but I don't tell Mr. Wang that as he'll get mad at me for wasting his money. I still eat the food we buy, just not everything for breakfast.

Mr. Wang doesn't know I've kept writing in here. Only you know, journal, okay? He can just see the books I copy, though I need to find something better to copy than poems. I think I'm going to hide you inside my pillowcase.

On that, I like this new sleeping arrangement I have here. Mr. Wang does not have beds. Instead, he has a raised platform with a big bamboo sheet on top. It used to be his bedroom, but he's given it to me. I sleep directly on the bamboo sheet with a pillow and a thick blanket on top. It's perfect. He says he prefers the sofa bed he has in the studio, so he's sleeping there now. I'm okay with it; I like having my own room again and I am so glad that I don't have to share a room with everyone anymore.

When Chi-Yue learned to escape from her crib, she would sneak into my bed in the middle of the night and I would find this little girl curled up next to me. I kicked her out the first time she did that and she fell on the floor pretty hard. Her crying woke up both Mary and Liang-Chun. They were, of course, upset with me and since then, I let Chi-Yue sleep with me. I wasn't happy with it, but the little one could get away with anything, and I'd wanted Mary to love me like she used to before Chi-Yue came along. Was that too much to ask? I didn't think so, but Grace thought so. She lectured me non-stop that whole day.

I remember her huffing and puffing while we sat on the beach after school. She wouldn't sit down and kept mumbling to herself before turning and shouting at me. I had never seen Grace so mad. She said I could have hurt my sister, and how could I have kicked her out? I'd tried to defend myself and said that Chi-Yue could fall on the floor in the worst possible way and still bounce right back up from it. I'd seen it happen after all. She'd fallen off a chair, landed on her face, cried, had a bleeding lip, but was fine some ten minutes later. I promise—that's exactly what happened! Therefore, me kicking her out of the bed was no big deal.

But Grace wouldn't hear of it. She thought I was cruel. When she was still talking to me, she said I'd gotten meaner with each sibling that came along. I used to be thoughtful, she'd said, but now I wasn't.

I have no idea what she means. Why would she say such things to me? Doesn't she know that what she said hurts? Especially after I had found out that Mary was not my real mama, and that my baba was this person who came to find me from America. Instead of consoling me, Grace just kept yelling at me. I don't understand.

I saw Grace leave school the other day. I started to follow her and I know she saw me, because I could hear the others around her pointing at me and whispering my name. I was almost next to her when she sped up and hurried away. She didn't even turn to say hi. If that's how Grace wants it to be then fine; I won't talk to her either! Let's see how she likes that. I can ignore her too. I can!

"That was so much fun!"

I jumped at the intrusion, and next thing I knew, Victoria

was flopping down on the bed right next to me. I blinked, bleary eyed, and realized it was morning. I must have fallen asleep while reading Harrison's journal.

Victoria climbed into the bed and pulled the covers over our heads.

I noticed what she was wearing. "What in the world? You're still in yesterday's clothes. Did you just get back?" I asked.

"Yeah. I haven't had that much fun in a long time. Those rich people sure know how to party. And you're one to talk—you're still in yesterday's clothes too."

"Please don't call them rich people. And at least I was at home in my own bed."

"Oh right, you're one of them now too," Victoria said with a laugh.

"Yeah, I am, and I'm nothing like them."

"Anne, they're not all bad. Even Isabella behaved herself all night. Well, she avoided me and I avoided her, so I think that was pretty good behavior for the two of us. I also did pretty well and kept my thoughts about her to myself."

"Good for you," I said, sighing with relief. The last thing I needed was my best friend to cause a scene, especially since I was hosting Lauren's bachelorette party in Hawaii tomorrow.

"What have you been up to?" she asked.

"Aren't you the least bit tired?" I countered.

"No. My blood is rushing through me so fast right now that I can't sleep. Tell me what you've been up to."

"Did you have coffee? You know how caffeine affects you when you've been up all night."

"I did. We were all up talking and dancing, and then Lauren made coffee—and Anne, it was the best coffee I've ever had!"

"Don't let Cook hear you say that."

"You should try it some time. They use beans that have been flown in from Ecuador, specially processed to a certain blend that Lauren's parents like. They actually worked with the coffee producer and got the exact taste they wanted. Can you believe that? She lives in such a different world whereas I'm happy if Starbucks doesn't run out of Big Bang."

"I'm guessing there's no stopping you this morning then," I said, hiding a sigh.

"Nope, so you should get up and keep me company. I'm probably good for another four or five hours."

"All right, all right, I'm up." I emphasized this by flinging back the covers.

"Yay! I can't wait to tell you more about Lauren."

"Yippee," I whispered under my breath. Just what I wanted to hear about first thing in the morning.

CHAPTER 14

"Lauren really is starving herself."

"What do you mean?" I asked. "You saw how she swallowed those fish and chips as if they were the last meal she'd ever eat."

"She is!" Victoria insisted.

We were lounging in the sunroom with the floor to ceiling windows wide open. I was hoping the cool spring air would make Victoria want to snuggle under the blankets and go to sleep, but it seemed to be doing quite the opposite. She was chattier than ever and I was starting to think that Lauren had rubbed off on her.

"Okay, that makes no sense. Everyone eats," I said.

"Technically, she must. But I saw her put only about three bites of lettuce in her mouth. We had the best dinner! It was cooked by this celebrity chef her parents know, and all she ate was the lettuce! I don't understand."

"Maybe she ate on the side when no one was looking? Maybe she doesn't like the way she looks when she eats?"

"Yeah, I considered that, too, but I was with her the whole night. It was uncanny. I ended up right by her side the whole night; part of her inner circle, you know. Isabella was there, too, but like I said, we were civil with each other. The weird thing was that Lauren seems to really love Isabella and vice versa. The two were inseparable, and everyone else respected that. Lauren is the only person I have ever seen who has been allowed to touch Isabella. She was draped all over her by the end of the night, and if it wasn't for Isabella, Lauren would have been a puddle on the floor."

"Wow, it sounds like you had a blast."

"It was so much fun! I wish you had joined us."

"Do you really think it would have been my scene, though?"

"Hmmm . . . when you put it that way, maybe not. I'm glad you didn't go then or else you could have been disappointed. I like Lauren, though."

"Yeah, she's very likeable."

"No. I mean, she really seems genuine and a very nice person. What we saw yesterday was the same person I saw last night, even when she was drunk. Your true self comes out when you drink and she didn't change at all. If anything, she became more vibrant. People gravitated toward her. I didn't think that was possible until I saw it with my own eyes."

"Hmmm . . ."

"Well, I'm coming with you to Hawaii, so Isabella will have to go through me if she wants anything to do with you."

"I'm glad you're coming. I'm way out of my element with all this."

"Oh!" Victoria sat upright so fast that I jumped and ended up falling off my chair and landing flat on my face. I could hear Victoria laughing hard behind me.

"You could come and help me up," I said.

"Oh, you're fine. That was spectacular."

"Thanks . . ."

"Are you okay?" She was still laughing.

"Aside from a bruise on my hands and face, and my ego being impaired if any of the staff here saw that, I'm fine."

"Good." But she kept laughing.

Goodness, she was way too happy for me this morning.

"Really, though, come here. Let me see your face," she said, her laughter finally subsiding.

I sat down next to her and she tenderly poked at my face before proclaiming that I would survive.

"Why did you sit up so quickly?" I asked, trying to get the conversation back on track.

"I just remembered that Lauren had asked me if I knew of a good florist for her wedding. I told her I didn't but that you did."

"Why? She has tons of people who can help her find a florist."

"You would think, but they've already gone through two of the best florists already. Apparently they have money, but not money like some other families do, and the florists keep getting poached for other jobs. At this point, Lauren says she'll be happy if she can just have a florist at all."

"Why is she asking you, though? What about her friends and Isabella, who were all there last night?"

"I asked her the same thing. She said she couldn't trust her other friends there because a couple of them are also engaged and she didn't want to be in a floral war with them."

"She can't trust them? But they're . . ."

"I know. Can you believe it? Living a life where you can't trust your friends! They were all nice enough and I think a couple of them are helping her with other parts of the wedding, so it's not like she hasn't asked them for help too."

"That is just so weird, though."

"So, will you help her with the florist you know?"

"Sure. I'll give Lucia a call."

"Now?"

My mouth dropped. "Right now?"

"Yeah, I kinda told her that you would be on top of it as soon as I told you. I really talked you up. Let's not disappoint her."

The look on Victoria's face was so pleading that I couldn't say no. I sighed and pulled out my cell phone to dial Lucia's number. Thank goodness she picked up after the first ring. Victoria had her hands on her face and her elbows on her knees as she leaned toward me expectantly.

"Hi, Lucia, this is Anne."

"Anne! Oh, darling, you need to come by more often. I miss seeing you. How are you, sweetheart?"

"I'm doing well. Life is good right now. I miss seeing you too. Maybe we could meet for coffee sometime."

"That would be fantastic. Do you like the roses Sebastian gets for you?"

"I love them, Lucia. I'm looking at some right now." And I really did. Lucia always picked fresh ones straight off the truck for Sebastian, and she always picked out the best ones to put in the bouquet.

"How can I help you today?" Lucia asked warmly.

"I have a friend—Isabella's cousin to be exact—who is in need of a florist for her wedding. I wondered if you did that sort of thing?"

"Of course I do! I would love to do a wedding for your friend."

"Are you sure? You don't want to hear more of the details before agreeing?"

"Darling, any friend of yours is welcome here. Sebastian thinks so highly of you and I would trust him with my life."

"Thanks, Lucia," I said, blushing.

"Anytime, sweetheart. Why don't you come along with

your friend so she can tell me what she needs and we'll go from there? When is the wedding exactly?"

"That's the thing—it's in a couple of weeks."

"Well, that does put a tizzy in the timeline but nothing we can't work with. Can you come by today?"

"I'll ask L—"

"Yes! She can come by today," Victoria said, pulling my phone toward her so that her mouth was right next to the speaker.

I pulled the phone back and gave her a look. "I'll call Lauren and see if she's free," I repeated slowly to Lucia.

But Victoria yelled again, "She's free!" before collapsing back on the lounge chair.

"Okay, darling," Lucia said with a laugh in her tone. "Just let me know. I'm here until five o'clock."

"Thanks, Lucia."

"Anytime, sweetie."

CHAPTER 15

Lauren was indeed free. She apparently had managed to have a great night's sleep and was awake and ready to go as soon as I called her.

I wondered how she was able to stay so alert given they had stayed up late. But with all the money Lauren must have, maybe she had a next day concoction that made her feel like she had eight hours of sleep? I could hear Victoria telling me I was stereotyping, which I absolutely hated. I shook my head to clear the thought and told myself to be more open. I knew all about how stereotyping could hurt; I didn't want to go down that route.

Victoria was already asleep before I hung up. I left her lounging in the sunroom with a blanket over her. Then, I went up to my bedroom and entered my closet, picking out some suitable clothes that weren't lounge wear—clothes I would feel okay to be seen in when going to a florist with someone I hardly knew.

Why wasn't Victoria helping me with this? Ugh. Fine, I'll admit to myself that I was a bit jealous of how much fun she'd had.

How could my best friend let people in so easily? What magic did she have that allowed her to do that?

"Anne, the car is ready for you," Ben said, suddenly appearing in my doorway and disturbing my thoughts. Thoughts that I knew were taking me down a rabbit hole.

"Thank you, Ben. I'll be right down. Keep an eye on Victoria if you don't mind. She might be really hungry when she wakes up. And could you have some Advil and water available for her too, please?"

"Will do."

I got changed and exited the house, climbing into the waiting vehicle. The car was familiar now and I had gotten used to being driven around. There were a couple of times that I insisted on driving myself, just to make sure I hadn't forgotten how to drive, but otherwise, I got driven. I knew the staff still worried they would not be needed and possibly fired and whispers that their jobs were in jeopardy was the last thing I wanted. They went through enough of that last year.

Lauren was waiting in front of her house by the time I got there. She looked perfect, as usual, and slid into the car smelling of lilies. It was like the spring air had slid in right alongside her.

"Anne, it's so good to see you," she said, leaning over to give me a hug.

"It's good to see you too." Funny enough, even with all my humming and hawing about wanting to help her, it really was good to see her. Lauren radiated happiness and it rubbed off on me whether I liked it or not.

"You trust this florist we're going to?" she asked,

although I noticed she wasn't looking me in the eyes like she usually did when she asked the question.

"Absolutely. It's the place Sebastian has been going to for a long time. He's the one who brought me there to get roses the very first time he took me out. The owner, Lucia, is wonderful."

"That's sounds great."

Lauren's hands seemed to be tying knots into her dress. "Is something worrying you?" I asked her.

"Oh." She immediately stopped fidgeting with her hands and laid them flat on her legs, smoothing out nonexistent creases in the material. "No. Nothing for you to worry about. It's just, well, you know, Isabella."

"I do." A foreboding feeling passed through me.

"It's nothing; I'm sorry I mentioned it. Isabella is great, she's so nice to me."

"Lauren, you can tell me. I promise I won't say anything to Isabella."

"No, I'm okay. I just got in a fight with Stephen this morning. It has me a bit rattled." She looked at me for the first time and gave me the most dazzling smile, but I could tell she was holding something back. Her eyes had a worried look to them.

"Okay, I'm here if you need to talk."

"Thanks, Anne." She turned to look out the window just as the car slowed. "Oh, are we here?"

The car had stopped right outside Lucia's floral shop. I had forgotten how charming the store was. It looked very welcoming and from memory, I knew it would smell fantastic.

"Yes, this is Lucia's floral shop," I said.

"I love it already."

Lauren definitely wasn't as chatty as she usually was.

We exited the car and walked into an aroma of a dense

flower garden. The shop was tiny, and Lucia was behind the counter tying up some orders.

"Anne, so good to see you," Lucia said, walking around the counter to give me a hug.

I returned her hug, pulling away to say, "Lucia, this is Lauren. She's the bride I was telling you about."

"So nice to meet you, Lauren!" Lucia gave Lauren a big hug as well and I could have sworn I saw tears forming in Lauren's eyes. I wondered if she and Stephen were okay.

"Would you like a look around to see what we have?" Lucia continued. "Or do you already have something in mind?"

"I know what I'd like," Lauren confirmed.

"That's great. Let me get some paper and I'll take your order."

Lauren bit her lip and asked suddenly, "Are you able to get this done in the next two weeks?"

"It depends on what kind of flowers you would like," Lucia explained.

"I'd like an open prairie feel. Blues, whites, and greens. I want the one I carry to be large with flowers dripping down two-to-three-feet below my hands. Large flower arrangements for each table, and a garland of flowers across the awning that we'll be married under."

"What kind of flowers?" Lucia asked, all business.

"Any you can find."

Lucia nodded. "I can do this. Why don't you come in later this week to see some samples that I'll put together?"

"That would be fantastic. But are you sure you can take this on so quickly?"

"Yes. I never go against my word. You can ask Anne."

"I trust you. If Anne and Sebastian trust you, then I trust you. Thank you." For the first time today Lauren seemed genuinely happy.

"It's not a problem. You came from a very good recommendation," Lucia said while looking at me.

I'm sure I blushed. I felt guilty for having hard feelings for Lauren when she had been nothing but nice to me.

"I'll come by on Friday to see the samples," Lauren confirmed. She then went to give Lucia a hug, which I was surprised by, but Lucia wasn't fazed. They hugged for longer than I thought appropriate for people who didn't know each other, but I also wasn't the type of person to be all lovey-dovey.

"Perfect, sweetheart. You just let me know what time when you know it."

Lauren turned to look at me and said, "Anne, do you mind if your driver takes me home and then he can come back and get you? I just need some alone time."

"Of course."

When she left, the sound of the bell at the top of the door woke my senses and I wondered why I had said yes. Lauren's demeanor today was not the Lauren I knew. Her fight with Stephen must have really shaken her up and I wondered what it could have been about.

"She seems like a very nice girl," Lucia said from behind me.

"She is. I really don't know her well, though, as I just met her this week. However, she's very different than what I imagined Isabella's cousin would be."

"Isabella has her moments," Lucia said, but didn't care to elaborate.

"I'm hosting her bachelorette party this weekend in Hawaii," I said. "I only just found out this week, but apparently all the arrangements have already been made by Isabella."

I suddenly realized that I'd been holding a grudge because this felt similar to the stunt that Isabella had pulled when she'd tried to redecorate the house earlier this year.

Lucia didn't seem to notice my frustration, but it wasn't from lack of attention—she hadn't taken her eyes off mine since Lauren had left. "Anne, something is bothering her. She seemed subdued."

"Yeah, she's usually very chatty. That wasn't like her at all."

"Maybe she needs someone who can be there for her now —a new friend."

"Her? She has tons."

"If she has so many friends then why were you here with her?"

It was like Lucia could read my thoughts. "Well, when you put it that way . . . ."

"I know from what Sebastian has told me that you could use some more friends too."

"Sebastian said that?" I resented that. I didn't need more friends; he and Victoria were enough for me.

"I worry about you, Anne. Sebastian is like a son to me, and therefore, you are like a daughter to me. He loves you very much and he worries about you."

I think I turned a slight pink hearing all about that love coming from Lucia. My heart ached for Sebastian at that moment, more so than normal. When was he going to be less busy? Maybe we should go on a trip together again soon without work in the way.

"Just think about it, Anne. It might be good for you, too, to get to know Lauren a bit more. She's part of the Wilkens family, right?"

"Okay . . . and yes, she's part of the Wilkens family. You and Cook should really get together sometime. Between the two of you, no one can keep their thoughts to themselves."

She only laughed and gave me some tasks to do around

the shop. I helped Lucia until my ride came back to pick me up. This had been the oddest day.

I was winding down for the day when my phone rang. I picked it up to hear a familiar voice on the other end.

"Anne!"

"Mom? Where are you?" I could hear the loud sounds of trucks and people on the street.

"I'm in Oakland! I flew here the same day you sent me the address. I've been going to Harrison's house every day to say hi, and today he finally let me in! There is so much good food here. Now I know why your trip to California was so long—you stopped to eat!"

I could hear Mom laughing at her own joke and that made me smile. I hadn't heard her this happy in a long while. "Mom, where are you staying now?"

"Grace has lent me a room in their house. Did you know you have three cousins? Three cousins, Anne!"

"Wow! Have you met them all?"

"Not yet. Erik is the oldest and lives nearby. Leslie lives in San Jose, and she wants to meet you too. They're so excited now that we've met. Their youngest actually lives in Portland. Isn't that fantastic? I'll try to get his contact information so you two can meet."

"Mom, are you really okay with this new family and everything?"

"I'm great, Anne. I really am. Harrison will take some warming up to, but Grace is lovely. We've hit it off. I'll call you later, okay? I just wanted to let you know where I was and I didn't want to say anything until I had news to share."

"Thanks, Mom. I'm so glad you've met your brother."

"Thank you, sweetheart. And you have that bachelorette party coming up, don't you?"

"Yes."

"Enjoy it, Anne. I know parties aren't your scene but try to have fun, okay?"

"I will. Don't worry."

"That's my girl. Look, I'll talk to you later! We're going to R&G Lounge tonight for dinner. It's supposed to be delicious. I'll let you know how it is."

I looked at my phone after Mom had hung up. At least one of us was enjoying ourselves.

CHAPTER 16

THE BACHELORETTE PARTY CAME QUICKLY AND before I knew it, Victoria had us packed and at the airport before I could put up more of a fight. It didn't help that she had enlisted Ben and a couple of other staff members to help her. Also, because I still didn't own that much stuff, she just threw most of my clothes into a suitcase. I had received a dozen roses from Sebastian with a note saying that he hoped I had a fantastic trip and that he would be thinking of me. I missed him terribly, and it wasn't the first or second time that I wondered what had him away for so long.

Lauren and her three bridesmaids, Isabella, Gillian, and Amber were all at the airport when we arrived. Amber's parents had a private jet that somehow fit all of us, and Victoria and I piled in with everyone.

"I'm so excited all of you are here!" Lauren cried. "It's going to be so much fun and I can't wait to see what you all have planned for me!"

I swear she was glowing. If a person could sparkle, it would be her.

"Let's do quick introductions," a girl with long brown

hair to her waist said. She had on what looked like a blue jumpsuit with spaghetti straps and three-inch heels. Large sunglasses, ruby red lips, and gold jewelry on her neck, ears, and wrists was finished off with a purse that looked more expensive than anything I owned. "I'm Amber. This is my parents' plane, and no one is allowed to throw up in it. I will get in so much trouble, so limit what you drink while we're in the air."

Did Isabella just roll her eyes?

Isabella and Lauren were dressed similarly, and I was so glad the last girl there was not. She was in a summer dress that I had seen in Old Navy, a big straw hat, and sandals.

"And we're so thankful to your parents," Isabella said, not sounding impressed. "Now, let's hurry this along. I want to get out of the sun. I'm Isabella, but you all know that. This is Gillian," she said, pointing to the girl in the summer dress. "And this is Anne, and her friend, Victoria. Okay, everyone good? Let's get strapped in and get ready for takeoff!"

The plane was like any other plane with row seating and an aisle, but that's about where the similarities ended. The chairs were all leather and some could swivel so you could face the person behind you. Little desks folded out of the walls so you could place your drinks on it, eat, work, or whatever else you needed it for. There was also a stereo system, and Amber must have installed the disco ball in the middle of the plane because I couldn't imagine her parents would need that. Finally, there was a bedroom in the back where we dumped all our bags.

I can't say I didn't enjoy it. The seats were more comfortable than a commercial aircraft, and there was a server who came and took our drink orders right when we got on the plane, during the flight, and just before landing.

"She seems quite happy today," Victoria said, looking out the window at the view below.

"Lauren?"

"Yes, who else?" Victoria laughed.

"There's all these other girls here too," I explained.

"You know who I was talking about."

"It's weird, Lauren was so subdued the other day," I confessed. "I don't know what to make of it. She mentioned Isabella, but didn't say any more on the subject except that she and Stephen had gotten in a big fight, but I feel like there was also something else—something she didn't want to say."

"Let's just make sure she has a great time at her bachelorette party then, shall we?"

I nodded. "I'm so glad you're here, Victoria."

"I know." Victoria leaned over and gave me a huge hug.

I couldn't do this party without her. I would ruin the whole thing by sitting off to the side because I had no idea what to do with myself.

They played music during the flight and I watched while Victoria and some of the other girls danced most of the five-and-a-half hours from Portland to Kona, Big Island. By the time we were ready to land in Kona, we were all psyched and ready to have a great party for Lauren.

A limo came to pick us up. I ended up sitting on the edge of the seat by the door. The girls were so loud that I was glad I was on the side. I left the window open a crack and looked at the beautiful volcanic scenery rolling past us.

"I've stayed there before," Amber said while we drove by Waikoloa Village. "I remember thinking it was really nice. Are we going there, Lauren?"

"No, it's further north. Great Uncle Anthony wanted privacy away from the tourists in the village."

"But why here?" Gillian asked. Out of all girls in the limo, Gillian seemed the most down-to-earth. I got the feeling that in another life we might have become good friends. Maybe this weekend I might hang out with more than just Victoria after all.

"Yeah, there are so many better islands to be on—like Maui. I love Maui. I could spend the rest of my life there," Amber said, looking as if she'd go there right this instant.

"Many of us have asked the same thing," Isabella said, talking for the first time since we got into the limo.

"But we all agreed that we love this place as much as he did," Lauren piped in.

I saw a look pass between Lauren and Isabella and I wondered what that was all about.

"Did you get to come here often?" Gillian asked.

"Oh yes. Great Uncle Anthony was very generous with his home," Lauren answered.

I caught an eyeroll from Isabella, but seeing how she was on the other end of the limo and everyone was focused on Lauren, no one paid her any attention.

"The house would rotate through all of Anthony's siblings. Grandma used to have the whole family down for the holidays. Christmas was my favorite time to go. We would have all my aunts and uncles, all my cousins, my grandparents, Mother, and Father. It was magical. We'd get to have Christmas here every few years."

"I thought your grandmother had lots of siblings. How'd you get to come every few years?" Amber asked.

"Oh, well, it was really Grandma Catherine, Great Aunt Bernice, and Great Aunt Geraldine. The brothers had no kids. They were invited to celebrate some of the holidays with us, though. It was so much fun. Some of my fondest memories were spent here. I'm so glad Anne said we could use it." At this, she looked over at me and so did everyone else. I'm sure I turned a deep red.

"Anne was the person who inherited my Great Uncle

Anthony's estate, including the Hawaii property," Lauren explained.

"And the Taiwan property," Isabella piped in.

I saw Lauren give her a look, and it dawned on me what that look earlier was about. They must have had a disagreement about me joining this trip. Part of me became a little bit happier at being here. If I was making Isabella uncomfortable then that was a plus in my book.

"Wow, you must have done something big for her great uncle to let you inherit everything," Gillian said.

"Actually, it was—" Isabella started to say.

"Really not something that needs to be discussed right now," Lauren cut in, shifting her weight like she couldn't wait to get out of the limo. "We're almost to the house and before we get there, I want to propose a toast. I want to thank every one of you for taking the time to come here with me to celebrate my bachelorette party. I really just want to hang out with all of you, especially because I haven't seen some of you in ages." She gave Gillian's hand a squeeze before continuing, "And thank you to Anne for letting us have my party at a place that is so dear to my heart." She raised her glass at me and everyone else did too.

It was quite moving and a part of me started to thaw. This trip might not be half bad. I had Victoria with me and Isabella was somehow being muted by Lauren. It was just a weekend trip. I'd be home by Monday. What could go wrong?

CHAPTER 17

I WASN'T THE ONLY ONE IN AWE WHEN WE ARRIVED at the house. Everyone had a slight gap between their lips when they saw it. The house . . . well, it was a house. A house you might see in a regular, middle-class, suburban neighborhood. One that would fit three beds, two baths and maybe a game room, a kitchen big enough to accommodate two-to-three people, a backyard for two kids to run around in, and two trees in the front, symmetrically placed on either side of the main entrance. To say this wasn't what we were expecting would be putting it mildly. The drive in had been grand in the sense that we were surrounded by ten-feet-high hedges, each groomed into a perfect replica of the one next to it. They were so dense you couldn't see anything behind them. I could, however, hear water trickling like a waterfall.

None of us dared utter a sound. Lauren and Isabella were already halfway in the front door before they noticed that the rest of us were still standing ten feet away, wondering if this was all a joke.

"Why are you guys standing over there? Don't you want to come in?" Lauren asked.

"They're surprised that this house doesn't look bigger than we made it out to be," Isabella said, and I could see a smile forming on her face.

"Oh, yes, it's much bigger inside, trust me. There will be plenty of room for all of us to spread out. You'll each have your own room. Come on in. It's really nice and comfortable here."

Sure enough, as soon as we walked into the building, we realized our mistake. The front façade might have looked like a normal middle-class house, but the inside was definitely not like that. A big, open foyer greeted us and there were skylights galore in the entranceway, the sitting area, our rooms, the bathrooms, the kitchens, and even in various little nooks hidden here and there throughout the house. The sunlight streamed into the maze of rooms and hallways—just like the maze in the backyard of my home. Although this time, instead of an outdoor maze garden, Anthony had internally built the whole house like a maze. There would be all sorts of nooks and crannies to explore here. My sense of wonder piqued and suddenly, I thought this trip might not be so bad.

I unpacked my items in the main bedroom and spun circles on the carpet. The room was as big as my own at home, but decorated in a very masculine way. It included a four-poster bed with actual canopies on three sides, and a boxy, solid wood side table with a porcelain lamp and an ash tray.

I wandered over to the table and lifted the ash tray up. Did that have Anthony's initials etched into the bottom? But he didn't smoke. Could it be his dad's? The thought of owning a family heirloom was a mystery to me. Ah Po didn't really leave much for Mom or me. I'll have to explore more while I'm here, but for now, I was amazed that I owned this place too. It was all mine and I could do whatever I wanted with it.

Putting the ash tray down, I looked around the rest of the room. Its light green tones on the walls, chairs, and bedspread made it feel inviting, and I knew that I could stay in this room for the weekend. There was no need to interact with the rest of the group.

I was just about to lay down on the bed when I noticed the curtains on the wall were not covering a window but rather a set of French doors that led out to a balcony. Sure enough, when I stepped out, the sea air rushed over me and I took a deep breath in. The salty air calmed every cell in my body. I could get used to this.

But the sound of giggling drew me away from the quiet respite. I looked over the balcony and saw a few of the girls in their bathing suits running out the back door and around the corner of the house. I had a pool? Of course I would have a pool!

I heard a scream of joy and looked toward the sound to find it had come from Lauren. By the look of things, Lauren had just gotten something she had no idea was coming. I started to lean out on the balcony to see if I could catch what had caught her attention, but at that moment, Victoria came into the room, dressed to go swimming.

"Why are you still in your flight clothes?" she asked, looking me up and down.

"Why shouldn't I be?"

"If you would have looked at the itinerary Lauren sent us, you would know there's a toast party at the pool right now. We're kicking off the event by having a volleyball game in the pool."

"A volleyball game? Can I just watch?"

"No, you can't. You are getting changed and joining in the fun." While Victoria was saying this, she had already taken out my swimsuit and was pushing me toward the bathroom to change.

"I can just meet you there." Anything to give me more time before I had to face everyone again.

"I am waiting right here until you change and then I'm dragging you to the pool."

"Okay, fine."

This was a pool straight out of a movie. It was a solid fifty-yard pool, five lanes wide with a bridge over the middle. I couldn't believe that there was an actual stone bridge leading to other paths in the garden! I knew before I came that I had fifty acres of land here in Hawaii, but I'd thought that would comprise open land with no neighbors around for miles, not landscaped woods and a pool with a stone bridge across the middle!

"Oh yay, Anne made it," Isabella said from the lounge chair next to me. I looked down and there she was in all her perfect glory: white bikini, tanned skin, hair in a fancy braid, big round sunglasses, and a sun hat. She looked very chic. I, on the other hand, was in a one-piece; a nice lay-by-the-pool one-piece, but still a one-piece. Victoria clearly had also gone shopping for me because the last I remembered, I had owned an old one-piece speedo and that was it.

The decorator Lauren had hired had called me prior to our arrival to see if I had any input in how the house was to be presented. Of course, I didn't, and she had done a spectacular job. There were Christmas lights all around the pool and tiki torches were lit. An open bar was to the right of the stairs I had just descended, and there was a huge spread of hors d'oeuvres. I could see cheese, pate, crackers, fresh bread, fruits . . . and was that lobster? And filet mignon?

I filled my plate with a little of everything, especially the lobster and filet mignon—I wasn't going to pass that up. Victoria gestured to me from the other side of the pool and I walked over, trying not to spill my food and drink all over the immaculate pool-side deck.

"So, she just inherited the whole property?" I heard a girl with a dark bob hairstyle say as I drew closer to the group. I saw Amber nudge her right before I joined the circle, but she didn't even look ashamed to be talking about me.

A very excited Lauren started speaking before I could introduce myself. "Anne, this is Sara, one of my college friends. Can you believe it? I thought she wasn't coming when she didn't show up for the flight."

"Hi, Anne," Sara said, sticking her hand out for me to shake.

"It's nice to meet you, Sara."

"I wasn't able to make the party at Lauren's place last weekend, and I overslept and missed the flight with you guys. But I made it—here I am." She laughed, clinking glasses with Lauren and Amber.

"Sara has always been like this. Good thing her father has his own jet too," Lauren said with a laugh, clinking glasses with the girls again.

"Lauren was just updating me on who you two were," Sara said, indicating Victoria a few feet away. "It's amazing that you inherited everything, Anne. I wish I had a benefactor who would look out for me like that."

"Anne and Victoria are so down-to-earth. I can already tell, going by the one night that Victoria hung out with us, that we were all going to be besties," Lauren said, reaching over and squeezing Victoria's hand.

What was this? Victoria didn't seem taken aback at all. *Am I the only one who feels like this whole conversation is really odd?*

"I know all of you are going to get along so well this weekend," Lauren said, beaming at all of us.

"Anne made herself right at home as soon as she got the inheritance, didn't you, Anne?" Isabella said, sauntering over from where she had been lounging.

I saw Lauren visibly scowl at the jibe. It made me feel good that none of the other girls seemed overly excited to see her join us.

"Izzy, come sit next to me," Lauren said.

As soon as 'Izzy' sat down, I watched as Lauren leaned over and whispered something to Isabella. It was only a quick whisper and I seemed to be the only one who had noticed because the other girls were deep in their own conversation, including Victoria. *It's only for three days. It's only for three days.*

"Anne, you're so tense. Are you okay?" Lauren asked, leaning over to put a hand on my knee.

"I'm fine."

"I know you don't know everyone here very well, but you know Isabella and me, and of course, Victoria. I really hope you have a great time this weekend."

"*I* should be wishing *you* a good time this weekend. It's your bachelorette party." A sense of guilt hit me and I could see Isabella staring at me from behind Lauren. I really needed to not be so me, me, me, and focus on ensuring that Lauren had a good time. Besides, it was only three days and Victoria was here.

"Oh, well, I plan on having a good time and I know everyone. We're going to have a blast. I just know it. On that, I want to propose a toast." At this, everyone stopped talking and Lauren actually stood up.

Shouldn't Isabella be giving the toast? Stop it, Anne. Just focus on Lauren.

"I'm so glad all of you were able to make it here. It really means the world to me. Isabella, you have been by my side since I can remember. You've always been there at my lowest, and you're always there to throw me the best birthday and celebration parties. This one is no exception. I can't wait to see what you've planned. And thank you so much, Anne, for letting us use the house. You didn't have to but I'm so glad you did as this house means a lot to me. The fondest memories from my childhood were spent here. And Isabella too," she added, looking back down at her cousin, "as she would sometimes come with my family to celebrate the holidays."

"Lauren, let's not get all sentimental now," Isabella said, standing up and raising her glass too. I couldn't help but think that she didn't want Lauren to reveal more than she already had. Isabella continued, "Here's to Lauren, who's going to have the best time this weekend before getting married to Stephen."

"To Lauren!" everyone said in unison.

Right at that moment loud music started and acrobats came tumbling from around the house. But that wasn't what Lauren started squealing about. From the back of the house above the staircase, twelve girls came walking out and all of them had a huge smile on their face. Lauren couldn't run fast enough toward them and she literally disappeared into a mass of arms and jumping girls all squealing that they were so happy to be here.

"Who are they?" I asked no one in particular.

"They're our cousins. I got all of them to come and surprise her. Lauren is very much about family even though I could have done without some of them here."

I turned in shock to see Isabella right next to me, talking to me with no hint of sarcasm. If anything, she looked sad while looking at her family.

She noticed me staring, but before I could turn away she was back to her old self again asking, "What? You don't think I can talk to you?"

"Not at all. I just—"

"Look, Anne, I don't like you. I never will. But I can be civil. Can you?" And with that she walked off to say hi to her family.

I stood there a bit shocked at what she said until Victoria nudged me. She hadn't heard the conversation and I could see why when I started to look around.

The light in the pool had changed to a magenta color and the Christmas lights had been turned on even though the sun hadn't set yet. A fountain I hadn't noticed on this end of the pool had also been turned on and all of a sudden, there were mermaids too.

"Oh. My. God. This is going to be the best party ever!" Victoria said, squeezing my arm and jumping up and down.

"Yeah . . ."

"Come on, let's go see what that is!" Victoria said.

"What what is?"

"That," Victoria said, pointing with one hand while pulling me with her other.

I looked at where she was pointing and couldn't help but think, *I'm going to enjoy myself just fine tonight.* The circus had literally landed in the backyard of the house. A couple of the girls were already standing by the stairs watching the trapeze artists swing from huge swings that could hold ten people standing close together. In this case, one person was keeping the swing swinging and the other was leaping from it to another swing six feet away. The action was mesmerizing. I'd seen these types of performances on television and in live shows but this was something else. Here, I could walk so close to them that I could almost reach my hand out and touch them.

All of a sudden, a hand slapped mine. I hadn't even noticed that I'd actually been reaching out.

"Don't get any closer!" a voice hissed. "If you cause them

to have an accident, you'll take responsibility for the payment and fines associated with it."

I turned to see Isabella standing next to me again. She had a look of annoyance on her face. The "civil" Isabella had gone and the one I knew had come back.

"I have no idea why Lauren has taken such a liking to you, although I'm not too surprised," Isabella continued. "That girl can take a liking to a hyena if she wants to. You better not ruin any of my plans this weekend as Lauren means a lot to me. I don't know why she bothered to invite you and your friend—I told her not to."

"If you like Lauren so much, why would you say something like that about her?" Victoria asked. I could tell in the raising of her voice that she was holding back her anger. It wouldn't hold out for long.

Isabella stared at Victoria for what seemed like a long time. Long enough for me to start sweating and wonder who was going to lash out at the other first. But then Isabella gave a sigh and a look of loss passed across her face.

"You wouldn't understand," Isabella whispered.

"Try me," Victoria said.

"There she goes again," Isabella said, looking over at Amber, who was trying to give one of the jugglers a hug while giggling nonstop. "Just don't touch the acrobats or their props."

"Great to talk to you too," Victoria said really loudly while Isabella walked away to assist Amber. "I hate her," she said to me.

"Ditto."

"Look, let's forget her and find Lauren. She seems to be having a blast—that's where I want to be," Victoria said, already heading in that direction.

"I'd like to stay here a little bit more if you don't mind."

"Okay, have fun. I'm in for what looks like ice cream and half naked men."

I watched while Victoria danced her way over to Lauren. As soon as she was embedded into the group, I refocused on the trapeze performers. They were astounding. And when I tired of watching one artist, I moved on to another. I made myself comfortable on one of the lounge chairs as I looked at the performance happening around me. There were jugglers walking around, and I suddenly noticed they had set up a bar in the pool, and above that bar were two ladies entwined in silk rope, twisting themselves into moves that made me gasp every time they rolled down fast or did tricks high above us.

Somehow, when I wasn't looking down, Lauren, Victoria, and Gillian had gotten into the pool and were being served drinks from the bartender who had set up his bar in the middle of the pool.

I noticed a couple of girls coming my way and I realized I had nowhere to hide. "Hey, you're Anne, right?" one of them asked.

"Yes. I'm sorry, I didn't catch your names?"

"I'm Amanda and this is Catherine," Amanda said. "We're Lauren's cousins. Lauren told us about you; she's gushed about how kind you've been letting her have the party here. I'm not big on parties, but Lauren has a way of always persuading you without trying."

"Yeah, I've noticed," I said, chuckling. I liked Amanda; she seemed very straightforward. I looked at Catherine and asked, "Are you named after your grandmother?"

"I am," she said with a smile. "How did you know?"

"Lauren has told me multiple times now how much she loves her Grandma Catherine."

She smiled warmly at me, whereas Amanda—the more talkative of the two, though nowhere close to Lauren—asked, "Would you like to join us? I saw you were sitting here by yourself. I promise we don't bite, and not all of us are upset that you inherited the mansion. I loved visiting the place, but if you had asked me if I had wanted to own it, I would have said no. It's just too much to keep up and I like things simple."

I really liked Amanda now. Part of me wanted to go and join their group, but I saw Isabella was among them and decided not to. "I'm okay here for the moment. I'm enjoying watching all the artists perform."

"Well, you're welcome whenever you want to join," Amanda said warmly.

They walked back to their group, and I commenced watching the performances. At one point someone gave me a handful of sparklers and told me to follow along. So, I did. I had no idea what I was doing, but next thing I knew, we had formed a conga line and were all going around the pool and up and down the stairs, cheering and laughing. It was the most fun I'd had in a while.

This reminded me of who I was when I traveled: I let myself go, I made new friends, and I took risks—not like the person I became in Astoria and Portland. I realized that this was what life should be like, not sheltered in my home by myself. Sebastian was off doing what he did, although I wasn't quite sure what his mission was about this time. He was very hush-hush about it. I was still a tad annoyed by our discussion before he left, but I was missing him more and more the longer he was gone. Tonight, however, was a night to be free of all those worries.

The night just got better and better when there was a big boom and fireworks exploded, lighting up the sky with a shower of colorful lights. My favorites were showcased, too, including weeping willows, hearts, and stars.

Then there was another booming sound behind me, and I realized there were even more fireworks going off around me!

Really huge ones, too, that seemed to cover the whole sky. I couldn't turn fast enough to catch them all. I quickly glanced down to see if I could position myself at a better vantage point and saw Victoria sitting with Amanda on one of the lounge chairs, looking skyward. That position was perfect for a nighttime show. I made a mental note of where they were—not quite twenty feet past the bend of the pool—and headed in their direction, not taking my eyes off the sky.

There were shapes I had never seen before, including a heart with an arrow through it and a smiley face! Then the sky emptied, and you could feel the sudden anticipation in the air. Two entwined circles shot up into the air. *Oh! Maybe that was meant to be two wedding rings?*

I started hurrying so I could tell Victoria my epiphany when I felt my left foot start to slip. The next thing I knew, I slid onto my butt, let out a yelp, and fell into the water. I was mortified. I let myself sink to the bottom and stayed there for as long as I could. But before I could push myself to the surface, I felt arms around me, pulling me up. I tried turning around to tell them I was okay, but whoever had me was strong and I was unable to do anything but be towed along.

I felt myself being pulled out of the water and heard, "Anne, are you okay? You could have drowned! Have you been drinking? Victoria said you rarely drink. I didn't think you would. I told the staff not to give you any if they thought you couldn't handle it. What was I thinking? Oh my goodness, you could have drowned!"

My eyes were starting to clear and I saw that I'd drawn a lot of attention. Lauren was bent over me, crying. Her mascara was smudged around her eyes and running down her cheeks. She looked petrified.

"I'm sorry." I felt horrible. It was her night and now here she was, soaking wet and scared for me. "And I wasn't drinking. That wasn't the issue; I was just clumsy."

"I think maybe we should call it a night," one of the girls said.

"Yes, yes, I agree," Lauren said while still fussing over me.

Fireworks were still going off, lighting up the blunder I had created. I scrambled to apologize. "Lauren, I'm sorry. I really am. I don't know what happened. You should stay and enjoy the rest of the night. I'm fine."

"I'll help her to her room," Victoria said. Victoria helped me up and began to drag me toward the stairs while the other girls comforted Lauren. I felt horrible.

"Are you okay?" Victoria asked.

I could tell she had been just as worried as Lauren, and I felt bad for ruining their night. "I'm fine. I was just really happy and didn't want to take my eyes off the fireworks . . . and then I misjudged where I was walking."

"Your moments of clumsiness are few and far between but when it hits you, it hits you hard," Victoria said with a laugh and ushered me inside. "On a different note, let me ask you something—and I'm not trying to berate you, okay?"

"I wouldn't think you were." I looked at Victoria with some confusion, not sure where she was going with this.

She released a breath before facing me and said, "Do you want to be here? Like, really want to be here, or are you only hanging out here because I'm making you?"

"I . . ."

"You've been by yourself most of the night," Victoria said pointedly.

"I was in the conga line!" I protested.

"Yes, but only after I told one of the girls to give you sparklers and ask you to follow along. I noticed a few girls walk up to you a little earlier, but they left you pretty quickly. I know you and you probably declined their offer to join them, right?" She turned and we continued walking into the house. The whole building was lit up with all the lights on like everyone was inside, even though no one had entered the house since we'd gone straight to the pool on arrival.

Darn, she knew me too well. I looked at Victoria. She had that look on her face like she knew she was right.

"Some of the girls have asked me if you were doing okay. Are you, Anne?"

"I'm fine. You know I'm not outgoing in places like this."

Victoria just looked at me, not saying anything.

I sighed. "I don't know what to do. I'd just mess things up if I joined any of their little groups. They all know each other."

"And yet you can let loose when you travel! Well, you traveled here, right? We're all the way in Hawaii. Anne, this is your chance to make a good impression. You own this house—you're the host. Lauren and Isabella might have spent time here during the holidays, but you own it now. You were the one who said yes to Lauren hosting her party here."

Victoria was not helping. I was getting more and more anxious the more she talked. We were now at my room and as we walked inside, I cried, "I didn't ask for any of this! I'm sorry I scared all of you. I was distracted by the fireworks and having fun in my own way. You know I don't know how to act around others in a party scene."

Ignoring my outburst, Victoria continued, "We both agreed on the plane to make sure Lauren had a great time this weekend, right?"

"You're more worried about Lauren?" I couldn't help it. My thoughts were becoming scattered. The last thing I'd thought would happen was my best friend telling me I was being a bad guest or host or whatever I was! I was here, wasn't I? I flew to Hawaii.

Victoria had led me into the bathroom, thrown in some pajamas, and closed the door. I tried to grasp what had happened today, but all my brain wanted to do was shut down. It had been a stimulating day and I was ready to go to bed.

When I came out with my pajamas on, Victoria grabbed me by the shoulders and looked me in the eyes. "I am not just thinking about Lauren! I really do think that getting to know Lauren more would be a plus for you. You would see a different side of the family. But that requires you to hang out with her and her friends and family. You are also the host, and Isabella is here, too, remember? She's the one who's trying to take everything away from you. Therefore, you should act like a host and prove to her that that will never happen."

This was too much for me right now; I couldn't take it all in. "I can't follow you right now. I'm going to bed."

"Fine. Just think about what I said," Victoria said, tucking me into bed.

I felt like a child who had played all day and was now exhausted. How did I keep this up when I traveled? The last thing I remembered seeing was Victoria standing at the door with a worried look on her face.

CHAPTER 18

The next morning was torture. My butt and back were throbbing from my fall into the pool and all I wanted to do was stay in bed. The smell of roses finally made me open my eyes—that smell had not been in my room yesterday.

Sure enough, when I pried my lids open, there were a dozen red roses sitting on my bedside table. A card was sticking out of the stems. I opened the card to find that Sebastian had written a note for me. Just me. I curled up in bed and read his message over and over again, imagining him standing right here telling me in person.

Anne,

I miss you so much. I'm sorry I haven't been around a lot, but this case is super important and I want to make sure it's taken care of. I still can't tell you the details, but I hope to be home soon. Here's a dozen roses for you. I think about you every day.

Love,

Sebastian

. . .

He had always been able to at least tell me where he was going. But this time it felt worse because I knew it involved me somehow. I missed him so much.

My back twinged again as I moved to put the card on the bedside table. I felt like I needed some medicine, so I made myself get out of bed and dig around in my purse for some Advil. This was going to be a long day.

"Good morning," Victoria said in a singsong voice as she charged into my room.

"You could have knocked."

"When have I ever knocked with you?"

True. "Why are you in such a chipper mood? My back is throbbing. Could we tone it down a bit? I want to go back to bed."

"I refuse to allow you to ruin this wonderful weekend! It's not every day that we get invited to such a big event by people who can afford so many extravagant things."

"Oh . . ." I groaned. "I don't even want to know. I just want to lay here for the rest of the weekend and not move."

"No! You are getting up, getting dressed, and coming down to join the rest of us. Lauren is beside herself thinking that you were really hurt. I know your back is throbbing, but some Advil will make that go away. And you need some food in you." Victoria came over and held my shoulders as she looked me in the eye. "Don't give Isabella more reasons to try to take your inheritance away. You need to show these girls that you belong here. I don't know about the other girls, well, except Lauren, but I know Isabella will walk all over you if you let her. Besides, what happened to the girl who stood up to Isabella and Sebastian when they wronged you? What happened to her?"

"She shriveled up and is in hiding." Because even I could

tell I was throwing myself a big pity party. "I remember everything you said last night—no need to go on and on about it."

"Well, get up and I'll stop nagging you. Everyone's downstairs having breakfast. I'll give you ten minutes to get dressed. Rinse your mouth a bit cos it stinks and get your butt down there."

"Ten minutes?"

"I'm counting."

Victoria had that determined look on her face. I knew that when she got like this there was no saying no. I forced myself to get out of bed and shuffled my way to the bathroom. It wasn't until I peered in the mirror that I realized how awful I looked. How was I going to show my face downstairs after embarrassing myself last night? Victoria was right; I was a recluse.

"Put on the floral dress," Victoria urged. "We're going to the beach today and you'll love it being so flowy and comfortable."

"I don't own a . . . Wait, did you go shopping for me?"

"I sure did. Your wardrobe is pitiful."

"Thanks, Victoria."

"Don't mention it. Just hurry up; I can smell breakfast tacos and I am not about to miss out on them."

"I'm coming. I'm moving as fast as I can."

I shuffled out of the closet, only to have Victoria attack me. She dragged me back into the bathroom and applied some makeup to my face so that I didn't look like a zombie. Well, at least that's what she told me.

Downstairs, the girls were all awake and in their own comfortable, flowy dresses. I went straight to Lauren, who had stood up as soon as I entered the room.

"Anne, how are you feeling today?" she asked. "I feel just awful about what happened last night. Are you okay this morning? Is there anything I can do? Anything you need?"

I could feel the other girls staring and I knew they were judging me. I didn't want to care, but I felt like I was back in high school and I didn't belong.

"I'm okay, Lauren. I really am. Nothing Advil won't help with, and I've already taken them."

"Well, okay, if you say so. I'm really glad you're okay. Isabella found the best chef to cook for us today. He's making breakfast tacos with chorizo, which is my favorite, and they're almost done."

"Yum! I love them," I said, putting on my best smile. I needed to get through today and tomorrow. That was it. Not even two full days. I could do this. I would be in my own bed soon enough and then I could hide from the rest of the world.

However, before we could all get some food, we heard a commotion at the front door. I heard her before I saw her.

"Where is my favorite granddaughter? Where is she? Come give your Grandma Catherine a kiss. Oh! There she is. Oh, sweetie, look how gorgeous you look! Only a bride-to-be could look so pretty."

"Grandma Catherine!" Lauren squealed. "You made it! Oh, I thought for a second that you might not come. I know you don't travel as much as you used to."

Lauren went running into the arms of the lady wearing the brightest colors I'd ever seen. She wore a light pink top with a big ribbon running along her collar bone and a pair of purple, flowy pants. The plum blossom brooch her brother had given her was pinned exactly where Lauren said she liked to wear it. Catherine must have gone to a salon before arriving because I couldn't see how else her hair was so perfect after getting off a plane. Big, round, black sunglasses and a wide rimmed sun hat finished off her look. She looked chic and comfortable.

Isabella, on the other hand, did not look pleased. I watched as she directed her foul face at another older lady who had come in after Catherine. I sucked in a breath when I realized who it was. Victoria grabbed my arm and pulled me in close when she, too, caught sight of her.

"And you brought Grandma Geraldine too!" Lauren said, running over to give Geraldine a hug.

"You haven't changed, Lauren. You're still as chatty as ever," Geraldine responded, giving her great-niece a peck on each cheek.

Geraldine was standing there staring at me like she would like to light me on fire right then and there, and Isabella was doing the same to her. I didn't have time to think about why Isabella was so upset at seeing her grandmother when Catherine came and gave me a hug.

"Anne, so good to see you. I've been wondering about you and if you've been doing okay all alone in that big house of yours. We used to have lots of kids living in that house. I have no idea how Anthony lived there by himself all those years. It used to be bustling and now I can only imagine how quiet it is." This whole time she had both of my hands in hers and her palms felt so warm and inviting. Her whole demeanor calmed me down, even with the fact that Geraldine was standing not that far away from me. "You remember my sister, Geraldine, and also Isabella's grandmother? She's been anxious to see you again too."

Really?

"Grandma, I thought you never flew anymore?" Isabella asked Geraldine with a look that wasn't what I thought an adoring granddaughter would give.

"Only for special occasions, my dear," Geraldine said, giving Isabella's hand a pat while not taking her eyes off me.

"What about Great Aunt Bernice?" Lauren asked, oblivious to the tension in the air.

"Oh, you know her, pouring over some research that she can't get her head out of. Waste of time, I say. She could have done anything with her life but all she cares about is books," Geraldine said.

"That's a bit harsh, don't you think? She's created a very good life for herself," Catherine said, giving Geraldine one of those sisterly looks of admonishment.

"Sure, if you think what she has is a life."

"Geraldine." Catherine was suddenly very rigid.

"Grandma, why don't I show you to your room?" Isabella said, taking Geraldine by the elbow and leading her toward the stairs.

As her sister left the room with Isabella, Catherine turned to Lauren. "Oh, sweetheart," she said, giving her granddaughter another hug. "I am so excited to be here with you. Have I got the best surprise for you or what!"

Was no one fazed by what had just happened? And what did just happen, anyway? Having had no siblings of my own, I didn't understand how they could say such mean things to each other. I had always wanted a sibling, and it hurt me to see siblings fight.

"What did you get me?" Lauren said with a squeal.

I had never seen her so happy. She and Catherine definitely had a relationship that Isabella and I did not have with our grandmothers. *Whoa! Isabella and I have something in common?*

"Come on, girls. Your present is outside on the patio, Lauren," Catherine said.

"Oh, yippee, yippee!" Lauren said, bouncing out the door while holding onto her grandmother's arm. All of us followed.

Outside, the scene in front of us was not at all what I was

expecting. It was the setting of an obsessed workout fanatic, not a bachelorette party.

"This is going to be fun!" Victoria cried.

I clamped my hands over her mouth. I knew her well, and this scene was something she loved.

"Anne, it's an obstacle course!" Victoria squealed from behind my hands.

"That is not an obstacle course. That is a military style training ground." In front of me was what looked like a gladiator training facility.

"I know! I'm so excited!"

This time I put my hands over my ears as I allowed Victoria to get all her excitement out. Next thing I knew, she and Lauren were jumping up and down holding hands, squealing together, and running off to what they thought was the most glorious place to go.

Okay, maybe that was a bit too romantic. I did not want to work out; I never had and I didn't plan to start now. When did they even have time to set this all up, anyway?

Before anyone could stop me, I snuck back inside and headed for my room. It wasn't that I was ignoring what Victoria said last night; my back did hurt, and I had seen a voicemail come through from Mom this morning that I wanted to listen to. I promised myself that I would start being a better host after this exercise gauntlet was done.

On my way to my room, I ended up stopping at the kitchen. Couldn't go relax without a snack, could I? I was deep in my own thoughts, now rejoicing that I was able to escape that I didn't realize who was in the kitchen until I almost ran into her.

"Well, if it isn't the Orient," Geraldine said, looking at me like I was a piece of garbage. "I'm actually Taiwanese American—"

"Whatever," she interrupted. "You all look the same to me. Can't tell one from the other."

She started to stand up and lost her balance. I made to catch her. "Don't touch me! I don't want to get infected!" she screeched.

Infected? What in the world? She was so close to me that she was breathing into my face. There was a distinct smell of chocolate and wine, and I willed myself not to pinch my nose.

"Look what you made me do!" Geraldine cried.

With no idea what she was talking about, I looked down to find that when she had lost her balance, she had knocked some of her cake off her plate. She was staring at her cream, silk shirt, which now had a distinct dark brown smudge on the front of it. I fully expected her to scream at me some more, but instead, she grabbed something from the shelf under the counter. A wine glass, full to the rim, suddenly appeared in her hands. She reminded me of the witches in *The Witches*—properly dressed, prime members of society that were keeping a secret only they knew of. I wanted to giggle at this absurd thought, but the idea of her turning me into a mouse stopped me short.

I decided to be overly nice so that I could get away without much of an incident. Plus, I was the owner of this house. There was no way this woman—or witch—could harm me here. "It's nice to see you again, Ms. Leach."

Thank goodness Andy had made me memorize the family's names when I threw the Christmas Gala.

"At least your mother taught you some manners. And call me Geraldine. I want nothing to do with that husband of mine. His last name should be his first name." She took a deep drink.

Was she going to be this nasty the whole time she was here?

Geraldine lowered her glass and said, "I want you to know that I know what you're up to."

"What am I up to? Please enlighten me."

"A back-talker—I knew it! Your kind infiltrated our borders. My grandfather and father should have never hired your kind to work on our railways. You better understand this, missy—you are not entitled to my family's properties, money, or lifestyle. I will make sure of that."

She's crazy! That's the only explanation for what's going on right now. "I—"

At the same time, Geraldine said, "I don't think you—"

"Grandmother!" Isabella suddenly exclaimed, coming into the room. "What are you doing?"

Geraldine and I swiveled to face Isabella, and I never thought I would be this happy to see her.

"Isabella, my dear girl," Geraldine said, recovering smoothly. "Why are you here when you should be outside enjoying yourself with your wonderful cousin?"

At these words, Isabella's smile faltered and lines formed on her forehead. I had never seen her face make such an expression before.

"Cut the crap, Grandmother. I asked the question first."

I felt my mouth drop open. *Did Isabella just disrespect her grandmother?*

"It must be this girl," Geraldine sneered while pointing at me, "that has made you learn to talk back to me."

"Even if it was—which it's not—you still haven't answered my question."

"I don't need to tell you," Geraldine said sharply, then commenced eating her cake and drinking her wine.

"You're not supposed to be eating chocolate cake!" Isabella exclaimed. "And are you drinking wine? You know you can't have that either."

"I'll eat whatever I want and it's none of your business

what I drink, Isabella," Geraldine said, putting the wine glass back under the counter.

"It sure is when I'm the one responsible for you. And I already saw the wine, Grandmother! Mother will kill me if something happened to you." Isabella made to take her glass away, but Geraldine stood up to block her way.

"And when did you care so much about what your mother thought?"

I'd thought Isabella adored Geraldine, but the scene playing out in front of me was saying otherwise. In retrospect, I should have taken this time to leave the kitchen, but part of me wanted to see what happened, and I was also afraid that the slightest movement would make them notice me again.

Sure enough, as soon as I shuffled on my feet, Isabella's focus turned to me.

"What are you looking at?" she snapped.

She had a scowl on her face and looked as if she was ready to pounce on someone. She definitely wasn't going to attack her grandmother—at least, I didn't think so, but would she take her anger out on me?

"I just came in to get a drink," I managed to say.

"Well, get it and leave then. Unless you're in the habit of gawking at family members when they're arguing."

"No . . ." I should just leave. I grabbed a cup of water and as I was walking out of the kitchen, I heard Isabella say to Geradline, "Why did you come, anyways? You hate family gatherings, and Mother said you refused the invite I sent you."

I couldn't help it; I hesitated on the stairs, waiting to hear more.

"If you know I hate parties then why would you send me an invitation?" Geraldine asked waspishly.

I heard a groan come out of Isabella. "Grandmother, you know I always want to invite you to everything."

"Hmph. You should have at least sent the family plane to pick me up. I had to fly first-class with Catherine. Did you know she almost made me fly economy? Me, in economy! I still haven't forgiven her. That's why I'm eating this chocolate cake."

"You know we don't have access to that plane anymore. It was Anthony's."

There was a snort of discontent before Geraldine said, "That girl—you need to get rid of her. Do you understand me?"

Geraldine was seething at this point. I could hear the evilness in her voice. What did she mean that she wanted Isabella to get rid of me? Was it more than what Isabella had been doing already?

I didn't wait to hear more. I headed upstairs before my legs wouldn't move. I didn't want to be caught eavesdropping, and Mom's voicemail was calling. Hopefully it would take my mind off Isabella and Geraldine.

As I headed to my room, I could hear the girls whooping and yelling. At least the bride-to-be was having fun.

CHAPTER 19

In my room, I checked my phone and realized that Mom had left me three voicemails. I listened to the first one.

Anne, you're going to love your new family. Harrison has really warmed up to me now. He's not as odd as you thought he was; he's just shy and doesn't trust people when he first meets them. Given his history, I can't blame him. He sent you a couple of surprises that I think you'll really like, and he's written up a letter for you. Make sure you sign for them. I believe they'll arrive when you get back from Hawaii. You'll love them, Anne. Oh, and Erik's little girls are so cute. They're so bright and funny. I've also decided to extend my stay a bit. Oh, I have to run. I cannot wait for you to meet them! I love you.

That message sounded awesome. It made me extra happy that Mom was over the moon about getting to know her brother, and that Harrison had opened up his home to her.

As Mom said, maybe he wasn't the same person who had come to visit me almost two weeks ago.

I pressed the button for the second voicemail.

Anne, I forgot to mention something: What do you think about a family get together at the mansion next weekend? Nothing fancy. They all want to meet you and they've been meaning to come up and see Paul and explore Portland. Why not have everyone stay at the mansion? Please say yes. I think it'll be fantastic, and Grace said this will be a healthy change for Harrison too. He's refused to face his past and this will allow him to see the house again and maybe form a new, happier memory from it.

Have everyone at the mansion? My first thought was that the place hadn't been cleaned in a long while, but it would be fun to meet everyone.

I pressed the third voicemail.

One more thing, Anne, and I promise this is the last. Grace mentioned that someone had come over to their house a couple of weeks ago asking about the Taiwan property. He was being nosey and making her feel really uncomfortable, so Erik threw a vase at him because he refused to leave without an answer. Do you know anything about this? She didn't tell Harrison because she doesn't want him to worry, but we got to talking the other night and she confided in me. Anyways, I just wanted to put it on your radar. I love you, Anne, and I can't wait to see you! Oh, and have you been in touch with Paul? I texted you his phone number. Grace said he's always reading books and working in the lab. He could use a friend. I think you could use more friends too. Anyways, that's enough mothering from me. I hope you're having fun in Hawaii! Say hi to Victoria for me.

. . .

I collapsed back on my bed and shut my eyes. This was just too much. Someone was harassing Grace, Mom was having heaps of fun with her newfound family while making plans for me to meet them, and I was in Hawaii, stuck with my enemies in the same house for the weekend.

I reached over and grabbed Harrison's journal. While everyone was sweating, I could dive back into the sorrows of a thirteen-year-old boy. Opening the journal, I sent a fervent wish that Harrison was taking care of my Ah Po's journals.

51年1月3日 (Wednesday, January 3, 1962)

I was awake last night thinking about my mama standing in the bakery with her husband and daughter. They looked like the perfect family without me in it. I wished the wind could have blown me away. I wished Anthony hadn't come to get me, and I could have just walked away and disappeared. It would have saved me the trouble of going back to my father's house, back to where that girl, Geraldine, lived. She's a monster. She started telling me stories about Anthony and the seamstress, about the evil doings of my mama. But Andy was always there to shoo her away, so I never heard a lot. It was kind of weird how Andy was always around. It was like he was keeping an eye out for me.

When I first arrived at the house, I thought I had won the grand prize. I was going to become a prince and live in wealth and luxury. My imagination had no boundaries. There was no thought of ever returning to Taiwan if I lived in a place like this.

But Anthony's baba, who is my Ah Gung, was cold and unwelcoming. He made me feel like a servant. I avoided him at all costs.

Anthony's mama, my Ah Po, was nice, but she treated me

like a foreigner and not like family. She would have breakfast with me and ask all sorts of questions about being a "Chinaman" but not really a "Chinaman." She was curious about life in Taiwan but not the day-to-day stuff. She wanted to know about what the women were wearing and what the latest trends were. I was twelve! How would I know? I couldn't treat them like family either. Their skin was white like ivory, their eyes were big and bright, their clothes were fine, they always had hot food available, and servants were always there to help with anything. I was not used to this sort of living. Every morning there were plates of scones, pancakes, toast, or whatever else you wanted for breakfast. The food felt heavy inside me. Lunch and dinner were big meals too. Whatever they wanted they got. The amount of food was too much and seemed a waste. It went against what Mary had taught me about valuing what I already had and not wishing for more.

Then there was Geraldine. She was in her twenties and I remember wondering why she wasn't married. She didn't look like she did anything around the house, and her eyes scared me. She seemed to pop up in places someone shouldn't be.

One day a closet in the hallway opened in front of me. The door swung toward me, providing a natural space to hide behind. Geraldine then stepped out of this door and walked down the hallway in the opposite direction, not looking back to see if anyone was there. When I looked inside the closet, there were just cleaning supplies like a big vacuum and mops, nothing of significance really. When I heard her come back, I turned to make it look like I was walking the other way. But she didn't seem to notice; she was focused on something in her hand and reentered the closet. I tiptoed back and peaked in the door to see her moving the cleaning supplies out of the way and clawing at something on the back wall. To my amazement a door appeared, and she pried it open and disappeared through it. My curiosity took over and I followed her. It was an old tunnel and she had lit a couple of torches along the path.

Geraldine was talking to someone and I followed her voice. She wasn't too far ahead, and I saw her put something down on the ground. She stepped to the side and I saw that she had put a mouse in a jar. She was listening for something and shaking a bag in front of her. Then, I heard a meow. I had never seen a cat in this house before and wondered where it had come from. Next thing I knew, she had opened the jar and the mouse came running out. But it didn't run straight. It had heard the meow, too, and had turned around and come running back in my direction. I tried to run back to the door before Geraldine saw me, but it was too late. She ran after me, yelling about privacy. I was able to get through the door and back out into the hallway, but she caught up to me there. Her eyes were crazed, and she called me a lot of names I had never heard before, but I knew they were not nice words and they made me feel like trash, which I imagined was her goal. No one was home that day except her and I. No one else heard her screaming except the staff, and I had learned they kept to themselves—except for Andy and Cook, who took care of me. Besides Anthony, they were the only ones who were nice to me.

Andy had heard the yelling—either that or someone had told him—and he came to my rescue. He told Geraldine to leave me alone or he threatened to tell Lord Anthony. Then, I was brought to Cook, who gave me some warm soup and cake. I am not used to their cake. It is heavy and too sweet, but I didn't dare say no. They were nice to me. I valued that.

I didn't want to admit it, but I felt a little bit better after their kindness. I have not told anyone about my experience in Portland, or about meeting my white family. It was not a good experience. It was scary and I never want to see them again. Maybe there is something to writing things down as I do feel better for sharing that. I'll see what else I can remember tomorrow.

51年1月4日 (Thursday, January 4, 1962)

I've been looking at the picture of Grace and me; the picture we took when I was still living with Mary, and the one we took in private without our family knowing. It was right before I left for America. Grace was excited for me. She looked at it as a chance to meet my new family. So, she wanted to have a picture taken to remember me in case I didn't come back. She's smiling with her head leaning toward me. I'm an inch taller than her. We were the same height in elementary school but in the last year, I have started growing faster.

I need to ask Mr. Wang for some money to buy new clothes. My pants are getting a bit short. My sleeves are, too, now that I look at them. I roll them up all day, so I don't usually notice them. I wonder if Mr. Wang will give me money. We haven't talked about payment, just learning and food and a room to sleep.

51年1月5日 (Friday, January 5, 1962)

I wrote a note to Grace. I told her I was sorry. I told her I couldn't go back but that didn't mean I didn't miss her and that I wanted her back in my life. I explained about how I was feeling, and that I was writing in my journal. I dropped the note under the big rock in the front of her house and left a mark on the rock so she would know where it was. It's the same place that I've left notes for her in the past. I hope she gets it. Guess I will have to wait and see. I'll come back in two days to check if she leaves a return note for me under the rock.

51年1月6日 (Saturday, January 6, 1962)

So, Mr. Wang confirmed that I will receive no payment, just food and a place to stay. I guess I should not be picky. I did run away from home after all. The big news today is that I do not have to check if Grace left a note under the rock tomorrow as she came to the studio to see me! She said she missed me, too, but she was still mad at me. She says Mary is still looking for me. I told her that I don't want to see her. I trust Grace; she won't give me away. We talked for a long time. Mr. Wang did not bother us or ask me to get back to my work. I think he was glad that I was talking to someone my own age, especially Grace. He had been wondering why she wasn't coming by anymore.

She brought me food her mama had cooked. She saw what we were eating and said she'll bring more when she can so that I have something healthy besides the street food Mr. Wang and I eat. I love her. I think she feels the same. We are like two magnets—we can't stay apart even if we wanted to.

51年1月7日 (Sunday, January 7, 1962)

Mr. Wang gave me money to buy two new pairs of clothes, some socks, and a pair of shoes. I also saw Mary today. She was shopping in the same market as I was. I almost came out to say hi, but I hid behind a stall until she walked away. She looked older than I remembered. Like she had cried every night since I last saw her. My heart broke but I couldn't talk to her; I'm set in my decision to stay away. I went back to the studio, forgetting half of the things that I promised to buy and cried all day. Mr. Wang was frustrated with me because my tears kept mixing with the paint, making it too watery. He said I'm wasting his supplies and I will need to do extra chores to make up for it. I don't care. I miss Mary. But I am still so mad at her.

51年1月18日 (Thursday, January 18, 1962)

I've made a decision. I told Mr. Wang that I am no longer going to write in this journal. It's wasted my time and his. Instead, I could spend the time working on my art, which would be a better use of my time. He said my strokes and overall control of the brush was improving, so he agreed that I didn't need to write anymore. He also sat me down and said there were easier ways to make a living besides being an artist. He had inherited a plot of land and he said that I could live on it and become a farmer, then I would have crops that I could sell and earn a profit from. He explained that there was no guarantee anyone would like my art and I might not ever sell a single painting. But I said there was also no guarantee that I would ever be able to grow anything on his farm.

I told him Ah Ma tried to teach me how to take care of an orchid one time, but the plant started wilting under my care. It took a lot of love from Ah Ma to make it come back. Mr. Wang said if this was my choice then I had to stick with it. I was not allowed to go back on my decision and I had to apply myself to my art every day. I said yes, and we made an agreement that I would not cry or mope around the place anymore. I would take my art studies with him seriously and apply myself until I became a master too. I want to one day show my art in an art gallery and have people buy them to hang up in their homes. Mr. Wang said if that is what I want, then I have a long way to go. He said that everyone has this dream, but few will make that dream come true. But I'll show him. When I set my mind on something, I stick with it.

It looked like he used the journal as a sketch book for a while. There were no more entries for probably ten pages. Then it started up again five years later.

54年4月12日 (Monday, April 12, 1965)

It's been a while since I've written in this journal and a lot has happened since my last entry. The biggest news is that I'm eighteen this year. The other is that Mr. Wang used one of his connections to land me my first art show. I have signed all of my paintings with a plum blossom. It's my one tribute to Mary, something to remember her by, and people won't associate them as my paintings either. I made an agreement with myself that I will never contact Mary or anyone in the family again. I am my own man and I will keep it that way. No one will get hurt any longer.

Mr. Wang has been good to his word and trained me well. I can work on my art while traveling. Grace got accepted into an undergrad program in America, so we will go there first. It's a place called Berkeley and it's very hard to get into, but I believed in her. Of all people, Grace could get into any school she wanted to, and the only one who didn't believe that was her. She left me for a year saying it was too hard to keep my location a secret from Mary. But then she came back. We are like magnets; we cannot stay away from each other. She told me she loves me, and we intend to start a new life together.

54年7月13日 (Tuesday, July 13, 1965)

We are here! We are in America! Grace and I, just the two of us and no one else. We arrived last week and have already tried spaghetti, pizza, crepes, and so much cheese. We have made some new friends in the apartment we rent. Grace can walk to campus, and provided I am not bothering other people, I am allowed to set up my easel and paint wherever I want there. I paint scenery on campus, but I also paint from memory. Mainly Taiwan scenery and places that people here have not seen before as I find that more people stop to look at them and ask me questions when I'm painting scenes from Taiwan. I think that this will be a good life for us.

56年7月18日 (Tuesday, July 18, 1967)

Grace has asked me why I don't write in this journal anymore. I say it's because I am bored with words and I would rather be working on my paintings. But she insists that I write something down to mark today, so that is what I am doing.

We have been in the States for two years now. Grace is doing very well in school, and I am selling my paintings on the street and sometimes at fairs. Berkeley is a very fun place. I feel free here. Free to do whatever I want.

Grace and I decided today that when she graduates, we are going to travel. We will backpack through Europe like our new white friends do and see the world. I hope she's happy that I have written this down.

She says this journal has been good for me as she saw a change in me after I wrote the long entry about my Portland visit. Maybe this has helped. Who knows? Regardless, I am glad I have Grace. She is the one who saved me.

59年7月6日 (Monday, July 6, 1970)

We did it! We have been in Europe for a year now. I have eaten so much cheese that I think my body is made of cheese now. It is my favorite food. We have ridden trains, met so many different people, and learned new words that I have trouble remembering but Grace does not. I follow her every-where. Wherever she wants to go, I find a way to make that happen. We have seen Paris, London, and all the little cities in between. There is still so much to see, though, and we have made new friends—friends who are generous with their couches and their food. And the best news is that I proposed to Grace at the top of the Eiffel Tower! And she said yes! We are going to have a small wedding with friends in Europe, even though Grace really wants to go back to Taiwan with her family.

This is the life. I am so happy!

59年8月12日 (Wednesday, August 12, 1970)

The news just keeps getting better. Grace's family actually want to come to Europe for the wedding. They said that since we are here, we can show them around. It'll just be her parents and siblings. I am so excited that I agreed to let Grace send an invitation to Mary. If Mary comes, I will apologize to her. I miss her. But what if she doesn't come . . . ? I guess I'll know that she didn't care about me as much as she said she did.

60年6月5日 (Saturday, June 5, 1971)

I can't believe today is the day! I have to record what's about to happen. This journal has become our record of big events. One of our friends is letting us get married in his family's vineyard, so we invited about twenty friends to join us. Our guests also include Grace's family, who are finally here. Mary never responded to her invitation but I'm still hoping she shows up today. I really want her to come.

This entry is much later on . . . and Mary didn't come. She didn't come! I was so upset but I didn't let it ruin the occasion. It was a beautiful day. Grace was like a fairy. She had her own glow that shined brighter than anyone else there. She made me very, very happy today. Her family has also made her very happy by attending. She misses them and I feel guilty about not wanting to go back to Taiwan.

Her mama talked to me about my silence with my family, but she said she would not interfere. She's not happy that her daughter does not live in Taiwan, but Grace has always been independent. I don't know what Grace has told her parents about me and Mary, but I'm grateful that they don't try to control our lives.

Grace has rare parents. She has said many times before

that her parents have always let her do whatever she wants. Within boundaries, she always adds, pointing a finger at me. Yet she has always known what freedom is and now she has shown me what it can be too—free from traditions and obligations, free from my past, and free from people who don't want me.

A handwritten note appeared here.

Grace never got her big banquet in Taiwan, surrounded by her family. I owe her this.

60年10月1日 (Friday, October 1, 1971)

Grace is pregnant! And we're going to have a boy! She made me wait to record it here until she'd passed the first three months mark. We are so excited. Grace is glowing. She has never looked more beautiful.

61年3月28日 (Tuesday, March 28, 1972)

Erik Lin was born this morning. He's perfect. We are so in love with him. Ten fingers and ten toes. I have no idea what I am doing but Grace is a natural mama. Our family is complete.

62年2月14日 (Wednesday, February 14, 1973)

I took Grace out for a romantic dinner for Valentine's Day today. This is a tradition we have also picked up from the Western world. During dinner, we talked about our family. Grace wants more kids and to move back to Berkeley. Her parents also want to move to the States to be with us.

I told her I don't understand why she wants to change our lifestyle but really, I do. I just don't want to admit it. It has been hard living from place to place with a child, but we made it work. However, now Grace wants stability. She wants to settle into a neighborhood and put down roots.

Her parents moved around when she was little and she hated it. She also said that if we moved back to California, we'd be that much closer to Taiwan if we ever wanted to go back. I think she's hinting that she wants to but I'm not ready for that just yet. I don't know if I ever will be. My paintings are doing well, though, and now might be the time to go back to Berkeley. Maybe I can open a store there.

Happy Valentine's Day.

64年4月7日 (Monday, April 7, 1975)

We have a boy and a girl now. Erik is three and Leslie is almost one. I told Grace we are done now, and she said, "Maybe."

I opened a postcard store, or that's what Grace calls it. It's really my art studio but I wanted to sell my paintings on items that people walking by might want to grab too. Plus, this allows me to sell other items if I choose.

We found a house in Oakland, and I have to say it's nice to be back in Berkeley. I also found a word that explains my life very well: outrageous. I like this word 'outrageous.' I have always known the word but haven't spoken it aloud before, especially like I heard this man say it recently. He was walking down the street toward me, pointing his fingers at everything and everyone and repeating "Outrageous!" over and over again. He was clearly mad about something or someone. I walked across the street to avoid him, but I kept watching him as he continued down the street.

Since then, the word has gone round and round in my head. I think it describes my life very well. Outrageous.

69年2月14日 (Monday, September 8, 1980)

Paul was born today. He's a healthy boy with ten fingers and ten toes. I love him just like the other two, but this really is our last kid! I told Grace so. I said "This is it. No more."

I'm super happy, but there will definitely be no more kids. This time she agreed.

70年5月6日 (Wednesday, May 6, 1981)

I learned about a new gallery in Taiwan. It's called The Living Art Gallery, and it's for artists who are still alive. I sent some paintings over for their consideration and I just received a letter back that they want more. This could be my big break! They are going to showcase my work as a Taiwanese artist even though I don't live there anymore. They promised to keep my identity a secret. Maybe if this all goes well, I can take Grace back to Taiwan. Her parents have lived near us for five years now, but maybe we could all go back for a visit. I know that would make Grace happy. The kids should also see Taiwan and where their parents are from.

Thoughts of Mary make me pause, but I don't have to see her. She might not want to see me either. Who knows if she's even still around or how to even get in touch with her? I still think about her a lot. I don't tell this to Grace anymore, but I do miss her. It has been too long.

100年4月19日 (Tuesday, April 19, 2011)

A lot has happened since I last wrote in you. Paul found you on the shelf, stuffed behind some canvases. He's so quizzical, always looking for things and digging where he shouldn't be digging. He asks so many questions that my head hurts. He's always been like this since he could talk. It drives me crazy. But Grace does not mind. He definitely takes after her.

I flicked back through the journal after I found him reading it, and I realized I never did take Grace back to

Taiwan. I had the best of intentions, yet she never said anything. I should really bring Grace back with me some time soon.

I've been thinking of throwing this journal away, but then today, I got an email from a girl named Anne. She says she's my niece. How she found me after all these years I don't know, but Grace told me that I should sit down and write about it. She thinks that writing it down has always helped me, and she also said that I've become a grumpy old man. I'm not a grumpy old man! I just like my privacy.

But how do I know if this Anne is even my real niece? Her email has brought back a lot of memories I'd thought were gone forever. I had locked them up tight, but they are now pushing themselves to the front, wanting my attention after all these years. It's like they are begging me to sift through them—and I don't want to! How dare she open up this wound again?

100年4月20日 (Wednesday, April 20, 2011)

I made the mistake of telling Grace about the return email I sent back to Anne. I can't keep a secret from Grace; she knows everything about me. Well, as I should have known, Grace got mad at me. She said I was acting like a child, no better than Madison when she doesn't get what she wants and she's six. I resent that. I do not act like a child. I just like to have a little fun, and I also don't like the memories that this woman, Anne, has brought up.

Much later on . . . I have been brooding on this matter all day. Why is my past following me? I moved on. I live in America with the family that Grace and I created. We have grandchildren now. We live a happy, simple life.

But Grace made a good point today. She said that I'll never be truly happy if I don't make peace with my past. I told her that that was a sappy Hollywood ending and she gave me her knowing stare. She's right. She's always right. I don't know why I bother arguing with her except that I wish I was right on this point.

I don't want to face my past; I've done a really good job of running away from it. We've lived a good life, but I can't deny that my heart wants to know what this Anne has to say.

My painting of Mama is already at the gallery. I'm flying there tomorrow night. Bettie will be surprised that I will actually be showing up. It's fun to keep her guessing. Maybe I'll see this Anne there and find out what this is all about. Maybe.

100年4月22日 (Friday, April 22, 2011)

I saw Anne. I didn't do anything—didn't approach her or meet her, but she did catch a glimpse of me. In that moment, she looked upset. Is finding me that emotional? I struggle to believe it. I'm nobody. I'm old. She looks about the same age as Paul, and has features like Leslie. I can tell she grew up in America.

What am I to do? I can't deny I'm curious but seeing her in person has made it all too real.

On another note, Taiwan has changed so much. It doesn't look anything like I remember.

100年4月29日 (Friday, April 29, 2011)

Grace is forcing me to end this. She does not want me going in circles again. She's right—again. I need to figure out what is going on or just put it to rest once and for all and be happy with my grumpy self. She says I'm driving her crazy. I'm driving her crazy? What about her, pushing me all the time to address my past. What does she think is going on in my head? I feel like a tornado has picked up my brain and won't let it settle. I don't know what to do.

That was the last entry in the journal, but there was a note scribbled at the bottom.

Anne, as you know, I showed up at your house and here we are. You now know more about me than you probably ever wanted to know. I'm going to let you choose if you want to get to know me more or if we should just let whatever this is rest. Even my own children don't really talk to me. Their mama is the angel in our relationship; the one who keeps us all together. If not for Grace then I would be happy to live by myself, painting and selling my art, and never having to talk to another person again.

I promise I will send you back your Ah Po's journals when I am done reading them. Do not worry. I might be a grumpy old man, but I am not a liar.

Harrison

CHAPTER 20

MY BED WAS SO COMFY THAT I HAD A WONDERFUL
nap. I loved that I could stretch out in all directions without
hitting anyone. When I woke up, I saw the journal sitting
next to me on the bedside table. What a tortured young soul
Harrison was. I couldn't imagine how he had lived with that
loss all these years, never seeing or being with family he
loved. He'd held onto hatred for so long that he didn't know
how to overcome it.

I never wanted to be like that, and I wasn't going to let
Geraldine or Isabella stop me from hanging out with the
others . . . which meant that I shouldn't be hiding in my
room when I'd been invited here for Lauren's celebration.

At least Lauren was happy, and that was all that mattered.
For the life of me, I couldn't figure out what she saw in
Isabella, or how they could be so close. They were complete
opposites.

I freshened up and went downstairs to see what I had
missed when Lauren accosted me in the hallway.

"Anne! You missed it. Victoria was awesome! She was the
fastest through the obstacle course!"

"That's wonderful! How did you do?"

"I was right behind her the whole way," she said, beaming.

"And you're okay with that?"

"Of course! I don't mind losing to her. You don't know how lucky you are to have Victoria. She sings high praises about you and she's such a good friend."

"Wow . . ."

"Come and join us when you're ready, okay? I would love to get to know you better." Lauren gave me a hug so tight that I thought I was going to be squeezed in half. The girl was strong. "Oh, Grandma Catherine wants to talk to you too," she added, finally letting me go. "She mentioned it this morning and I totally forgot. She's in her room. It's the third door down the hall if you want to talk to her now. See you soon, okay?"

"Okay." I couldn't help but smile. Lauren did that to people; she was like a ray of sunshine.

As Lauren walked away, I decided to get this talk with Grandma Catherine out of the way and headed to her room. The door was ajar, and when I knocked, a strong voice told me to come in.

"Anne, dear, come and sit with me." Catherine was seated at a table applying her makeup, and I found a stool next to her and tried to make myself comfortable.

Catherine turned to look at me. This was the first time that I'd been this close to her, and I could see the wrinkles in her face and hands. There were streaks of white in her gray hair and her skin was soft, yet there was a strength to her. Her eyes sparkled with life, and her hands were steady as she applied her lipstick to her still full lips. "Is my sister being nice to you?" she asked.

"Geraldine?"

"Who else? We both know she hates your guts."

Catherine started chuckling. "Geraldine was the most spoiled of all of us. My father adored her; he let her get away with everything. Do you know that she used to have a cat? She found him wandering around the garden one day. She started feeding him and eventually brought him into the house where he tried to destroy the sunroom. It was comical.

"My mother and I were walking by at the time and you should have seen my mother's face. I had never seen it go that shade of pale like it did then. That was the one and only time that Geraldine got in real trouble. They made her get rid of the cat. We never saw him again, but she once mentioned a tunnel that she used to explore. She took me there once, and I bet she took all of us siblings at one point. It looked like it hadn't been used in a long time. She had put torches in the walls to light the path, and there were a few other hallways and rooms coming off the tunnel.

"It looked like a place for storage and smuggling. No one really knew what things my grandfather used to do in there. Well, maybe Father, but I wouldn't put it past him to have been the one to show Geraldine the tunnel so that she could hide her cat in one of the rooms there."

I now knew where Lauren got her talkative streak from. Catherine was still going.

"The cat had made a friend! Did you know that? Geraldine was showing off her tunnel to me, which I thought was kind of creepy, when I heard all this meowing. She didn't try to hide the cats. You have to understand that she's our youngest sibling. Anthony was right about what he said in his will—Geraldine didn't get enough love while growing up. We all loved her but didn't have time for her. I probably played with her the most because I was the next in line, but she and I couldn't be more different—as you've probably noticed just by the way we dress." She smiled at this and patted my leg as if acknowledging that I was still there.

"What was I saying? I can't keep track of my thoughts as well as I used to in my old age."

"The meowing?"

"Oh yes. Geraldine took me to a room in that tunnel, and what should I see but a family of cats and kittens! There were four grown cats and about ten kittens wandering around in there."

I must have had a horrified look on my face because Catherine was quick to add, "She wasn't hurting them. There wasn't even a door to the room and it was pretty spacious. The animals were free to come and go. They also had access to food, because I saw a couple of dead mice. I truly think Geraldine loved them, and I know they gave her unconditional love in return because all of them came up to her and rubbed their heads on her leg at one point while we were there. Now, you must be wondering why in the world I am telling you all this?"

"Well . . . yes."

"Geraldine might seem like a grouch, but she's still capable of caring. She's not a monster like I'm sure she has become in your head." Catherine was looking at me with some seriousness now, and I tensed involuntarily. "How she treated Rose was awful. There are times where I wish I had stood up for Rose more. I really liked Rose, and I think we could have been friends if we were teenagers in today's world. But back then, a friendship with a Taiwanese woman, especially a servant, was a big no no.

"Geraldine persuaded me to give her my voting rights on the family trust. I didn't think anything about it at the time. It's not like it would change anything, but I did not realize she would become so fixated on getting you out. She's always felt Rose was the reason for Father's and Anthony's break. She thinks Anthony could have been a better man if your grandmother had never appeared."

I started to object, but Catherine held up her hand and continued, "I do not agree with her and no matter how much I talk to her it doesn't seem to make a difference. You see this plum blossom brooch on my collar? I see you're wearing yours too. Isn't Lauren the best? I think she's the most like me, even more so than my namesake, her youngest cousin. Anyway, this brooch is my way of telling Geraldine that her fixation is silly.

"I know your Sebastian and Jack are working on something. You have a good man in Sebastian, Anne. I just talked to him last week and I told him a lot of what I'm telling you. Make sure you hang on to him."

Sebastian was working on something with my inheritance? I wondered if he'd made any headway. I was still confused why Catherine was sharing all this with me.

"Don't let Geraldine step all over you," she carried on. "And don't hide yourself away from everyone because of her, or even Isabella. Yes, yes, I know how Isabella can be. We are family, after all. She takes after Geraldine a bit too much for my liking but it's not for me to say. Goodness knows, Geraldine and Isabella's mother have given me enough of a talking to that I know I need to butt out. We're not all like them is what I'm trying to say. In fact, very few of us are like them. And Isabella, I think, can still change for the better if she got the chance. I still hold out hope for that girl. Anyone Lauren loves that much must have some sort of nice bone in her, right?" By now, the sparkle had returned to her eyes.

"Keep your head up, Anne, and make sure Lauren has a fantastic weekend," she continued. "Reach out to me or Jack if you want to see a saner side of the Wilkens family too. Now, you better be off to join the others before they think you've left."

"Yes, ma'am." I didn't know what else to say. That was more about Geraldine than I had ever heard before.

I headed out of Catherine's room in a daze. Geraldine had raised a family of cats? Didn't Harrison's journal mention that he'd seen her going into a tunnel in the hallway as she'd been trying to entice a cat? She must have been crazy and super lonely. I couldn't imagine being in a big family and not getting any attention from anyone. Deep in thought, I almost walked into one of the girls sitting on the floor in the living room.

The whole lot of them were nestled under blankets and pillows watching Kate and Leopold while drinking hot chocolate. I felt a little guilty that I had pulled myself away from the party. I could have at least cheered the gladiator exercise on from the sidelines.

"Anne, come here," Victoria said from across the room, patting a spot next to her.

I winded my way through the girls and nestled down next to Victoria, getting some smiles from the rest of the girls.

"I found you fast asleep in your room but thought you might wake up in the middle of the movie, so I saved a hot chocolate for you. It's cold now, but chocolate is chocolate."

"Thanks, Victoria."

"Your back doing okay?"

"It's only a little bit sore now. The nap did it good."

"Good. No more skipping out on activities, okay?"

"Definitely." And I vowed to be more involved for the rest of the weekend.

The next day consisted of sailing, and a run that I did out of guilt for not participating in the obstacle race. The problem was: I did not enjoy running at all. Plus, it was so hot I could hardly catch my breath. At first, Victoria wouldn't let me stop running. I'd slow down to a jog, but she would then keep pushing me to go faster. Eventually, even she got tired of me holding the group back, so the party went on ahead and only Gillian stayed with me. She jumped right in with questions as soon as we were alone.

"So, how has it been inheriting Lord Anthony's properties and all that money?" Gillian asked.

"Um . . ." What was I supposed to say? I didn't know how close she was to Isabella. Even then, Gillian wasn't family, so why was it her business to even ask?

"That well, huh?" she said.

I turned to look at her and was surprised to see sympathy written all over her face. At the very least, I was expecting her to laugh at me. Isabella really had done a number on me; I expected the worse out of anyone who was related or even close to the Wilkens family.

"It could be better." I left it at that, but clearly, she didn't get the message.

"Lauren is the nicest person you'll ever meet. She is the epitome of niceness. I've known her since high school when I moved to Portland."

"That's how long I've known Victoria. She moved to Astoria when we were in high school," I said, latching onto the subject.

"How wonderful! Yeah, if it wasn't for Lauren, I don't know how I could have gotten through ballet camp, or school for that matter. There were too many spoiled rich kids who looked down at me."

"I get what you mean. It was super nice to have a close friend like Victoria who understood me through high school."

"Yeah."

Our simple conversation made me bold to ask her something that had been weighing on my mind. "This is a fantastic party," I puffed out, slowing my pace even more to accommodate our conversation. "I don't know how you got all of these events put together in such a short time."

"Money speaks and Lauren's parents spared no expense."

"Yeah . . ." Why was it always about money? "You must know her really well, then."

"I do, and I think I know where you're going with this." Her mouth turned slowly upward in a knowing smile.

"How are Lauren and Isabella—?"

"So close?" she cut in, panting.

"Yeah, I mean, they're totally different people."

At this, Gillian started laughing. "They are, aren't they?" She shook her head and laughed for quite a while. "Sorry, it's a subject Lauren and I have touched on from time to time," she continued. "I'm not very fond of Isabella, and after watching your interaction with her this weekend, I'd say you're not too keen on her yourself."

I nodded my head in acknowledgement, finding that was quite hard to do while jogging.

"Isabella is—how do I say it? An acquired taste?"

"You can say that again."

This insinuated more laughter from Gillian. When she finally calmed down, she said, "Lauren is very protective of Isabella. She's told me a little about how hard Isabella's life has been, how her parents weren't the best. Worthless is how Lauren put it. They grew up together, you know. Isabella was always at Lauren's house having dinner with her family once a week. She won't say much about Isabella, not even to me, but from the little that I've gathered, Isabella saved her from something, and she has been loyal and protective of Lauren's secret ever since. It's not a subject Lauren likes to talk about much, so I haven't dug deeper, and Isabella doesn't usually hang out with Lauren when I'm around, so I never really got to know her that well either. Isabella's always been aloof but very put together. I have no idea how she does it."

I nodded my head; I couldn't help but agree. "I'm always amazed at how good she looks whenever I see her."

"Isabella was the queen bee at school, that's for sure. There were always people around her, and everyone knew to never cross her. There was a rumor that she had a mean streak and that she had someone do her dirty work. Like, she'd dig up your secrets so she could use them as blackmail." Gillian stopped to drink some water. "Though I don't know how much blackmail you could get out of kids, but I guess many of them did since most of them had parents with infinite amounts of cash. So, I guess to answer your question, I don't really know why Lauren and Isabella are so tight, except that something big happened and Isabella helped Lauren out with it, and then that sealed their bond."

"That's more than I knew."

Gillian took another swig of water, then she lowered it suddenly. "Oh! I just thought of something I think you should know, but you didn't hear it from me."

"Okay . . ."

Gillian gestured at me to start walking, and I realized that time was getting on. We were no doubt lagging way behind now. As I kept pace beside her, she said, "Last night, I overheard Isabella and Lauren talking."

"Is this something I'm going to regret hearing?" I asked quickly.

"Maybe . . . but I think you should know. I overheard Isabella asking Lauren if she could talk to you about giving up your inheritance. She said something about letting you keep the Taiwan condo if that was necessary because you're Taiwanese and most likely will want that one." Gillian gave me a little shrug when she caught my expression. "Don't give me that look. I have no problem with you being Taiwanese, but Isabella does and always has. I thought you'd like to know instead of being ambushed by Lauren later—if she ever brings it up, that is."

"So, she's using Lauren now," I said under my breath. I decided that it was best to ignore the comment about me being Taiwanese. After all, it wasn't the first time I'd heard something like that.

"Oh, she's always used Lauren," Gillian replied, clearly having bat ears. "I don't like how Lauren acts around Isabella, but like I said, the two are bonded."

"Well, thanks for letting me know." *I think. Should I be looking over my shoulder to see if Lauren will be coming at me soon to discuss giving up my inheritance?*

"Here's the first stop!" Gillian said, jolting me out of my thoughts.

My stomach plummeted. "What do you mean 'first stop'? There's more?"

"Oh yes, this goes on for quite a bit. You going to be okay?"

I felt faint but I wasn't going to show any weakness, so I took a deep breath and followed Gillian to the cooler that was sitting on the rocks. At least the view was beautiful.

"I'm so thirsty. I finished my water bottle already," Gillian said, showing me her empty bottle.

She filled up her bottle with some water from the cooler, and the two of us stared out at the open expanse, each lost in our own thoughts. After a while we started up again. We made it to the end of the trail eventually, and I swear my legs would have fallen off if they weren't attached.

That night, someone had set up a campfire in the backyard. A huge smores kit was sitting close by, ready for our consumption. We sat around the fire and listened as the girls shared stories from their childhood—stories of parties, beer pong competitions, boys, and other sentimental moments that had brought this group of girls together. Even Isabella shared a couple of stories.

I hated to admit it but I was enjoying myself. The fire was warm, I had helped myself to some wine, and the company wasn't too bad. Even Isabella seemed relaxed. She was on a lounge chair and had a decent smile on her face. Catherine and Geraldine had retired early, saying they were too old to hang out so late.

One by one, the girls excused themselves and went to bed. Even Victoria said she was beat and headed on up. Before long, it was just Lauren and me. We were both sitting on the lounge chairs facing the pool. I started to get up to head to bed when Lauren started talking.

"I hope you're enjoying yourself," Lauren slurred, turning her head to look at me. She had a happy glow about her.

"I'm having a great time. Thank you for inviting me."

"Anytime, Anne. I really like you. You're so simple."

I wasn't sure how to take that but seeing how Lauren had never been malicious toward me, I took it as her just being inebriated and not being able to find the right words.

"I must look like a mess," she continued. "I tend to let loose when I drink too much. Isabella usually takes me to bed, but I guess she's had enough of me too." She said this last part with some sadness.

"It's your bachelorette party; you should enjoy yourself. I wouldn't look too much into Isabella's actions."

"You don't think much of her, do you?" Lauren asked, trying to sit up so she could talk to me more directly.

"Well, she hasn't—"

"I heard about the bombing earlier this year," Lauren suddenly blurted out. "I really don't think Isabella did it. She can be nasty but she isn't into killing. Now, her grandmother on the other hand . . . Have I told you that even Isabella thinks she's a witch?"

"No." I wasn't sure what else to say to this.

"We got in a fight earlier today . . . before we met up with the rest of the group. You know she's like a sister to me, don't you? I would do anything for her, but I'm just so tired. She's so domineering. It's the reason why Stephen and I got in a fight recently when you took me to see the florist. Do you remember? He's so tired of me doing Isabella's bidding."

Lauren sat up, leaned over, and grabbed my wrist. "Isabella really is a good person, Anne. She really is." She collapsed back on the chair as if saying that took some effort. I couldn't tell if she was laughing or crying. There were tears running down her face, but she was still smiling and laughing and sipping her wine.

The subject changed again. "You know I'm a lightweight? Always have been. Isabella knows that, you know? She knows everything about me. And I want to believe I know everything about her, but who knows with Isabella. Her family is so good at keeping secrets that I think it's like an ingrained gene that gets passed down every generation. Or, you know, it could just be Grandmother Geraldine. She, you need to be careful of; she's racist." Then, she burst out laughing like that was the funniest joke anyone had ever made. "I said it out loud, Anne! I did, didn't I?"

I could only nod. I didn't know if I should take her upstairs and put her to bed or let her fall asleep here. It was a warm night, and to tell you the truth, I liked laying here, too, and didn't really want to move.

"Isabella loved Grandma Geraldine when she was growing up. They were each other's favorites. Isabella's mother hated it. She tried to severe the relationship at one point, but she was too distracted by her friends and charity events to do anything serious about it. Grandma Geraldine had all the time in the world. I don't think she's ever worked in her life, so Isabella has really learned from the best, you know. Grandma Geraldine is really good at manipulating." At this, Lauren got so sad that it was my turn to console her.

Noticing my movement, Lauren cried, "Anne, you really are the sweetest! I saw you and Gillian talking during the run. Isn't she the best? She's the total opposite of Isabella, but they're both so good at heart. They really are."

I didn't know if she was trying to persuade me or herself about Isabella's caliber. But what I did know is that I was starting to get sleepy and the drone of her voice was incredibly soothing.

"Did I mention Isabella and I got in a fight this morning?" Lauren continued. "Over the same thing Stephen got mad at me about when I went to look at the roses with you. You were invited, Anne, because I wanted you here. Your friend, Victoria, is awesome. I'm really so happy the two of you could make it here. Oh, I guess this technically is your house now anyway, so you should be able to come, even without an invite."

I felt like I should interject. "You're always welcome, Lauren. I'm very glad you invited us. Victoria and I are having a fantastic time."

"That's so good to hear," she said in a half-asleep voice.

I noticed she had put her wine glass on the table and had curled up in a fetal position. A last coherent thought flashed through my head and I asked quickly, "What were you two fighting about?"

"Oh, it was about you," she whispered. "Isabella has her heart set on getting everything back from you. At least, I think she does, but she doesn't seem as certain as she usually is on things. I think if she really wanted to take everything away from you that she would have already done so. It never takes Isabella long to get what she wants. You know that's how she saved me, don't you?"

Lauren was almost asleep, but at this point, I was more awake than ever. I needed to hear what she had to say so I reached over and poked her until her eyes opened again.

"Did I fall asleep?" she asked all of a sudden, eyes now wide open. "I told you I'm a lightweight, right? You're going to stay close, right? Don't leave me alone. Isabella usually would but she's still mad at me that you're here this week-end. She's the one who wanted the party here in the first place. I don't know what she expected. I mean, I couldn't host it here and not invite you."

"Lauren, how did Isabella save you?" My feet were on the ground and I was leaning forward, waiting to hear what she had to say.

"Oh, I was stupid and naive in high school. I thought Rudy really loved me; he said he did. I believed him and thought he was going to ask me to marry him in our senior year. Our families are really good friends, you know? Anyway, I grew up with him and I always had this crush on him, but he dumped me the day we graduated. We hadn't even changed out of our graduation outfits! Turns out he met a girl when he went to his college orientation and he realized then and there that he wanted to start a relationship with a more sophisticated girl. Can you believe it? I gave him everything. I was so heartbroken." There was silence for a little bit before she continued, "Anne, have you ever been treated poorly by a guy?"

"I have," I whispered, but Lauren heard me.

"We're like sisters, maybe in a past life," Lauren said, reaching out to hold my hand.

"But what did Isabella do?" I pressed again.

"She saved me. My parents were so mad at Rudy that our family relationship almost fell apart. And that would have been very bad for business seeing how my family provided the fashion contacts that Rudy's family needed to run their business." At my quizzical expression, she clarified, "They resell couture outfits that designers don't want anymore. Oh! I could take you there one day and you could pick a couple of dresses out for yourself. They're beautiful, even if the designers thought they were flawed."

"But why . . .?" I had been poking her awake this whole time, and to give Lauren credit, she wasn't complaining.

"Isabella smoothed everything over," she finally explained. "She even said something to the girl Rudy had started seeing, and she dumped him before he'd even moved into his dorm. It was the best day when he called me and said it was all my fault and why couldn't I just let him be happy. Can you believe it? He asked *me* why I couldn't just let him be happy! I owe Isabella a lot, but I do think that she's taking advantage of that old incident by still asking me for favors. And I'm tired, Anne. Did you know Isabella was the one who wanted the party in Hawaii? And she pushed to have it earlier rather than later. I just wanted a simple party in Portland with my girlfriends.

"Anne, you have no idea how lucky you are to not have grown up with a family that has all this money and influence. You're so down-to-earth." This time, Lauren seemed to be finished, and I watched as her eyes slowly closed. But then her brain seemed to catch up, and she suddenly sat back up and said, "Oh, I've said such terrible things about Isabella! Don't tell her, okay? She'll be so mad." At this, she put her finger to her mouth and said a loud, "Shh!" Then, she added, "I want to be with Stephen; start a new life. You know he doesn't like Isabella? He thinks she's a bad influence on me. And he's the sweetest guy. I don't want to lose him, but I do love Isabella too. She really isn't a bad person, Anne. She really isn't."

By now, I had stopped poking her, and I just watched as this time, Lauren fell asleep. I decided to lay back down on the chair and close my eyes as well. Confusion fogged my mind and what better way to clear it up than to sleep on it? Maybe tomorrow would be better and I could make more sense out of what Lauren had shared tonight.

She mustn't have been fully asleep because out of nowhere, she asked, "Will you be my friend, Anne? I'm envious of what you and Victoria have. I'd like to be your friend."

I didn't answer because when I looked over, Lauren's arm had slid off the chair and she was breathing deeply. But I knew that if she asked me again, I would say yes.

CHAPTER 21

THE NEXT MORNING, I WOKE UP TO FIND MYSELF ON the lounge chair with Lauren still asleep beside me. It was a bit chilly in the morning air, so I found a blanket to put over Lauren and tiptoed back into the house.

Once again, the only person in the kitchen was Geraldine. She was the last person I wanted to be with. I turned to leave before she saw me, but halfway through the door, I remembered what Catherine had said: "She's not a monster."

Catherine had almost humanized Geraldine. Besides, this was my home now and she was a guest. I decided to turn around and look for some breakfast, even if she was going to give me the stink eye the whole time. While rummaging through the pantry, I could feel her eyes boring into my back.

"Anne, we got off on the wrong foot yesterday," I heard her say from behind me.

I turned around and looked at Geraldine. There wasn't a smile, no shining eyes, no sign of her playing a trick on me. Did I hear what I thought I'd heard?

"Anne, come here and sit next to me," Geraldine said, patting the chair next to her.

I couldn't help it; she was like a siren drawing me in. My curiosity piqued, I walked around the island and took the seat next to her.

"We got off on the wrong foot yesterday," she began.

"So you said." I could feel the hairs on my arms standing on end. What was she playing?

"I received something today. Something that has me very concerned for you."

I felt my mouth gape. "You're concerned for me?"

"Isabella has told me how you're like a fish out of water and struggling to fit into our world. I apologize for my outburst yesterday. I got a good talking to about it and I promise it won't happen again."

It truly looked like she meant it. *Was this even the same person from yesterday?* What was she up to?

"What do you say we start over?" she continued. "I'm Geraldine Wilkens, Anthony's youngest sibling. I knew your grandmother, but you know that already. My brothers and sisters tell me I was spoiled, but I like to think I knew how to enjoy the finer things in life, which was how we were brought up. Isabella is my protege. Did she tell you that? I love her dearly."

I could now feel the hairs on my legs rising up in warning too.

"Isabella mentioned that you've hired the private detective she uses—Nick, isn't it? She mentioned something about looking for your uncle. How is that going?"

I was surprised that Isabella had mentioned it. "He found my uncle, and my mom is spending time with him as we speak."

"How nice. Brother and sister reunited. You do not have any siblings?"

"No, I do not."

"That's a pity as they keep life interesting. Someone who

has known you your whole life is the most comfortable person you can be around. It makes me sad that you will never know what that feels like."

"I think my life is going just fine."

"Speaking about your life," she said, pausing to pick up her tea. "Nick was also doing some investigating for me. Please do not take this the wrong way. I know it does not seem like it, but we have your best interests at heart. There are things . . . about Sebastian's past that you do not know about."

Ah, so here it was. The trying to get me away from Sebastian trick. Well, let's see what you've got.

"Isabella tells me that you and Sebastian are quite close these days," Geraldine said.

"Yes, but that's none of your—"

She held up a hand to stop me. "Sebastian is like a son to me. Did you know I took care of him when his parents didn't? That I helped him find information on his biological family? Did you know that?"

"No, but I'm sure there's a reason—"

Once again, her hand shot up to stop me. "The Donaldson family—do you know them?"

I shook my head, not bothering to say anything this time.

"They're very influential, as big as my family. Their daughter was rumored to have had a child with their gardener. It was very scandalous, you must understand— someone of her standing stooping so low. I'm glad none of my children ever did a thing like that. Well, as it was, Sebastian was that child. She was forced to give him up, and he grew up with two very ordinary parents who raised him to be a nice young man."

"Why are you telling me this?"

"Just wait. It'll become clear soon." She took another drink of tea. "Did you know his mother passed away during his senior year of high school? That's when Isabella met him. So, you see, Isabella and Sebastian have been together for a long time. I've molded Sebastian so that he is what a man should be: strong, independent, well-groomed with impeccable manners, and with the ability to carry himself in our society. I have a vested interest in knowing that he will have a partner in life who will meet his standards."

Was this a threat? She was even worse than Isabella. This whole time, her features had been either neutral or loving when she spoke about Isabella or Sebastian.

"Isabella has been telling me that Sebastian has not been acting like himself recently. She was very distraught by it, so I asked Nick to follow him. It was only for my own piece of mind, but I just received some photos that might concern you, and I couldn't not share them with you."

Really? She couldn't not share them with me. If I could roll my eyes even further back into my head, I would.

I watched as Geraldine pulled her phone out and rifled through whatever files she was searching for. She didn't say a word while she turned the phone around so I could see the image on the screen.

At first, I wasn't sure what I was looking at. Sebastian was sitting at a cafe with a lady. She had wavy brunette hair with kind eyes that looked like she was or had been recently crying, and she wore a business suit that matched Sebastian's. They both looked well-dressed and I assumed they were coworkers. I didn't know why Geraldine was showing this to me, but on closer inspection, I noticed how he leaned in toward her, how his hands wrapped around hers as if to offer comfort, and how close they were sitting next to each other. Without a word, Geraldine scrolled to the last picture, which illustrated Sebastian holding her in his arms.

"Her name is Sarah," Geraldine said. "She works at the same law firm as Sebastian, and she's been there for years.

I've always felt uncomfortable with Sebastian working at that law firm with all those other females. I think girls should be home tending to their own affairs. But that's beside the point. I tried to warn Isabella, but this was one area where she would never listen to me. So, I'm letting you know now as you and Sebastian are together. You do with the information as you wish, but don't say I didn't warn you. I ask you, Anne, do you really think you know who Sebastian is?"

I didn't know what to think. All I knew was that I needed to get out of here. Away from Geraldine. There was no way that what she was sharing with me was for my own good. She was up to something and I didn't want to know what that was right now. Instead, I needed to go to my room and pack and get ready to leave Hawaii. I started backing up.

"Are you okay, Anne? I'm sorry if I scared you," Geraldine said, and this time I thought I saw the hint of a smile. But it could also be my imagination.

Once again, I couldn't be happier when Isabella walked in. "What are you two talking about? I didn't know you two liked each other now."

"We don't," I managed to say.

"Anne and I were just having a bit of a heart-to-heart, weren't we, Anne?" I saw her fingers tap on her phone and turn it face down on the island.

"Yes. I'm going to go now. I have a plane to catch with Victoria."

"Oh, I just saw Victoria. She was looking for you upstairs," Isabella said with her face turned into the fridge— probably looking for champagne to celebrate how Geraldine had scared me.

I couldn't get out of the kitchen fast enough. Thank goodness Victoria was in our room already packing. I followed her example and threw everything into my luggage.

CHAPTER 22

I GOT HOME. WITHOUT VICTORIA. THERE WAS A last-minute change of travel plans, and Victoria left with Lauren and the gang for Italy. Just like that. So and so had a family villa, someone else had a private jet, and everyone apparently had time to jet off for a couple of days, so off they went. They, of course, wanted me to join, but I couldn't abandon Mom when she had made so much progress with Harrison.

So, here I was, back in Portland and all by myself, throwing myself another pity party. Even Sebastian hadn't answered his phone since I'd arrived home this morning. Like a good girl, I waited at the mansion to sign for the package that was supposed to arrive today. I was brooding, pacing back and forth in my room about what to do with myself when the doorbell rang.

Good thing I wasn't wearing socks because I almost slipped down the stairs in my rush to get to the door. Any visitor would do, as long as it was someone who cared about me and who could tell me that everything would be okay.

The person at the door was not who I thought it would be.

"Hi, Anne."

I couldn't form words in my mouth. Why was he here? At my house?

"Can I come in?"

"No," I said without thinking. "I mean, yes. Wait—no! Why are you here?" I walked out and closed the door to make sure Brian couldn't come in.

"I meant what I said in Taiwan—I've missed you, Anne. I really want us to work, and I thought what better way than to come here and see you. Was I wrong?"

"No . . ." Where was Victoria? I needed her here and she was off with Lauren, her new best friend. "Brian, there's nothing to work on. You dumped me. It was a nice surprise to see you in Taiwan, and yes, it brought back good memories, but you were a jerk to me."

"Yes," he said loudly with his arms raised in surrender. "I was a jerk. I didn't know what I was doing. But, Anne, you're the one. After all these girls—"

"All these girls? Do you even know how you're coming off?" I was starting to feel a bit heated. He just decided that one day he wanted me back and thought I'd say yes? Was I really that compliant when I was with him? It reminded me of what Victoria had said about me following him around and doing what he wanted with no thought of my own needs.

I heard the sound of a car driving up the driveway and was about to turn around to see who it was when Brian leaned in and planted a kiss on my lips. I was so taken aback that at first I didn't push him away. My initial thought was how nice it was to be kissed again. But logic kicked in after that and with one shove, I tried to push him off me.

But Brian grabbed my hand and held me close, whispering, "Just think about what I said. You saw how well we gelled in Taiwan. You couldn't possibly have that type of chemistry with Sebastian."

Then he turned and left. Just like that. I was left on the front porch in a stupor as he got in his car and drove off down the driveway.

"So, you don't have any feelings for Brian?"

I turned to find Sebastian looking at me with sad eyes and tight lips, arms laden with roses and a picnic basket where the top of a wine bottle was sticking out. He looked so good with his worn jeans, a button-down shirt that had the top unbuttoned with the sleeves rolled up to his elbows, hair thick and tousled, and a morning shadow across his jaw.

His timing today, however, was turning out to be a sore spot.

"It's not what it looks like," I began to say.

"Of course it doesn't; you just lingered on that kiss a bit longer than someone who wouldn't have welcomed it." I could hear the spite in his voice.

"Are you accusing me of having feelings for Brian?"

"Maybe I am."

"That's big of you to say seeing how you and Isabella—"

"Isabella and I have been over for quite a while. I quit my job for you!"

"Big deal quitting your job! You didn't even like working for them after Anthony passed away, anyway. You're still just as busy, and I'm still not able to spend much time with you."

"Really? That's how you feel about it?"

I pushed on. "Plus, Geraldine showed me pictures of you and a brunette cozying up to each other!"

That got his attention. His back went stiff, straight as a board, and his eyes narrowed. I could see his fingers tightening around the roses and the picnic basket.

I'd gone too far but I was so ramped up. "Did you not trust me when I said there's nothing between Brian and me?"

I threw out in exasperation, hoping the change in topic with me at the center of it would ease his anger.

But Sebastian was not to be deterred. "What brunette? And when did you and Geraldine get so cozy?"

"She knows things about you, and apparently you come from a super-rich family. You never shared that with me. What other secrets do you have up your sleeve?"

I got no response back. Just a steely glare that sent shivers down my spine. In slow motion, he placed the basket down at his feet and lay the roses carefully on top. Then, he walked toward me until there was only an inch between us. I could smell his mustiness, and my anger immediately subsided, but I could tell that his was not coming down any time soon.

"Listen to me, Anne. I came here to surprise you, to welcome you home. Instead, I'm just going to say this: Stay away from Geraldine; she's dangerous. Even Jack is on edge about her and she's his own sister. She's used that same tactic of showing pictures of me with another girl to Isabella too. The only brunette I know of is Sarah from work, and she's going through a breakup and might lose her son. You know me, so you decide what you want to believe from Geraldine. I, for one, have never trusted her." He paused and looked as if he might kiss me. I wanted him to. I wanted to forget this whole stupid argument, but all he did was take a deep breath, close his eyes, turn around, and walk away.

My adrenaline was high, my heart pounding at what just happened. I could only stand there and watch his car drive away, taking my heart with him. *What in the world just happened? What in the world just happened?!*

In a daze, I managed to walk back into the house and find a seat in the sitting room. I stared at the TV. *Did that really just happen?* The two boys in my life, who I have each had a close relationship with just met on my porch at the same time. What were the chances of that?

My thoughts wandered to Geraldine. What did he mean about Geraldine? The bombing flashed through my head, and I wondered if Sebastian had found any evidence. It couldn't be her. Isabella was the younger, more manipulative one whereas Geraldine was just plain mean. I got the feeling that she played mental games with people, and maybe that was what she was doing in the kitchen on that last day in Hawaii. Before I could dive anymore into my thoughts the phone rang.

"Will you accept a collect call from Mom?" asked the bored voice on the other end.

A collect call? What happened to her cell phone? I didn't even know people could still make collect calls. "Yes," I said in a rush. "I accept."

"Putting you through now, miss. One moment."

The line clicked. "Mom?" I asked.

"Oh, Anne!" She sounded out of breath. "I know it's silly that I called you by collect, but Harrison and I left the house without our phones, and I had to share this with you as soon as I found out. We'd like to throw a party at your place if that's okay? Harrison's whole family will be there—including his kids and grandkids. I had mentioned in my voicemail that it would just be a family get-together. Isn't this great? Two of the grandkids have birthdays soon, and we thought we could put together a party at the mansion. I have Harrison right here." Her voice got quiet, and I could somewhat hear her asking Harrison if he wanted to talk to me. I chuckled, thinking about the two siblings at a pay phone.

Mom came back on the line. "He's so excited, Anne. Anyways, more on that later because Harrison is going to show me the view from the Headlands now."

"That sounds great, Mom."

"Fantastic. Okay, we'll see you soon, sweetie."

For the first time today, I felt a smile come over my face. I was happy that Mom and Harrison were bonding. It had been a long time coming. I wondered what his kids were like. Mom seemed to like them, but would they like me? After all these years it was weird to think that I now had cousins. Legit cousins by birth, and not ones you just called 'cousins' because you desperately wanted them when everyone else went on vacation to see their extended family for the holidays.

And a birthday party to welcome Harrison and his family? Well, that would be a fantastic distraction from what had happened this morning.

CHAPTER 23

Mom called later in the day to share more details of what she had planned for the party. She was intent on making sure Harrison and his family felt like they were 'coming home' rather than feeling like guests.

She said we should hire a professional cleaning company to clean the entire house. We'd air out all the rooms and Cook would make a Taiwanese feast with a whole roast pig, fried sticky rice cakes, and many other wonderful delicacies. I had to throw in other food, too, including carrot cake, duck confit, and enchiladas. And, of course, an extra chocolate cake because there were two birthdays to celebrate!

It'd be a smorgasbord of food from all over the world. It wouldn't be as fancy as the Christmas Gala, but it'd be close to it. I thought Harrison and Grace would appreciate that since they had traveled so much. I couldn't wait. This was going to be more fun than the Gala, because this function would just be for immediate family—a nice intimate group.

I rolled my eyes. *Who was I kidding?* I was a nervous wreck. I'd only met Harrison once, and Grace sounded nice enough, but I didn't really know them or their kids and grandkids. Would they like me? Just because they were also Taiwanese didn't mean we'd get along. They were total strangers from San Francisco—big city people. Would they expect more than I could offer? I had the money to provide an amazing family reunion, but I didn't know what they would like to do that weekend. What if I messed everything up and they didn't enjoy anything I'd planned? Would they want anything more to do with me?

"Anne?" Ben asked, poking his head into the library.

Thank goodness he came in right then. I could feel the spiral that I was descending down slowly unwind. "Ben, you're just the person I wanted to see!" I paused at the hesitant look on his face. "Oh, but it seems you wanted to ask me a question first."

He seemed embarrassed all of a sudden. "No, Miss, please continue."

Conscious that Ben took his job seriously, I asked in my gentlest voice, "Ben, what was it that you wanted to come and ask me about?" I had vowed to not be the kind of person who took staff for granted.

"Well, I . . ."

"Ben, you know you can ask me anything."

"Yes, I just . . ."

"Spit it out." I started laughing. I couldn't help it. But when I saw this was making him feel more embarrassed, I pulled it back quickly.

"My mother's birthday is coming up and she hasn't been feeling well. I was wondering if I could take a few days off," he finally confessed.

"Oh, Ben, of course! Take a week. You haven't gone home in a while. I'm sure she'll love to see you."

"Oh, I couldn't take that much time off."

"I insist. When would this be?"

"Her birthday is in a week, so I could leave tomorrow and come back shortly after."

Right when I needed him to help with this party. But no, I wasn't going to be the kind of owner that held their staff back for their own whims.

"Of course, that sounds terrific," I said instead. "Say happy birthday to your mom for me."

"Thank you, Anne, I appreciate it. And what was it that you wanted to see me about?"

"Oh, nothing. It's not important," I said, trying my best to look carefree and as if it had been a trivial matter. But the look he gave me told me that he didn't really believe me.

"Well, let me know if I can be of help. There's also a large package that just arrived for you."

"Oh, fun! That must be the package from Harrison."

I ran to the foyer to see what it could be and I wasn't disappointed. The package was indeed huge. After locating a crowbar, we were able to get the huge staples out of the wooden frame and ply the top off. Inside was a bunch of packing peanuts and I mean a lot. I dug my hand in and felt something solid in the middle. Grabbing hold, I pulled out the inner package and took out what looked like a painting wrapped in layers of bubble wrap. Unwrapping the bubble wrap exposed the backsides of two paintings, both of which were framed with gilded flowers, just like the ones you'd see in a museum. I pulled the two paintings apart and tossed the cardboard that was between them away.

"Ben, can you help me prop them up?"

With the help of other staff, I managed to get the two paintings propped up against the wall so that I could properly view them.

"Miss, they're beautiful!" I heard Ben say from behind me.

I turned to see Ben and the other staff members looking at what all the fuss was about.

"I'm glad you like them," I said, beaming.

One of the paintings was a smaller version of the one I had seen in Taiwan—Harrison's masterpiece of Rose and her child running in the fountain with the mansion in the background. I couldn't believe he had sent it to me. The other almost made me tear up. It was a painting of Mom and me with our arms around each other's shoulders, the Portland skyline behind us. I don't think anyone had ever done a painting of the two of us before. Mom had done a few fun ones, and other artists had completed some quick little sketches of us when I was little, but I had never liked sitting for them.

There was a note tucked under one of the frames and I went to read it.

Anne,

Your mama showing up on my doorstep was the last thing I wanted. But like you, she was persistent. I'm glad she was. We have gotten to know each other better over the last week and I'm happy to know that I have a sister now, one who can share with me stories about my mama, although, I have also learned a lot from the journals. I haven't thanked the people in my life enough, so I wanted to start with you. Thank you for letting me borrow the journals and for not demanding them back. Thank you for being patient with me. I saw how your home still looked and felt a lot like Anthony's, and I thought these paintings would be a start to warming up the place. I hope you enjoy them. I look forward to seeing you again this coming weekend and for the whole family to finally be together.

Harrison

. . .

I saw Grace had put in a note at the bottom of the paper too.

Anne,

What you have done means the world to me. Harrison is stubborn like a mule; he will never initiate anything. To see him so happy now makes my heart sing. Thank you for all you have done. We look forward to seeing you soon.

Grace

Ben left for his mom's birthday and a much-deserved vacation the following day.

I hated to admit that the first day he was gone did not go very well. The fire wasn't made when I came downstairs in the morning and even though it wasn't super cold anymore, there was still a nip in the air. Cook would send Lavender to remind me to have my meals, but if I even delayed by a few minutes, I would forget, and Ben wasn't there to remind me again. I realized how dependent on him I had become in the short time I had been here. I felt like a fraud and ended the day reprimanding myself for being someone I wasn't. I was not dependent on others, living the life of luxury and not wanting of anything in life. I'd become complacent.

I flopped myself onto my bed and groaned. This wasn't me. I wasn't someone who needed things and others to make them happy. I used to go and find adventure on my own. I took care of myself.

I pushed off the bed and came to my feet, catching sight of my dog watching me with inquisitive eyes, her nose on her paws. Taking my recent vow in stride, I said aloud, "Lady, you and I should go into town and have dinner."

I took her to Bowser's Lounge where Bowser himself was

a ten-year-old cocker spaniel. Bowser's Lounge was the best dog-friendly restaurant in town. The waitstaff had taken a liking to Lady the few times I had come with Sebastian or Victoria, so I thought it would be the perfect place to treat both me and Lady for a night out.

"Table for one?" the waiter asked.

I didn't like how he asked it—as if it wasn't obvious that I was by myself. "Yes, just me and Lady here."

He nodded. "Follow me."

On the other hand, with that response, he seemed like he couldn't have cared less. Was I being oversensitive?

There were plenty of dog bowls filled with water, and they even brought out some food for Lady. I ordered the fried chicken and waffle. Nothing would ever compare to Cook's or Mom's cooking, but there was something about treating yourself to a meal in a place that wasn't home. The food just tasted different, or maybe it was just all the grease they used so freely in restaurants. Whichever the case, the food was delicious.

The thought that I was spoiled for thinking Cook's food was 'just normal' did not escape me, but this chicken and waffle did taste extra good tonight.

"Well, you look like you haven't seen good cooking in a while," said a voice by my table.

I looked up to see Lucia, Sebastian's favorite florist. A huge grin broke out on both of our faces. I hadn't seen Lucia since Lauren and I had stopped by her shop to discuss the flowers for her wedding, which was happening this weekend.

I stood up to give her a hug. "Lucia, it's so good to see you!"

"Sweetie, it's great to see you too."

I motioned for her to join me, and she sat across from me, waving the waiter off.

"I could tell that he was going to have me sit at the far

end by the kitchen so I'm glad I saw you first," Lucia said. "How was Lauren's bachelorette party? Did you have fun?"

"It was great!" I said a bit too enthusiastically, even to my ears.

"That great, huh?" I could see there was no fooling Lucia, so while we ate our dinner, I filled her in on what had happened in Hawaii, and what had been going on since I had returned home. Lucia was a fantastic listener and let me tell the tale from beginning to end without interrupting. I knew I wouldn't have gotten through it if she had stopped me at any point.

"Seems like you did the right thing coming out to eat tonight," she finally said.

"Yeah, it felt freeing to come out and just do my own thing without any obligations."

"Have you had to follow the bidding of others for a while?" Lucia asked, concern written across her face.

"Oh, no! No, no, nothing like that. I just . . ." What was I complaining about? Nothing, that's what. I was just complaining for the sake of complaining. I jabbed at my chicken to see how many holes I could put in it before the crust flaked off.

"The chicken is already dead," Lucia said.

When I looked up, she was smiling—a motherly smile that relaxed me. "I don't have control of my feelings at the moment," I shared, then I held up a hand as I ticked off the following points on my fingers. "Sebastian is mad at me, he also warned me against someone who might physically hurt me, my best friend has gone off with my enemy to Europe, and I'm left here by myself."

"You did say you wanted to be friends with Lauren," Lucia reminded me.

"Lauren isn't my enemy. Isabella is on that trip too."

"Unlike others, I think it's okay to wallow in your own self-pity. For as long as you need."

"Thank—"

"But," Lucia cut in, "you must come out of it with some self-worth. You must look for your own ladder to climb, not someone else's. Not Sebastian's, not Victoria's, not your mother's, not anyone's but yours. Look at it like that party you said your mother wants to put on for your uncle."

"What about it? Wouldn't that be doing something for someone else?"

"Not necessarily. Yes, the party is for someone else, but why can't you make it fun for yourself and do something special while also making it inviting for your new family at the same time?"

A feeling of hope and excitement stirred in my chest. "I hadn't thought of it like that."

"Sweetheart, I know this whole inheritance thing hasn't been easy for you."

"You do?" I hadn't meant for it to come out so snarky, but if Lucia noticed, she didn't say.

"Sebastian comes and sees me from time to time," she said, smiling. "That boy loves you."

"You weren't there when he got mad at me," I returned.

"He had just caught you kissing your ex. How do you think he should have acted?" Lucia gave me a raised eyebrow, which from her was saying something. "I'd be more worried if he hadn't cared."

"That's true . . ."

"Give Sebastian a call," she encouraged. "Talk to him. Invite him to your family party."

"I plan to do that," I said, feeling the first real smile come over my face since dinner had started. "Thanks for listening to me, Lucia."

"Of course, dear! You're like family. And Sebastian is wonderful, Anne. He just needs some time."

I nodded and then asked, "Lucia, can I ask you one more thing?"

"Go ahead, dear," Lucia said, digging into the last of her sundae.

"Do you know if Isabella still—"

"Let me stop you right there," Lucia said, raising a hand in front of her. She paused and took a drink of water before composing herself and looking me straight in the eyes. It was a bit unnerving because Lucia was never one hundred percent serious. I mean, even during all her remarks earlier, she had kept a happy demeanor. But now, there was a certain steadfastness to her features as she said, "Isabella is—how would we call her? Unique, damaged, lost, spoiled—a sad little girl, maybe?"

A part of me was shocked at her description of Isabella that all I could think to say was, "Well, she's not that little anymore."

"She might look like a grown woman, but I can guarantee you that there's a scared little girl still hidden inside her, driving her through life. I'm sure Isabella has never gained control over that part of herself."

"You sound like you care about her."

Ignoring my question, Lucia continued, "Sebastian loved her dearly. The flowers he would send her were always the most beautiful ones I had. Some I had to specially order in for him, because no one else would ever spend that kind of money on flowers, at least not from my store.

"He came to my store for the first time when he was about twenty. He was just blooming into manhood and deeply in love with Isabella, and her with him. But he came in looking very sad this day. He told me a story he'd heard from Isabella about how her parents argue. She told him that they always fought, but this time she could tell something was different. Her parents went to their separate rooms, but her father came back out with two suitcases. He didn't even look at her when she came up to him to ask what was happening. Instead, he walked right past her and out the door without a word.

"When Isabella got to the front door, she saw him climb into a car and lean over the car seat to kiss another woman on the mouth. Now, how do you think a girl who grew up in a household like that would turn out? I'm sure that wasn't the only sad thing that ever happened to her while she was growing up either. Anyways, the point of this is that you shouldn't judge others until you have taken the time to get to know them. Everyone has secrets they hold dear to their heart, sometimes without even knowing."

"Even you, Lucia?"

"Even me, my sweet girl. But goodness, I almost forgot! Tell your friend, Lauren, that if she wants to switch out the blue roses for a lighter shade of blue then she'll need to give me a call. I finally got them in and I can have the bouquets made in time for her wedding if she wants them."

"I'll do that, Lucia. You're the best." I had a thought then and asked quickly, "Can I also order flowers from you for my party?"

"Do you really have to ask?" Lucia laughed. Her laughter was contagious and next thing I knew, I was laughing along with her.

This dinner out was definitely the best decision I had made for myself in a while.

CHAPTER 24

ISABELLA

"You imbecile!" I yelled as I whirled to face Nick. "Tell him he's an imbecile, Nick!"

"You're an—"

"Oh, you two!" I never lost my composure but these two were going to pop a nerve.

I had arrived home from Italy just this morning. Nick, of course, picked me up from the airport and updated me on all the gossip. He was giving me a foot massage when the doorbell rung. I opened it to find Brian on my front step congratulating himself on the great deed he had done by kissing Anne in front of Sebastian. He was sure he had won her over.

How full of himself could he be? Even I knew Anne was smart enough to see through his act. Then he had the audacity to ask me for payment, claiming that we had a deal!

"Let me put it to you in plain English, Brian: The. Deal. Is. Off. You were supposed to break them up in Taiwan, and that didn't happen. Therefore, there is and never will be any money coming to you."

"You never put a deadline on the deal, so as far as I'm

concerned the deal is still on. I expect money in my account by the end of the week."

"You haven't shown proof that Anne is not with Sebastian anymore," Nick chimed in.

"Boys! There is no deal anymore. End of discussion."

"We'll see about that," Brian said, and before I could get another word in, he turned and left.

I was too stunned to say anything. He walked out on our conversation? No one does that to me! I turned to Nick.

"Isabella—"

"You were no help!" I cried, cutting him off.

"Wouldn't it be the same if he broke them up now, though?"

"No."

"Why not?"

"It just wouldn't, okay!" I didn't like snapping at Nick. He'd always been by my side, but I really didn't want to talk about Sebastian and Anne anymore. I would have to deal with whatever Brian had done another time.

"Okay, okay, how did that call go with Great Uncle Jack?"

"It went fine."

"He never calls you, though."

"I wouldn't say never. It's just very rare."

"What did he want?"

"Just to catch up on Grandma Geraldine."

"What's up with . . .?"

"I don't want to talk about it. Weren't you about to make some drinks for us?"

"Yes. I'll be right back."

I watched as Nick walked back into the house. Finally, some quiet. Grandma Geraldine was my idol growing up, but lately something was nagging at me. Then there was Uncle Jack's phone call. I had a lot to think about.

CHAPTER 25

ANNE

The week flew by in a blur. I threw myself into preparing the party. Mom had said they would be here on Friday and that they intended on staying here for the weekend.

I wanted to show them that even though I was rich now, I was still down-to-earth. Of course, that didn't mean I couldn't throw money at their visit. As such, every room got a thorough cleaning from top to bottom. And I mean thorough. Me and whoever was willing to help took toothpicks to the carvings we could reach and dug out grime, dust, and whatever else had become imbedded in all the little crevices. It was kind of liberating. I felt alive and useful just cleaning the whole place. A cleaning crew was paid to do most of the cleaning, but even they couldn't and wouldn't get into every nook and cranny, and I really wanted to add my own sense of worth while giving the house a fresh start.

Some new throw rugs were bought to replace the ones that were thinning and unraveling at the edges. Rooms were repainted, some with the original colors and some to tone them down. One was all gray. I had no idea who would want a gray room, but I changed it to a nice warm cream.

Sheets were replaced, drapes were cleaned, the windows were opened to air out the rooms, bathrooms were polished, ceilings were combed for cobwebs, and Cook and I came up with a menu suitable for a feast. Mom had mentioned that Harrison and Grace missed the street food you could easily obtain in Taiwan. So, I found a whole bunch of recipes online and gave them to Cook who did her magic. We tested sample after sample until we got them just right. We nailed freshly squeezed soy milk, shao bing you tiao, dang bing, and luo bo gao. But of course, there was the main courses to attend to as well, and we decided to make xiao long bao. I knew Sebastian would love those as he still mentioned that he missed them whenever we ate.

Thoughts of him made me sad because I had tried to call him every day, but he never picked up or returned my calls. Luckily, Victoria came back midway through the week, and even though I was still a bit miffed she had jetted off with Isabella, I was so happy to see her that I couldn't stay angry with her for too long. True to our friendship, she threw herself into helping me get the house ready for my family and the party.

The whole time she worked, Victoria updated me on how fun her trip had been and what a great person Lauren was. She also mentioned that she might be wrong about Isabella. *Wrong about Isabella?* What Kool-Aid had she drank? But I knew deep down that I was starting to have second thoughts about Isabella too. Especially after what Lucia had said.

"Anne, you so should have come with us," Victoria said as we began to dig the dirt out of another carving. Then she stopped what she was doing and faced me suddenly. "Your family isn't even here yet and you're already overthinking this party. They aren't expecting anything; they just want to meet you."

"How do you know? You haven't met them either."

"Because anyone your mother loves are always nice people."

"Okay, true, but maybe she's wrong this time."

"Why are you being so negative?"

"I'm scared, okay? I'm scared they won't like me. If I think they aren't nice people, my expectations will be a lot lower."

Victoria gave me a long look. "You're right. I don't know, but I still think you're overthinking this party. But I know they're going to love you! Look at those paintings Harrison gave you! They're gorgeous! And it fits so well over the mantel in the sitting room."

I needed to get off the subject of my family. I knew Victoria was only trying to help, but I was getting more and more nervous the more she talked about them. "I'm glad you had fun in Italy," I said, deftly changing the subject.

"I do wish you were there. It just wasn't the same without you. I missed my old travel buddy," Victoria said, coming up to give me a hug. "I know how stressful it's been with finding Harrison, then your grandmother's journals being taken, not to mention Sebastian moving your journals in the first place —which we both know wasn't his fault—and . . ." She stopped suddenly and looked around. "Where is Sebastian, anyways? I've been home for two days—"

"We got in a fight."

Victoria stared at me with her hands on her hips. "You two are impossible. Fight, no fight, fight. When are you two not disagreeing and then making up?"

"He saw Brian kissing me." I turned away from Victoria to refocus on digging some more caked dust out of the wall carving we were working on. But after what seemed like ten minutes of silence, I turned to find that Victoria wasn't there. *She got so mad at me that she left?*

I was standing there feeling sorry for myself when she came back down the hallway with two bowls of ice cream. However, she walked right past me.

"Come and join me and spill all your secrets," she called over her shoulder. And with that, she disappeared into the sunroom, me following with my head down. Only Victoria could make me realize the feelings that I had pushed down.

"So, that's what happened the day I got home," I said as I finished up my tale to Victoria.

She sighed. "I always miss the juicy parts of your life these days!"

"You're . . ." I hesitated, waiting to see if Victoria was going to say more before adding incredulously, "not mad at me?"

"Of course not! You said you didn't kiss him back and I believe you. It's Brian that I'm mad at!" Victoria started pacing the room. "That lowlife is up to something. I just know it."

"I don't think—"

"Anne, you never saw him as someone slimy."

"Slimy?" I gave her a look. Was Victoria going crazy now?

"Yes, slimy. Brian is what you would call a snake. He preys on the innocent and then spits them out."

"What in the world?" I doubled over, laughing. Even for Victoria, this was a bit extreme. "Wherever did you start getting these ideas? You knew him in undergrad. He wasn't what you call slimy. Brian's a good guy."

"Oh, you know. Girls talk."

"What girls?" I got a little suspicious that this might have something to do with her trip.

"The girls were talking about boys they'd been with, and Isabella asked about you."

"Okay . . ." *Where was this going?* I had stopped laughing and was now sitting ramrod straight, hoping the stink eye I was giving Victoria was registering.

"I told them about Brian, and 'slimy' was how Isabella described him. I defended you, of course!" She held up a hand before I could stand up. "But now that you've told me what he did, I have to agree with her. I never really liked Brian; he rubs me the wrong way."

"Yeah, you've said that before," I grumbled. "And when did you start listening to Isabella, anyway?"

"I don't! But I do listen to Lauren, and we had a good talk about Isabella and how she's not such a bad person."

"Oh, really?" I was standing by this point.

Victoria held up her hands in surrender. "I'm always up front with you, Anne. I am worried about you—all alone here and without any direction."

"I . . ."

"Look, I don't want to fight. You said earlier that Cook wanted to go over the meals with you again. Why don't you do that and leave me here to keep on cleaning?"

I stared at Victoria for a bit longer, willing my heart rate to go down. "Fine, but I don't like what you said." I was never the best at comebacks.

"Love you, Anne," was all I heard as I walked to the kitchen.

Cook had a whole binder out when I sat down next to her at the kitchen table.

Without looking up or with even a hi, she said, "You're sure they're not picky?"

"No, Mom said they will welcome whatever you make." I hesitated a moment before voicing my next thought. "Cook, Victoria was telling me something earlier. We don't have to try so hard. I know I've been pushing this, too, but—"

"And not show off my skills? I don't think so. Here's the menu I've planned." She unfurled a roll of paper that was as long as my arm. "I'll have it printed so everyone can have a copy. I suggest you look over it to make sure it's as we discussed."

I looked it over and saw that Cook had added to to the menu, but everything looked delicious, and I knew my family would love it. I said as much and was quickly dismissed.

After spending the day with Victoria, the hallway seemed even more cold and empty than it usually was. But I was still mad at her, so I decided to go and find a room to clean that was far from the first floor. The last room I had been cleaning was the furthest room at the end of the hallway, just before the stairs to the third floor. So there I headed.

I could hear Victoria humming while she picked grime from the carvings in the library. She knew this was a futile task, as who would ever get through every single carving Anthony had done throughout the house in time, but something about the chore felt uplifting to me. It felt as though we were cleaning out years of sadness from this building.

When I got to the room, it was as I had left it. I was glad to see that no one else had come in to move anything. There was something about this room that I liked. It was a childhood fantasy. There was a four-poster bed against the right wall, with pink satin drapes on all three sides. Even the pillows and blankets were pink. The curtains were a soft beige that matched the carpet, and a vanity table with a mirror sat off to the right.

I had found an ivory-handled hairbrush that looked like it had been kept in there for many decades, and a boudoir at the far end of the room had a drawer in which I opened to find a poster of Elvis. It was rammed all the way in the back and had clearly been left there in a hurry as the ends were crushed. I wondered if it was because Elvis might not have been a parent's choice of idol for their kids back then. I had no qualms with him, though, so the poster was now hanging in my room. I wondered which of Lord Anthony's kids it had belonged to. Catherine was my guess as she was the one who seemed to cross boundaries the most. After that find, I was hoping to unearth more treasures in this room.

I headed to the walk-in closet, remembering I had seen the corner of a trunk hidden in the shadows. Sure enough, a big travel trunk with the most beautiful leather cover and binding sat in the back, with a big lock in the middle and two straps on either side. My heart raced when the lock came undone without any resistance. I quickly undid the straps and pried the top open, letting out a wave of dust. Next thing I knew, I was coughing and sneezing. After clearing the air, I spotted three beautiful, pristine boxes nestled on the top of some blankets. They looked like they were made out of the same wood that the rest of the house was built in, and far older than any of the Wilkens siblings.

Inside the boxes were old pictures, including scribbled notes and drawings, a wooden spinning top, and some play jewelry. They were all leftover pieces from a bygone era. Underneath the boxes, there were a couple of thick blankets that still looked in good shape. Maybe I'd put these on rotation on the various beds in the house? There was no point in having them sit here growing old.

There was nothing else in the bottom of the trunk, so I started to place the three boxes back inside, and it was when I was putting the third box back in that it slipped from my hand and landed with a thud at the bottom of the trunk. My first thought was, *What had I done?*

I went to pick up the box to see what permanent damage I'd made when I heard a click.

"Who's here?" I screamed.

It wasn't until I willed myself to calm down that I realized the room was completely silent. Slowly, poking my head out of the closet, I scanned the room to find it exactly as I had left it. To say I was unnerved was putting it mildly.

I went back into the closet and picked up the box I had dropped. Besides a chip of paint in the corner, the box didn't seem the worse for wear. However, at the bottom of the trunk where the box had landed, a small opening had appeared. I stuck my finger under the gap and slowly pried it open. Inside was a small wooden box, about four-inch by six-inch, covered in hand-painted flowers. Unlike the secret compartment that had appeared under my grandmother's trunk, this finding excited me more than it scared me.

Slowly taking it out of the trunk, I sat back on the carpeted floor wondering what could be hidden in this little box. But a quick glance around the edges showed there were no visible seams. My heart raced as I realized that this was a puzzle box and I would have to follow a specific sequence for moving the sides of the box in order to open it. I got to my feet and ran as fast as I could back to the library, hoping Victoria was still there.

"Victoria!" I screamed, bursting into the library. My heart sank when I didn't see her.

"Up here," she called out.

I looked toward the sound and saw Victoria in the very top corner between the bookcase and the curtains.

"You've been busy," I said, walking toward her.

"It's amazing, Anne! The carvings are literally all over the place and they're beautiful. Some aren't even blossoms.

There's a scene up here of a boat traveling across the ocean—the ocean being these curtains. The boat travels all around the library—look! I've also dug out so much grime that I don't think anyone has ever cleaned these since they were made."

"I wouldn't be surprised. Victoria, can you come down? I have something exciting to show you."

She raised a brow. "More than these carvings? You were super excited to clean these."

"I know, I know. Just come down. You'll want to see this."

Victoria took her own sweet time getting down from the ladder. I sat on the sofa, tapping my fingers on the box.

"What is so exciting that you have to show me now?" she asked, finally coming to sit beside me.

"Look at this box! I found it in one of the rooms. It was hidden in a secret compartment at the bottom of a trunk in the back of a closet."

Victoria's face lit up. "Oooooh!"

"I thought you might like that. But there's more—I can't open it. Look!" I handed her the box.

I watched as Victoria turned the box this way and that, and I could see her excitement build. "It's just like National Treasure!" she cried.

"I know! That's what I was thinking."

"Okay, we need to figure out the steps to open this box."

We spent the rest of the day trying to push in each of its four sides in different combinations, but to no avail. The box did not open. Just as we thought we had found a side that might slide out, I heard my name being called.

"Miss Anne?" It was followed by a light knocking on the door. "Miss Anne?"

I looked up to see Lavender hovering at the entrance.

"Sorry, Lavender, we're engrossed in trying to figure out how to open this box. Can I help with something?"

"An express letter just came for you. I signed for it but it looks urgent."

I got up to take the mail. At first I wanted to laugh and say that it was just junk mail, but when I looked closer, I saw it was from Schuster and Schuster Law Firm. My heart started racing and I stepped back, falling onto the sofa. *What was this?*

"What is it?" Victoria asked, coming to sit next to me.

"Another letter from Schuster and Schuster."

"Why don't I open it for you?" Victoria suggested. She took the letter from my hand and I watched in slow motion as she opened it, pulled out the letter, and read it. All I saw was a bunch of black and white. No words stood out.

"Anne, I'm trying to talk to you. Anne!"

I felt someone shaking me. Then I realized that Victoria had both of her hands on my shoulders and was trying to get my attention. "How bad is it?" I asked.

"It's not pretty."

My stomach plummeted but I forced out, "What is it they want?"

"They've frozen all your assets. This means your money is frozen, but you're still allowed to stay in the house."

"Who's initiating this? Did they say why?" *Thank goodness I already paid for the party and Cook went shopping for food already.*

"It only says on behalf of the Wilkens family. The letter says they have not had any formal confirmation from Harrison yet that he does not want the inheritance, and therefore, none of the money or the houses technically belong to you at this point."

"I was wondering if they had forgotten. Clearly not. But you mean just the Taiwan house, right?"

"No, it says here that they've recently found out that Anthony had left some of his money to Harrison too. But no one knew where Harrison was—"

"Please don't say any more," I said, dropping my head in my hands.

"There's one more thing. It's handwritten at the bottom of the letter."

"Yippee," I said between my fingers.

"Geraldine is coming to visit this weekend."

The silence was thick, and I realized that I had stopped breathing.

"Why?" I managed to say.

"I don't know, it doesn't say. Isn't your family coming—?"

"This weekend!"

The two of us stared at each other for I don't know how long. My first reaction was to start crying, but then a thought came into my head. Did Sebastian know about this? He might not be working for the Wilkens family anymore but he still worked for Jack. Maybe he had a heads-up and didn't bother to tell me.

I picked up my phone and dialed Sebastian's number. This time, he picked up after the first ring. It was like he knew.

"Hi, Anne. You got the notice?" Sebastian said, sounding very tired.

"Did you know?"

"Yes, but I thought I could stop it before they actually went through with it."

"How is this even legal?"

"It's not. You haven't done anything wrong, and just so you know, it's only Geraldine who's initiating this through Schuster and Schuster. She has powerful connections and she wants an investigation. One thing led to another and now your finances are frozen. I was able to convince them to let you stay in your house. I'm sorry, Anne."

"But haven't you been in Schuster and Schuster for a long time now? Even with Geraldine's powerful friends, don't you have some leverage there to put a stop to this?"

"I don't work for Schuster and Schuster anymore . . ." Sebastian said, sounding confused. "I told you I quit."

"I thought that meant that you just quit working for the Wilkens family, though."

"Quitting the Wilkens family is the same thing as quitting Schuster and Schuster, Anne. The family basically runs the place, or let's just say Geraldine does."

"I didn't know Sebastian. I'm—"

"No need to be sorry. I love you, Anne. We will ride this through. Just keep doing what you're doing."

"Do you need me to hire you? How are you getting paid? Are you doing okay? I've been such a jerk. I really didn't know." I had started breathing fast. How could I be so absorbed in my own problems that I hadn't known my boyfriend was jobless and yet still fighting for me? But Sebastian's reaction was not what I expected.

Laughing, he said, "Anne, I'm doing fine. Jack hired me. I'm also thinking of starting my own practice, which is something I've been wanting to do for a long time. It's freeing to not be under the Wilkens's wings anymore. So it's really a good thing and I'm doing fine. I miss you, though."

His words settled my anxiety. "Sebastian, I'm sorry about Brian. I don't know why he was here, and I didn't kiss him back!"

"I know. It was just hard to see."

There was an awkward silence while both of us tried to figure out what to say next. Thankfully, Sebastian took the helm. "Your family is coming tomorrow still?"

"Yes, and Geraldine will be there too."

"What?" Sebastian yelled.

"Yeah, the notice came with a note that she will be here this weekend." I heard a bunch of expletives and then a sudden bang like he had just punched something. Victoria must have heard it, too, because she sent me a startled look.

"Did she say when?" he finally asked.

"No, just this weekend."

More expletives before he said, "I can't come over till Sunday." More expletives.

"Where are you? I thought you said you'd be here for the whole weekend?"

"I'm with Jack at his place. We're trying to put something together."

"Something together?"

Sebastian was suddenly gone from the other end. I heard a mumbled conversation as he spoke with someone else before he came back on. "Shoot, I have to go. I'm sorry. Anne, I love you. Stay safe and have a fantastic time with your family—I really mean that. I will see you this weekend. I promise I'll get there as soon as I can." And with that, he hung up.

"Everything okay? I heard a lot of swearing," Victoria said, taking a seat next to me.

"Yeah, I wonder what he's up to," I said, deep in thought. *Putting something together.* I shook it off and smiled at Victoria. "Shall we make tomorrow the best party we can seeing how it might be the last one we hold here if Geraldine has anything to say about it?"

"Let's!" she said with a wide grin.

CHAPTER 26

IT WAS FRIDAY AFTERNOON, AND I COULDN'T BE happier at how everything came together. The food was prepped and we had enough for a large banquet. The house was also the cleanest I had ever seen it. All the linens were washed, pillows were fluffed, carpets shampooed, and every nook and cranny had been dusted. Fresh flowers were placed in every room, along with new towels and a full set of toiletries. I had bought presents for every single person, and I had even bought *Frozen* decorations because Grace had said that her granddaughters were obsessed with them and wanted a *Frozen* birthday party. Who was I to deny a little girl's wishes? This was going to be the best party ever!

"Anything else you can think of?" Victoria asked.

"No, I think we're ready. Now all we have to do is welcome my family with open arms." Then, with the realization that I had nothing to preoccupy myself with anymore, I felt my anxiety start to rise. "Victoria, what if they don't like me?" I began. "What if they've just been entertaining Mom so they can come and mooch off us?"

"Anne, deep breath. Remember, you've met Harrison. You said he seemed nice—"

"And flighty. He ran off with my grandmother's journals!" But he had sounded like an honest person from his journal entries, and I hoped the rest of his family were nice.

"I'm sure everything will be fine. Deep breath," Victoria repeated. "They're showing up soon, right? You said your mother called to say they landed about two hours ago?"

"Yeah, they—"

"Anne!" I heard Mom scream from the front entrance. My feet couldn't carry me fast enough; I was so excited to see her again.

I flew into her arms. "Mom, what happened? I thought you'd be here already."

Mom gave me the biggest hug. I had always been the one traveling, and to be the one stuck at home while Mom traveled made her homecoming that much sweeter.

"Look at you! Why are you so tense?" Mom asked.

"Because my extended family is showing up and I have no idea how I'll be received. Who knows if they'll like it here or if we'll get along?"

"We will all get along; they are wonderful! You'll see," Mom said, holding my face and giving me a loving look.

"You didn't answer my question about why you're late."

"Oh, they made us sit on the tarmac for forty-five minutes. Can you believe it? We got in early and didn't have a gate, so we just sat there and waited."

"Ms. Lin, it's so good to see you," Victoria piped up. "Where's your brother?"

Leave it to Victoria to remember why Mom was here in the first place. In the last few minutes, I had totally forgotten Harrison and his family were coming too.

"He and Grace are outside looking at the statue. You'll like them. Come meet your family, Anne."

I walked out with Mom while Victoria excused herself. Harrison was exactly as I remembered him: shy, awkward, and bald with a little bit of hair on the sides. He was wearing business slacks and a button-down shirt. His glasses were perched on the tip of his nose, and he shook my hand with lackluster emotion. Grace, on the other hand, was quite the opposite. When Mom called her name, Grace immediately turned and walked over to me with a warm smile, giving me a hug like she had been the one looking for me and had finally found me after all this time rather than the other way around. She had this serenity around her and I immediately relaxed in her presence.

"Ben can help take your bags to your room," I said, once Grace had let me go. "Oh, wait, Ben isn't here."

"It's okay, we can carry our own stuff," Grace said.

"Did you know that when I was here last time, it was the first time I had seen this statue?" Harrison said to me.

"No, I didn't," I said. "How did you . . .?"

"Paint it in so much detail in the painting?"

"Yeah!"

"Anthony sent the gallery a picture of the fountain when it was completed. They forwarded it to me, and I studied it every day for years. Then one night I got very angry and tore it up. It was then that I decided to paint it."

"But you ripped up the photo!"

"When you study something every day, you know it inside and out no matter if you can no longer see it."

"That's enough, Harrison," Grace said, putting a hand on his arm.

The way Harrison looked at Grace made me ache for Sebastian. I wondered when he'd be able to make it this weekend.

"I believe Harrison has something that needs to be returned to you," Grace now said.

"No hurry." Even though I was itching to get my hands back on the journals and confirm they were safe, I didn't want them to think that was the only thing I cared about.

"You are not good at lying," Grace said with a laugh.

"I've always told her that," Mom added.

What was this? My mom and her new sister-in-law ganging up on me?

"Fine! But it's only because I didn't know Harrison all that well the first time I met him."

"Yes, and I am sorry for that," Harrison said. "The journals are safe, though, and it has given me a better understanding and acceptance of my mama. Here, I'll show you." He opened a leather carry-on bag and inside it were Ah Po's journals, all laid out neatly and wrapped in bubble wrap. "I hand-carried them all the way to Oakland and back. They were well taken care of."

"Thank you, Harrison." And I meant it. He had taken care of the journals as much as I would have done. "I'm glad they brought you closer to your mom." Part of me kept forgetting that Ah Po was Harrison's mom too. That he was the result of a love born before its time. "But I'm being a horrible host! Everyone should come in. I'll show you to your rooms so you can get settled, and there are hors d'oeuvres set out for you to enjoy while we wait for everyone else to arrive."

I led everyone through the front doors, and you could hear the gasp Grace tried to hide. Part of me beamed. I was so proud of what we had done to the mansion in the past week. The house really shined. Mom and I let them soak in the foyer before moving them toward the sunroom. Inside, the doors to the gardens were swung open, and this elicited another gasp from Grace.

I decided to initiate the conversation this time. "Mom said you have two sons and a daughter?" I asked Harrison and Grace.

"Yes, Erik, Leslie, and Paul," Grace said. "They should all be arriving tonight. They live in different cities but Paul is actually here in Portland. He had some research he had to finish up today but he'll be here in time for dinner."

"That boy works too hard," Harrison mumbled, shaking his head.

I saw Grace give him a look as she continued, "He's met a really nice girl. She's so vibrant and she brings him out of his shell. I wish she could come today, but she said she had to be there for a friend."

"That's so sweet," Mom said. "Based on what you've told me about Paul, it sounds like having someone who is more of an extrovert is very good for him."

"I agree," Grace said.

"Hmph," was all I heard from Harrison.

I gave Grace a look. She just smiled and shook her head as she said, "Paul is very much like his baba, and it drives Harrison crazy."

"That does not drive me crazy," Harrison said, trying to sound mad, but I could tell he was becoming distracted from the conversation. His hand was rubbing the carvings on the wall. "You said that Anthony did these carvings. I understand better where they came from now, but I don't remember there being so many."

I nodded in confirmation. "The staff and I cleaned them all. Aren't they amazing?"

"Wow, there are so much more to be seen now!" Mom was twirling on her feet and craning her neck to see all the new designs that were visible given grime was no longer coating them. I couldn't be prouder of the work Victoria and I had put in.

Our contemplative silence was broken by a commotion at the entrance, soon followed by a high-pitched scream. We turned around to see a little kid, kicking and screaming in the arms of a man who looked like he had seen better days.

"Look, Madison! It's Ah Gung and Ah Po!" the man cried as he beelined straight to Grace, plopping the girl at her feet. He then turned and walked back to the entrance with his shoulders stooped. The girl, on the other hand, was on her back, full-on crying and flailing her arms and legs around.

I'd never been around little kids and I felt useless watching the scene unfold, but Grace bent down and picked up the little girl who, realizing it wasn't her parents, stopped for a second. Just long enough for Grace to plant a kiss on her cheek and start singing a song to her in Mandarin—a song I recognized, which immediately brought fond memories of Mom singing the same song to me. We all stood there, entranced by the two of them together.

I remembered in that moment that I had never had a grandmother who loved and comforted me. I felt Mom put a hand through mine, and I looked over at her and smiled. I couldn't have asked for anyone better.

The man came back in with an even younger child sleeping in his arms. I tried not to laugh because there was a line of drool flowing down the back of his shirt. A woman shorter than him, and who looked like a younger version of Grace, came in behind him. She went straight to Grace and put a hand on the older child's back and said, "She's been crying since we took off. It's been miserable, and the people on the plane kept giving us nasty looks. I think her ears are bothering her, and she was mad at us for not letting her stay at home. We forgot her lovie, and her best friend was having a birthday party this weekend. I feel horrible."

"Leslie, the child needs to learn that she can't act like this just because she doesn't get what she wants," the man said.

"Jonathan, she's six!" Leslie shot back, giving him such a stern look that he didn't say another word. Continuing to hold the younger child, he turned and walked toward us. That's when I realized Mom and I hadn't welcomed them yet.

"Hi, I'm Anne, and this is my mom, Josephine," I said, holding out my hand.

"Hi, Anne, I'm Jonathan. Yes, we met your mom while she was visiting Harrison." He gave me a lukewarm handshake, but I attributed that to him looking exhausted and awkwardly holding a kid.

"I'm Grace and Harrison's daughter, Leslie," the woman said. "I'm the middle child. These are my children, Madison and Ryan. Madison is six and Ryan is two." Leslie suddenly looked around. "Where are their cousins?" she asked no one in particular, most of her attention still on the older child who had calmed down now and was starting to fall asleep on Grace's shoulder. "I was hoping Erik and his kids would be here already so they could entertain Madison and Ryan."

"Erik and his family are coming after dinner. They decided to drive up," Harrison said. "I have no idea why, we said we'd help book them flights."

"Harrison, that's enough," Grace said in an almost whisper but it did the job.

"Paul said he had something coming up and would come when he's done, but that could be any time," Harrison said, giving another hmph that everyone ignored.

"That's just like Paul. I fly my whole family over to Portland and he still finds something else to delay him," Leslie said.

"Leslie, don't be too hard on him. He says he's onto something really important. And it won't take him long to get here," Grace said, now rocking the girl back and forth.

I watched all of them, mesmerized, thinking that this was *my* family—my own flesh and blood. Lady was having a field day with all the new people here. It wasn't until Mom nudged me and whispered the word "rooms" that I snapped back to the present.

"Your rooms are all made up," I broke in. "Would you like to go there now? I expect you would like to freshen up."

"Oh, that would be wonderful!" Leslie and Grace said in unison.

Ben startled me by coming up from behind and saying, "Please follow me. Your bags are already in your rooms."

"Ben!" What was he doing here? He was supposed to be visiting his mother.

"I got back shortly before your guests arrived," Ben said at the look on my face. "I knew you were keeping something from me, so I asked Cook. And before you ask, Mother is doing very well now. And I told her I'd stop by Sunday evening to see how she was."

I couldn't deny I was relieved. "Thank you, Ben."

My guests followed Ben upstairs to their rooms on the third floor as I'd wanted them to have a picturesque view of the back garden.

"Aren't they wonderful?" Mom said to me as they left. She was beaming.

I nodded. "I'm really happy they're here. It's just so surreal that they're our family. We went from just the two of us to now having aunts, uncles, cousins, and even nieces and nephews!"

"It's wonderful, isn't it?" Mom said again, glee written all over her face.

I couldn't help but laugh. "I'm glad you went to spend time with Harrison."

"I wish you could have come too. But you'll have a whole weekend with them and hopefully more down the road."

"Let's focus on this weekend first and not scare any of them away, okay?"

"Yes, one day at a time," Mom said, winking at me.

Who was this person? My mom was pretty laid-back, but this person was giddy. "Why don't we check on Victoria?" I suggested. "She went to see Cook to make sure everything was ready."

"That sounds fantastic. I can't wait to see what meals you've come up with."

What hadn't we come up with?

Dinner went just like I had imagined. I looked around the table at everyone laughing and smiling and thought that this is what a family should be like: loud and merry and happy to be in each other's company. It made me sad to know that Ah Po never had this, but I was glad that we had found Harrison, and Mom had persuaded him to come.

We were eating in the sunroom. The big doors leading outside were swung open and there were lights hanging above us and out in the trees. The sun was setting, and there was a happy glow in the air. I wanted to hang on to this moment for as long as I could.

Erik, Stephanie, and their two daughters, Caitlin and Ellen, had arrived right at the end of dinner. They were sitting at the other end of the table looking very tired from all the travel, but happy. They had stayed in Eureka the night before and had also stopped to visit the Oregon Coast Aquarium today. Both daughters, who I'd thought were twins at first, were hugging stuffies from their trip. I later learned that their eldest, Caitlin, was ten; and the other child, Ellen, was nine. Both girls were whining and refusing to eat, so dinner ended very soon after they arrived, and everyone went to their separate rooms.

Mom and I hung out in the library for a bit, and I

informed her that Geraldine would be arriving at some time this weekend.

"That woman is pure evil," Mom said, waving her wine in my face. She didn't drink very often and this was the first time I had seen her let loose. It was pretty fascinating to watch.

"I know. I kind of feel sorry for Isabella if this is the type of family she grew up in."

"Don't you go feeling sorry for her," Mom said, wagging her finger. "She has her own brain and wits."

I raised a brow. "Brain and wits, Mom?"

"I'm tired. I think I should go to bed now."

"I think that's a good idea. I'll come up with you." I didn't trust her on the stairs.

After I settled Mom in her room, I stood in the hallway just listening to the silence. There was a warmth in the air, something that hadn't been here before. A big grin spread across my face and I felt my heart swell. My family was here with me and I had never seen Mom happier. This weekend was going to be a good one, no matter what Geraldine had up her sleeve.

CHAPTER 27

I jolted out of bed, eyes wide, ready to attend to whatever the emergency was when some small part of my brain registered that Victoria was standing at the foot of my bed, and she didn't look panicked but rather excited. I mumbled something illegible and tried to slip back under the covers.

"No, Anne! You have to get up!" she insisted.

"What? I was having the best dream."

"Paul is here!" she hissed.

"Oh good, I'm glad he made it."

"No, you don't get it. Paul is here, like here-here!" Victoria's voice was so excited I made myself focus on her.

"Of course he is. His family said he'd come in late, but he never showed up last night. He had some research to finish up. I'm glad he's finally here." *Why was she so excited this early in the morning?*

"Right, he's your cousin, but what I'm trying to tell you is—"

My voice was firm. "Victoria, not to be rude, but I'm still waking up. I'm not sure which way is up at the moment."

"Right. Sorry about storming in like this. When you come down, you'll see." She left the room in a somewhat low mood. And after her initial excitement, her down mood seemed weird. One second, I was dreaming, and the next my best friend was storming into my room excited about a cousin I'd never met before. Of course, I knew Paul would be here and I'm glad he finally made it.

I took my time getting ready and headed to the sunroom where I was sure everyone would be for breakfast. Except when I got to the sunroom, there was no one there. I checked the library and knocked on Mom and Victoria's doors. No one was in the house. However, when I came back downstairs the second time, I noticed the hallway door was ajar. I went to close it when I heard a faint murmur from the back of the closet. Opening the door wider, I noticed that all the cleaning supplies were pushed to the side and there was an opening in the wall!

Could it be? Harrison and Grandma Catherine had mentioned a tunnel just like this. I hadn't gotten around to searching for it so now seemed like as good a time as any. *I'll just pop in, look around, and then go find my family.*

The air was musty and putrid like someone had used it as a bathroom and then closed it up for a long time. I pulled my shirt over my nose to block out some of the smell. Had anyone been in here since Geraldine was a young woman? And did she come back here at other times in her life?

I walked down a set of stairs for about ten feet. At the bottom of the stairs there was a long hallway, wandering off into the darkness. I could see other hallways branching off this main one, and there was a glow coming from the closest one to my left.

There was a voice coming from this lit hallway. It sounded like a woman was comforting someone. My curiosity took over and I ventured down it, heading toward the voice. The smell got stronger and I noticed what looked like cat poop on the ground. It wasn't until I came across another opening in the tunnel, close to where the voice was coming from, that I realized I was probably doing a stupid thing. I mean, who in their right mind would venture down a dark, unknown tunnel after a phantom voice?

But this was my house. I lived here. I should know who was in my house, what this tunnel was used for, and any other secrets it held. Right?

It took me a bit longer to psyche myself up, but I craned my neck around the corner. I almost yelped at what I saw. Good thing I swallowed my surprise before she heard me, because sitting in the middle of the floor and surrounded by five grown cats was Geraldine. She was singing to them, and they were climbing all over her, rubbing their heads on her arms and legs as she fed them something from her lap. The cats looked happy to see her.

The room was lit by the same electric lamps that were hanging from the walls in the hallway. I was happy to see that she was no longer lighting torches. I noticed a big pile of cat feces on one side of the room and saw a shovel and some bags next to it. That would explain the smell. Did she clean out their home every once in a while? How did she get in?

I heard footsteps behind me and turned to look back. I didn't see anyone so I turned to face the room again—only to see Geraldine staring right at me. The look in her eyes was enough to give me nightmares!

I hightailed it out of there and ran as fast as I could back to the main entrance. But I underestimated Geraldine's agility, and I made the mistake of stopping to catch my breath once I got through the closet and past the cleaning supplies. She came through the door, radiating anger.

"What were you doing in there?" she seethed.

"I saw the door ajar and heard a voice down there so I

went to investigate. I didn't know it was you." I wondered why I was defending myself. The question should've been, "What were you doing in there?"

I said aloud with more authority, "It's my house and I have the right to explore anywhere I want to."

We stared at each other for some time before she muttered, "We'll see about that."

I didn't wait to see what she did; instead, I headed straight back to my room. I needed to calm my heart rate down before meeting up with the rest of my family.

When I came back downstairs the hallway door was closed. I wondered if Geraldine had come here this weekend because she wanted to see the cats, not to see me. One could wish, right?

As no one was about inside the house, I ventured out into the backyard. That was when I heard laughter. Knowing it was from my family made me so happy that I rushed into the garden.

I walked down the path as the laughter got louder. That was when I saw Victoria standing next to one of the entrances. "Victoria, I—"

"Shh! She's on a roll," she said quickly, cutting me off.

"Who?" I turned to see Geraldine standing in the middle of the garden, gesticulating at the foliage around her and telling everyone the backstory on the construction of this "wonderful sea of green."

She must have closed up the tunnel as soon as I left as I wasn't in my room that long.

Everyone was enraptured. The adults were hanging on to her every word, laughing and asking questions. The four children were nowhere to be seen, but no one seemed overly concerned about it.

Then, Geraldine noticed me, and I swear a flash of hatred flashed across her face. But she masked it so quickly that I might have been the only one who saw it.

"What is she doing here? When did she get here?" I asked Victoria, trying to stop the quiver that was threatening to wobble on my lips.

"She just got here not long before you came out. Charmed them within a second. Harrison hasn't been here, though. You said he's met her before, right? I didn't have the heart to stop her, because everyone looked so happy when she offered a tour of the estate."

"I guess it doesn't hurt. I'm also curious to learn more about this house, even if it is from Geraldine. And Victoria, I have something I want to tell you later. It creeped me out a bit but I need to tell someone."

"Of course. Are you okay?"

I looked at Victoria and saw concern etched on her face. "I'm fine, I really am. Sorry, nothing happened to me, but . . ." I noticed that Victoria was holding hands with an Asian guy who looked like a younger version of Harrison. "Wait, you're Paul—Harrison's son! But . . .?" I looked back at Victoria to find she had a silly grin on her face—the kind you can't wipe away no matter how hard you try because you are so happy.

"Anne," Victoria began, "this is Paul. Paul, Anne. Paul is my boyfriend *and* your cousin. Isn't that cool? I only put two and two together this morning! That's why I ran into your room."

"Who would have thought!" I exclaimed.

I noticed some of my family were looking our way now, but Geraldine still had them mostly enraptured.

"I've been waiting so long for you two to meet," Victoria

said. "But, Anne, you've been so worried about your family that I didn't want to bring up my life."

"Oh, Victoria, I'm so, so sorry. I've not been a very good friend."

"I know." She laughed. "You have some making up to do all right. Like maybe taking me to a nice dinner, or even planning a spa day where we don't leave halfway through. I'll let you know what else I can think up."

Laughing, I said, "That sounds like a plan."

"You put up with Victoria quite a bit, I see," Paul said.

Victoria gave him a push, which made him put his arm around her and whisper what I guessed was something sweet into her ear. It made her blush, and I had never seen Victoria blush before. He turned his attention back to me, and I noticed he had a bookish quality about him. Not at all who I thought Victoria would end up with, but I couldn't deny that she looked the happiest I'd ever seen her.

"I would say she puts up with me more. I've been the stay-at-home and feel-sorry-for-myself type lately," I said.

"It was only for a little while," Victoria said, giving me a smile. "But I am so glad you finally have Harrison here. I don't know how much longer I could take if you hadn't found him."

I would have been offended except I could tell she was joking, kind of.

Jolting us out of our banter, Paul said, "Maybe we should join the rest of the group? It looks like they're moving on."

"Oh yes, that's a good idea." I saw that Geraldine was now leading them to the circular bench under the tree to where the statue of Rose was.

I focused on the rest of my family and heard Geraldine say, "My brother loved the garden so much that he kept up my father's work. Anthony's the one who had all these statues commissioned and you'll find them all over the property. They're supposed to represent a child who grows over time, except for this woman sitting under the tree. I think she was a lover at one point," Geraldine said, looking right at me. I could feel my heart racing and my hands clenched. I wouldn't let her get to me.

She added, "I find the statues kind of creepy, you know what I mean?" Some laughter ensued before she continued, "I talked to his wife once. Sally said she didn't mind them, she said it made him happy. We would always do anything to make my brother happy. Happiness is the most important thing in life, don't you think?"

That was enough. "Geraldine, I think you're here to see me?" I enquired in a loud voice.

"Oh, Anne, yes, so good to see you," she said, walking toward me with her arms outstretched in welcome, as if we didn't have that standoff in the hallway earlier.

I made no move to mirror the welcome, and I noticed that my family had quizzical expressions on their faces. Grace was the only who had an expectant look, as if she understood the tension in the air, and I suddenly wondered if Harrison had made himself scarce so he wouldn't say anything inappropriate to Geraldine.

Mom appeared at my side. "Anne, Cook said she made a nice aperitif for us to have before lunch. Why don't we all head back to the house, and then you and Geraldine can have a chance to catch up."

"That sounds like a grand plan," I said.

Mom and I led the way back to the house, everyone chatting behind us. I felt angry. This was my weekend with my newfound family and Geraldine had to come and ruin it. It was like she had planned it. I wasn't going to let this slide.

"What do you want, Geraldine?"

We had separated from the group when we got into the house. I was now sitting across from her in the library while the rest of my family were in the sunroom eating the delicious food Cook had set out. As we'd walked by it, I caught a glimpse of the beautiful display Cook had put together. The aroma coming from that room had almost made me tell Geraldine that we would talk later, but Mom had known what I was thinking and had nudged me back out into the hallway.

"I'm here to talk to Harrison," Geraldine said.

"That's it? Why were you in the tunnel, then? And how do you maintain it if you don't live here?"

"I don't need to tell you. Remember, I used to live here and I could come and go as I pleased. Anthony was my brother, and this was as much my house as it was his—and I intend to take it back."

"Why are you doing this, Geraldine?"

"Because you don't deserve all this. My family has worked hard to amass our wealth and you didn't have to do anything to receive it." She almost spat in my face while saying this.

"Your grandmother moved in fresh off the boat," she continued. "She inserted herself into our lives like she belonged here. Like she had always lived here! Cook, and that boy, Andy, took to her instantly." She paused and seemed to lose herself in the memory. Her face seemed to sadden and age all at once and her words were much quieter when they next came. "I was the only one of my siblings who knew what she was—a gold digger. My father knew to be cautious about hiring Orients. He only hired them for labor outside of the household, but Mother insisted on a seamstress, and Father didn't want to pay a lot of money for one. So they compromised, and your grandmother was welcomed into our home.

"But Father was right; Orients cause nothing but problems. I knew from the beginning that your grandmother would be trouble. I tried to warn the others, but I was only ten and the youngest at that. No one listened to me except Father. But look at what she did!" Geraldine pounded the table, making me jump. "Anthony was a solid man. My father groomed him to become the best person to run the family business."

"I think he still did a pretty good job of that."

Geraldine shook her head in denial. "No, he could have been so much more! He could have had kids with Sally, and carried on the family legacy by focusing on his connections to grow the business instead of just letting the board run it. Did you know that I have done more for the company than Anthony ever has? I'm the one who keeps it going.

"I see you have doubts but believe me when I say that you would not have so much wealth in your hands if it wasn't for me. It was never Anthony's inheritance to give away. I'm the one that should have been given the bulk share of it! I've done all the work—not my siblings, not my worthless husband, and not my children. Isabella shows promise, but even with her, I'm beginning to see some cracks.

"But Anthony was all about love. He tried to appease me once; gave me a wooden box in which he had carved a gorgeous plum blossom out of cedar. He said it would bring me happiness and protect my clothes at the same time. He said he'd done this out of love because I needed more love. He said that he was sorry that I didn't get loved enough. Anthony had never made me anything before, so I treasured it. I loved that blossom, and I took it everywhere with me— until I learned the history behind that flower. Your grandmother brainwashed him! She made him forget his place and family. We were a strong family before she came along!" Geraldine slammed her hands on the table again, making it shake this time. For a seventy-five-year-old woman she sure was strong.

"All I want is a nice conversation with Harrison. I'm sure he and I can come to an agreement. So, Anne, if you could just let me know where he is, I'll be on my way."

"You don't know where he is?" This whole time my heart was racing faster and faster, and I was barely holding myself back from screaming at Geraldine. But her question threw me off and I wondered again where Harrison was.

Right at that moment, Victoria ran into the room. "Anne, come quick! Madison is missing."

"What do you mean she's missing?" I asked, already out of my chair and following Victoria back to the sunroom.

I was bombarded at the entrance by Mom. "Anne, we've looked everywhere. Do you know of any secret places a little girl could have hidden?" she asked.

"When was the last time anyone saw her?" I returned.

How could we lose my cousin's kid on their first full day here? Leslie was full-on crying in Jonathan's arms while hugging Ryan to her chest so tight that there was no way the boy was going to escape, even though he was trying to. Erik and Stephanie were sitting with Caitlin and Ellen close by, all of them looking miserable. I wished I could wave a magic wand and make everything okay again.

"There are many secret doors around this property," Geraldine said, walking up from behind me like a snake knowing it had its prey in sight.

"Lots?" Jonathan asked.

I heard Grace gulp, and Leslie started to cry harder.

"I know of one place," I said. "Let's go check there."

"You wouldn't dare," Geraldine seethed under her breath, so low that only I could hear her.

I turned on her. "Don't you even start! This is a little girl we're talking about, not an animal. She's not an adult you can bully, and she's family."

"I won't allow it." Geraldine moved in front of me, using her body to block my departure.

Everyone else was looking at us like we were crazy. I thought Leslie was going to faint if we held out any longer. I had thrown out hope in finding Madison, and our next move had been paused because Geraldine was in my way. So, I did what I should have done all the other times I'd seen her—I walked around her and I didn't look back. She followed of course, throwing unpleasant names at me the whole time.

We reached the hallway where the closet door was and once again, I found it ajar.

"Who went in?" Geraldine yelled, but this time not out of anger but worry. She ran around me, through the door and down the stairs before I had registered what she was doing. Who knew a seventy-five-year-old woman could move that fast?

"Well, what are we waiting for? Let's follow her!" Jonathan said.

However, before we could start down, Harrison came out of the tunnel. His hand was on Madison's shoulder, and the little girl was holding a cat in her arms.

"Madison is okay. Let's all go to the sunroom. I still need to enjoy the delicious food that Cook has made for us," said Harrison, not missing a beat as he walked right past the stunned lot of us.

"Did you see Geraldine?" I asked, thinking the answer was no since Harrison seemed relaxed.

Harrison answered without turning around. "Yes. I think she went to check on her cats."

We followed in a daze, wondering what in the world had just happened.

When we got to the sunroom it was now Madison's turn

to be hugged by Leslie, and I had a feeling that she was not going to let the little girl out of her sight for the rest of the weekend.

"Can someone please tell us what happened?" Grace asked.

"Why don't we all grab some food and have a seat?" Harrison suggested, already heading over to grab a plate. "I'll tell everyone what happened while we eat because this smells too good to go to waste."

"Harrison Lin, you better tell us now or I'll make sure you don't get any food for the rest of the day," Grace said firmly.

We all stood there quietly while the two elders faced off against each other.

After a bit, Harrison relented. "Just know that I won't be able to tell a good story because my stomach is hungry, Grace."

"Harrison!" Grace was tapping her foot now.

"Okay, okay," he protested, hands up in the air. Lowering them, he began, "I was in the library reading when I heard Geraldine come in this morning. When she walked past the library doors, I slipped out and went to our room; I was going to avoid her if I could help it. Later, I heard you all come back into the house, and I knew it was because lunch would be ready. I was hungry so I came to meet you all, but on the way down I remembered about the secret tunnel from my childhood and I became curious. So, I went to where I remembered it was and sure enough it was still there. I thought it would be safe to explore the area while Geraldine was preoccupied with lunch, but who should I find down there with a bunch of cats but Madison! She had beat me to it." Harrison gave the little girl a smile, which she returned in kind.

"Dad!" Leslie said. "We've all been so scared that Madison was missing, and you two are just sitting there, smiling at each other? It's like you had no idea what was going on out here!"

"We didn't," Harrison said, shrugging. "Madison and I were having a great time until Geraldine ran in. I grabbed Madison and got out of there as soon as we could before the woman could say anything."

"And I got a kitty!" Madison said, beaming at the cat who was licking itself next to her.

"Okay, this still doesn't explain what Madison was doing there in the first place," I said.

"The kids were playing hide and seek," Grace said. "They couldn't find Madison."

Leslie had let Madison go, and the little girl was dancing around saying, "Yeah! I found the best hiding spot ever! The door was open, so I went in. I heard you, Auntie Anne, and another voice in there, but I stayed very quiet. I was so quiet! No one knew I was in there! I saw you two leave, and then I heard meowing and I knew what that meant, so I went to play with the kitties."

I could have smacked myself—it was her feet that I had heard when I was in the tunnels! "I'm sorry, Leslie, so sorry. I heard footsteps when I was in the tunnel, but I was distracted with Geraldine there so I didn't investigate."

"It's not your fault," Paul said. "My sister is a big worry wart."

This elicited a death stare from Leslie, who was about to go into a tirade on Paul when Grace sat down next to her and held her until she calmed down. She, in turn, took on the death stare aimed at Paul, who thankfully was smart and didn't utter another word.

I watched Victoria elbow him in the side. "You would be too if your kid was missing," she pointed out.

"I just know Madison, and she's always getting into trouble. She is never worse for wear by the end of it."

"Well, it's still nice to show some sympathy," Victoria said.

Geraldine came in at that point. How she still looked so put together was beyond me. She said curtly, "Harrison, I need a word."

"Hold on a minute. Our family is recovering from a missing child. Why don't you talk with Harrison later?" I asked, walking toward her.

Geraldine put her hands on her hips. "I came here to talk to Harrison, and I'm going to do just that. I can't help that the child wandered into the tunnel. She has a big Asian brain —if she had wanted to get out, she could have figured out a way to do it."

"What . . .?" A bunch of expletives were about to shoot out of my mouth when I felt a hand on my shoulder. I turned around to see Harrison.

"We found her, Anne. She's okay. I believe this lady is waiting to talk to me," he said in a very matter-of-fact way.

"Yes, I am. Would you like somewhere more private?" Geraldine asked, turning to leave the room.

"I should join too," I said, but Harrison put another hand on my arm.

"No, you should stay. Be with your new family, Anne, and get to know them. I'll be okay."

"But . . ."

"Come on, Anne," Mom said, pulling me away from Harrison. "Madison is found and the rest of us are going to go back outside for some fresh air. You should join us."

But even as she tugged on my arm, I couldn't take my eyes off Harrison and Geraldine. What in the world were they going to talk about behind closed doors?

CHAPTER 28

Like Paul had said, Madison didn't seem worse for wear. She was bouncing and running around just like the other children while her mom kept eagle eyes on her the whole time. Everyone seemed to be calming down.

We decided that now was as good a time as any to throw the birthday parties we had planned as we all needed a happy distraction. All of us chipped in. We threw up some *Frozen* decorations on the back porch, brought out the cakes, and sang *Happy Birthday*. And an hour later, all the kids were playing gleefully.

I, on the other hand, kept looking back at the house wondering what Harrison could be agreeing to with Geraldine. Would he give up his share of his inheritance so that he could finally be rid of all this baggage he had never wanted in the first place? I was in knots not knowing.

"Anne, have a drink," Victoria said, handing me a champagne flute filled with orange juice. I took a drink and smiled. This was my kind of orange juice, especially at a time like this. I said cheers with Victoria, and the two of us looked out at my family.

"This is awesome, Anne. You found your uncle and more."

"I did, didn't I? I feel so lucky right now."

"Have you been able to talk to some of them one-on-one?"

"A couple. But between it being so late last night and the fiasco this morning, I haven't really been able to get to know anyone well yet."

"Well, you have the rest of your lifetime now. That's something, right?"

"And who knows, if you marry Paul then we'll be related," I returned with a laugh.

"Oh, don't jinx it! But I do have hope, Anne. I really like him. And I hope you really are okay with me dating your cousin?"

"Of course I am! I just wish I'd put two and two together a lot earlier."

The back doors flung open then and out stormed Geraldine down the stairs in all her glory.

"All of you are a bunch of greedy gold diggers—that's all you are! Taking money from rightful owners! You're a disgrace to humans and should get on the soonest plane back to your country!"

We all stood there in shock just staring at Geraldine. She seemed crazed. Like legit crazed. Her eyes were wide, hands clenched, and I was afraid she might teeter off the stairs, she was shaking so much.

Harrison came out of the house behind her and tried to put a hand on her arm, but she swatted him away as she whirled to face him.

"And you!" she cried. "You're an abomination! You shouldn't even be alive! What my brother did was a disgrace to our family. My poor parents were humiliated. Humiliated! My mother had to explain over and over again that they had no idea to her friends. And my poor father had to explain to his work colleagues that he was not softening and that he had everything under control. There was never any need to justify their actions. They were esteemed people who never deserved what Anthony and that girl did to them. And the fact that you are walking around in this house as if you live here is sacrilegious!"

"That's enough, Geraldine!" a voice boomed from the house.

Shocked, we all turned to see Jack. I had never seen him so stern-looking before. He had aged since the last time I saw him.

"If it isn't the prodigal son; he who could do no wrong," Geraldine sneered.

"You've caused enough hurt all around, even to your own family, Geraldine. Haven't you had enough?" Jack asked while walking slowly toward her.

"Me? I've caused hurt? Do you not see the people who are in front of us? These people are the ones who have hurt our family—for three generations!"

"I would say they are the victims, especially Rose," Jack returned. "She did not deserve the treatment she endured."

"They've gotten to you too!"

"No one has gotten to me, Geraldine. No one is hurting us either. Our family is strong. The Wilkens are still invested in our family business. On a different note, we—all of us siblings—are planning a getaway and we want you to join us." He was a few feet from Geraldine now. "You've been fighting for so long, Geraldine. Why not stop and enjoy your life?"

Right then, something must have caught her eyes because she jolted to the left, picking up something from the floor. It was the small box that I had shown Victoria while we were cleaning the house, then completely forgotten about. Victoria must have been fiddling with it and left it out here.

"What is this doing here?" Geraldine asked, jerking around to face Harrison.

He just shrugged. She then turned to me and I could see tears in her eyes.

She looked so sad that I couldn't help but admit, "I found it in a room at the end of the second floor. It was in a trunk."

"My trunk? You had no right to go through there!"

"I didn't know it was yours," I said, moving backward even though she had made no movement toward me.

"Geraldine," Jack said, "is this the box Anthony gave you? The one you mentioned last week you wished you could find?"

"Yes."

"Well, why don't you open it? Maybe it's time to let go of the past; remember the brother we all loved and who loved you very much."

We all held our breath as Geraldine opened the box. I watched her fingers move around the edges and push imaginary buttons in the wood, as if she had opened the box so many times in the past that her fingers had memorized every movement. Sure enough, the right combination released the inside lock.

I saw a tear flow down her cheek as she pulled out a wooden plum blossom that still held its cedar smell. I watched as Jack put one arm around her, as if testing the waters to see if she was still volatile. When she didn't move away or make a sound, he enveloped her into his arms, and the woman who had exploded out of the house yelling at all of us was reduced to an old lady who couldn't hold on to her hate anymore.

I could feel a collective sigh flow through all of us. That's when I looked up to see Sebastian. He was standing at the top of the stairs, looking at me. He seemed exhausted but also happy. I walked past Jack and Geraldine, and up to Sebastian where he took me into his arms.

"I'm so glad you're here," I said, breathing him in as much as I could.

"I came as fast as I could."

"Why is Jack here?"

"Long story. I'll tell you after everyone has settled down. It seems like there was quite a scene here."

"Quite. Nothing like I expected this weekend would go."

We then watched as Jack escorted Geraldine out. She was still clutching the box in her hand. She didn't even look at me when she passed, which I took as a good sign.

CHAPTER 29

WE WERE ALL SETTLED BACK IN THE SUNROOM, everyone a bit shaken, including the kids. Cook brought out her infamous carrot cake, which was welcomed by all. With Mom's help, I distributed hot tea, apologizing for the fiasco that had recently occurred. I promised everyone that this was not normal and that we actually lived a very quiet life without drama.

Victoria and Paul had snuck off somewhere and it was just as well. I was so tired and all I wanted was to be with Sebastian on my own for a while. He must have read my mind because he took my hand and we sneaked out into the garden again to have our own private walk.

"Today sounds like it got a bit crazy," Sebastian said.

"It got out of hand really quickly. I'm still dazed about it all and not sure that today is still Saturday."

"I'm sorry, I got here as soon as I could," he said again.

"I know you did. Thank you." I stopped walking and looked up at him. A surge of love filled me and I could see he felt the same. He took me in his arms and gave me a much-needed kiss, one that we hadn't shared in a long while.

"That's the kiss I've been missing," I whispered against his lips.

"I've missed you, Anne. Let's not be apart for so long again."

"Deal."

Sebastian smiled and looked around the garden. He pointed to the spot where we had all been standing not that long ago. "Look, it's your Ah Po sitting under the tree."

"I know. Do you know this is my favorite spot? We shared our first kiss here."

"I remember." Sebastian took my hand and brought me over to the bench where he then pulled me back into his arms. "I've been worried about you."

"How so?"

"With Geraldine," he admitted.

I remembered that he'd mentioned something like this during our last phone call. "What have you and Jack been up to?"

"Jack received a disturbing letter from Geraldine a while back. Something about her doing harm to someone if things weren't put right. He became very concerned about her, and also about the family business. He knew Anthony had appeased Geraldine at one point by allowing her to sit on the board. She got kicked off in the end, but Jack believed she was still pulling strings in the background. He hired me, and together we've been trying to find out everything we can about Geraldine. I have to say it's been really hard on Jack. It's his own sister we've been investigating, and the papers we've found shows that she had more influence in company decisions than we thought.

"Anthony's signature was on all the paperwork, but emails and interviews with past clients brought her name to the surface more than Jack would have liked. I swear he's aged ten years since he hired me. I wish I could take his pain away. He doesn't deserve it. He's a really good man, Anne."

"What brought him here today?"

"He found out that Geraldine was in a mental institute when she was in her twenties. Lord Anthony's signature was on the paperwork. He also found out that she was sent back to the same mental institute ten years later, and then another twenty years after that. I'm not sure what the diagnosis was or the severity of her problems, but given recent events and how she's been behaving, Jack took it upon himself to find her a new place to stay so that she will be better taken care of."

"Is that where he's taking her now?"

"Yes."

I felt a sense of both sadness and relief. Poor Jack, having to take on the sole burden of his sister. "It was so fortunate he came when he did," I said to Sebastian. "Geraldine looked manic and ready to fly off the handle."

"I'm glad we arrived when we did too. I was so relieved to see that you were not harmed. Jack said that he went to talk to Geraldine last week, and she implied that she would be glad to blow anyone to smithereens if they got in her way."

My heart stopped. "Goodness! I guess that confession is as good as we're going to get."

"For now. We'll see what happens. I'm just glad you're okay. I drove here as fast as I could after Harrison called me."

"Harrison called?"

"Yeah, he called me this morning to say that Geraldine was here and that she didn't seem in her right mind." He must have seen my confused face because he said, "I'm getting ahead of myself. Let me rewind. I didn't want to get your hopes up, you see, because after Harrison took your journals and made it look like I was in the wrong for giving them to him, I was fed up. When Nick found his address, and your mother decided to be the person to go and see him, I took the opportunity to ask your mother to talk to Harrison on my behalf to see if he would meet with me. She agreed, and your mother is the best, by the way."

"I know," I said, beaming.

"She set up a time for Harrison and me to meet, and I was able to talk to him about the situation we were in with Geraldine and the inheritance. He then updated me that someone had been by their house while he was here in Portland, asking similar questions and getting aggressive with Grace. Apparently Erik threw a vase at the man. Then Harrison said someone had gone through his shop and made a mess of his office.

"It's still hard to believe that Geraldine went to all those lengths to gain control of her brother's estate. I apologized profusely for the mess she's made and I hope that with Geraldine now in safe hands, things will calm down some. Your uncle is a good man, Anne. He deserves happiness just as much as you do, especially given everything you've done to get this family together again."

"It's been quite a feat," I admitted, feeling every single step of the journey right then.

He pulled me in close, a look of pride on his face. "You've done good, Anne. Shall we go back and be with your family now?"

I smiled. "That's the best idea all day."

CHAPTER 30

IT WAS AN EARLY NIGHT FOR EVERYONE AND THE kids were asleep before their usual bedtime. I imagined the parents also fell asleep with the kids because no one came back downstairs that evening. Even Mom, Grace, and Victoria retired early. So it was just Sebastian, Harrison, and I in the library, sipping a strawberry lemonade and eating leftover finger sandwiches at seven o'clock at night.

"Here's to Harrison for standing up to Geraldine," I said, holding my drink up.

"It's the least I could do after taking the journals," Harrison said in his calm, quiet voice.

I considered him. "Sebastian said you called him this morning. When did you have the time to do that?"

"I'm up early, comes with age. I also heard Geraldine arrive this morning, and I knew she was a bad person after I'd met her the last time I came here with Anthony."

"I had forgotten Geraldine was here back then."

"She was one of the main reasons I left," Harrison confessed. "That woman is not in her right mind. Her parents did not raise her well."

"Jack was able to find a good mental facility for her, so hopefully she will now get the help she needs," Sebastian said.

"At her age, I don't know if a person can change," Harrison said. "I'm in my sixties and I am set in my ways. Her age is one reason that I am more at peace now."

"Why's that?" I asked.

"When I saw her in the tunnel just before, it was the first time that I had seen her since she was in her twenties. I always had this image of her as a young, powerful, and scary woman. But the old lady I saw today was none of those things anymore. Well, maybe still scary, but she couldn't hurt me. I had, and am, living a good life. There's no need for me to hang onto the past anymore. I have you and your mom in my life now, too, and I'm thankful for it."

"I'm so glad you think that." We sat in silence for a while, enjoying each other's company.

I thought of the paintings he had sent me and remembered there was something I'd wanted to ask him. "Harrison . . ." I began in introduction.

"Yes?"

"Why did you sign your paintings with a plum blossom?"

"Because it was the flower Mary gave me when I was small," he said simply. His face was grave as he asked, "I believe you still have it. Could I have it back now please given I've returned the journals?"

"Oh yes, of course!" I rushed up to my room and found the box holding the glass flower. And while I was retrieving the blossom, I remembered the painting Mr. Lu had given me. *Would Harrison want that back too?* I wondered if he even knew it had been sent to Taiwan. Without thinking more on the matter, I grabbed the painting and returned to the library.

I handed the box to Harrison first.

"Thank you," he said, accepting it with a soft look on his

face. "This flower means more to me than any of my other physical possessions. Not only did it mean something special to Mary, but I also used it as my signature on my paintings as a way of saying I was sorry. It wasn't until I read Rose's journals that I realized the real significance behind this flower. I never knew my first mama, and I did hate her for some time, but I've slowly let go of that hate. The journals helped a lot with that. They also connected me to her."

"Hear, hear to that!" Sebastian said, raising his glass. "To mothers who will do anything for their kids."

I squeezed Sebastian's hand knowing that he was thinking of his own mother too.

"Harrison, I have something else for you," I ventured.

"What is it?" he asked, a brow raised.

"When I was looking for you in Taiwan, I was introduced to a Mr. Lu. Do you remember him?"

"No. Should I?"

"Probably not. He was the security guard at the place where Anthony bought the condo."

"Let me guess—he's been looking for me too?"

"Not quite. He received a painting with a note from Grace."

"From Grace! What has she been doing behind my back?"

Harrison seemed a bit flustered and I wondered if this was a good idea. But I was committed now. Taking a breath, I said, "It was a painting for Anthony—one you had painted. She thought he might like it, but it never made it to him. So, Mr. Lu held on to it all these years. He gave it to me when I visited him, and I thought you might like it back." I handed the painting to Harrison, and for the first few seconds we all sat there staring at the wrapped painting in his lap. Then slowly, he unwrapped the edges and pulled the painting out. It was a painting of Harrison and Anthony.

"I always wondered what happened to this painting," my

uncle said. "Leave it to Grace to try to mend things for me. She has always been there to hold me up. I don't know what I'd do without her." Then, he looked up at me, but not with sad eyes; his eyes shined with purpose. "Anne, you keep this painting. Hang it up in this house. It belongs here, Baba and son together at last."

"Are you sure?"

"Yes, I have no use for it."

"If that's the case, I would like you to have the journals then."

"Really?" Harrison and Sebastian said at the same time.

"Yes, really. They are your mom's. I, at least, was able to meet her twice and grew up with my own mom. You deserve the journals. Please, take them."

This time there were tears misting Harrison's eyes. "That would mean a lot to me. Thank you, Anne."

"And Harrison . . ." He looked at me with so much happiness that I almost didn't say my next thought, but it needed to be said while we were having a heart-to-heart. "I think Mary would really love to see you again."

As expected, a shield came down over his features and I wondered if he was going to leave. But to Harrison's credit, he blinked a couple of times and looked me straight in the eyes.

"I don't think I'm ready." He put his hand up to stop me from responding and I noticed it was trembling as he added, "I don't think I will ever be ready. It has been so long."

"It's just a thought. We don't have to make any decisions right now."

"I owe Grace a trip to Taiwan," he murmured, so low that Sebastian and I looked at each other wondering if we had heard him right. But his eyes met mine again and he said, "I will think about it. I will not say no right now."

"Talk to Grace about it," Sebastian said, and then he

picked up the painting Harrison had put to the side. "Now, where should we hang this painting?"

"I think here in the library or in the foyer where everyone can see it," I said.

Harrison nodded. "I think in the library will be the best," he said. "This was his favorite room when I came to visit. He and I would hang out here the most."

"Then that's what I'll do," I said, beaming.

While in bed, I saw I had missed a call from Lauren. In all the fiasco I couldn't believe the party had only been a week ago. Today was her wedding and I had totally forgotten! I clicked on her voicemail and listened to her message.

Anne! Oh my goodness, I so wish you were here. If the guest list hadn't already been finalized, I would have added you, but now that I think about it, I should have just invited you and Victoria anyways! How silly of me to only think of that now. I would have insisted that they put two more place settings out for you two. Oh! But that's not why I called. It's because Stephen wants to meet you! I can't stop talking about you and Victoria. And he said I looked so much freer than I had in a long time since the bachelorette party, so he wants to thank you in person for letting me hold it in Hawaii. So, we need to find a time to catch up after we're back from our honeymoon, okay? Find a date that works for you. We'll be back in three weeks. I'm married, Anne! I'm married! And he's the most wonderful man in the world!

I then heard giggling before she finished with:

· · ·

I have to go. Stephen says I'm being too loud, and I think we're about to board the plane. See you soon, Anne!

I hung up and put the phone down before sliding under the covers to snuggle with Sebastian. It was impossible to be any happier. I fell asleep super excited for the next day.

CHAPTER 31

"Anne?" asked a woman's voice behind me.

I turned to find Grace and Leslie. The younger woman continued, "I just want to say that what happened yesterday is not a reflection on you. Madison can be so careless and—"

I reached for Leslie's hand, cutting her off mid-sentence. She grasped mine right back, looking me in the eyes as I said, "Leslie, you have nothing to apologize for. Your child was hurt, and you didn't know where she was. You're also in a new house. It's me that should be apologizing. I'm your host. I'm also your cousin, and I've done a terrible job of making you all feel welcome. It's been one disaster after another since you got here."

"Let's not go crazy," Grace said in her soothing voice.

We were interrupted by a noise at the other end of the room, and Leslie turned and started running, yelling, "Madison! Get off that shelf!"

I started to go after her, but Grace held me back with a hand on my arm. "Anne, please don't apologize, you have been very welcoming. Leslie is a high-strung person. She has always been this way. Madison takes after her baba and is a beautiful child, but she's a little daredevil and Leslie is always on her case. Maybe you could visit us one day and get to know Leslie a bit better? I think she would like that. From what your mama says, you are outgoing and I think you would be so good for Leslie."

"Of course! I would love to get to know her more, but I don't know about the outgoing part anymore. I haven't really been like that since I inherited this place."

"I'm sure you will find your way again," Grace said with complete sincerity. "And thank you for what you have done for Harrison."

"For Harrison?"

"Looking for him and dragging him out of the hole he dug for himself! I love him but he is so stubborn. He has wanted to find his mama for a long time, but he could never get past the wall he'd created. But you found him and gave him his mama's journals to read. It has offered him closure—which he desperately needed."

"I'm so glad to hear that." I held Grace's hand, thinking, This is my aunt. I have an actual Aunt and she cares about me! I'd also done something good for them. After all the worries I'd had to deal with on this journey as I'd tried to find my family, I couldn't believe we were all finally together now.

"Anne, look!"

I turned to see Mom. She was holding her phone out to me with tears in her eyes.

My heart skipped. "Mom, what's wrong?"

Both Grace and I walked over and helped her onto a seat.

"Everything's great. Read it." Mom pushed the phone into my hand.

Ms. Lin,
We are putting together an exhibit of Asian American

artists and your name was submitted to us by Harrison Lin. He spoke highly of you and we would like to meet with you if this is of interest. Please contact us at your convenience.

Sincerely,

Deborah Whittiker

San Francisco Museum of Modern Art

"Mom!" I gave Mom a huge hug and both of us were laughing and crying at the same time. I was so proud of Mom!

We finally separated to see that Grace was bringing Harrison over.

"Harrison, thank you so much," Mom said, wiping the tears from her face.

"It's the least I could do. After hearing about your show getting pushed out because of other more famous artists, I thought I'd try to help if I could."

Mom gave Harrison a big hug, and Grace and I laughed when Harrison's face started turning pink.

"I don't know if any one besides me has hugged him like that in a long time," Grace said with a big smile.

"Well, I plan on giving him more. He's my big brother," Mom said, giving him another hug.

A clinking sound came from behind us, and we all turned to see Sebastian standing in the middle of the room holding a champagne flute. I then saw Lavender passing around more flutes to everyone, and there was a soft murmur of curiosity circulating the room. What was Sebastian up to?

"I want to ask Anne something and I want to do it properly," Sebastian said, just before he got down on one knee.

Oh my goodness!

There was an audible gasp from everyone, and I could see cell phones were being taken out. Grace was still holding my hand and she gave it a squeeze. Mom let go of Harrison and put an arm around me.

On his knees in front of me, Sebastian pulled out a small box from inside his jacket and said, "Anne, I proposed to you in Taiwan during the midst of utter craziness. It wasn't ideal. Therefore, I want to propose to you today in a room filled with just your family—family that has been reunited, and which I can see brings you a lot of joy. I would love to create our own family to add to that happiness. So, dearest Anne, will you marry me?"

"Yes!" I squealed and launched myself at him. I couldn't get into his arms fast enough. I clung on to him so tight that I didn't want to let him go. With a huge grin on his face, he pulled away and opened the box. The ring he put on my finger was the prettiest, shiniest object I had ever adorned. It had a thin band that was laced with small diamonds, and a slightly larger stone in the middle was surrounded by small loops of metal that were also covered in diamonds. As I looked at the design, a dawning realization came over me. I looked up at Sebastian, my eyes wide.

"It's a plum blossom," he said in confirmation. "Knowing you, I thought you wouldn't want a huge stone, so I decided to decorate it with lots of small ones."

"Because that's less subtle," I said with a laugh.

"Well, I still want everyone to know that you're taken," Sebastian said with a smile, and he leaned in for a kiss.

There was cheering and toasting, then some more toasting. For a weekend that had started out as a disaster it was turning out to be quite a good one.

Sebastian eventually let me go and we looked into each other's eyes. I was going to spend the rest of my life with this man and I couldn't feel more fulfilled than in that moment.

I looked around me at all the smiling faces, knowing that Mom and I weren't alone in this world anymore. My thoughts turned to Mary, and I knew my next goal would be to reunite her and Harrison—and I wasn't going to take no for an answer.

Mom put a champagne flute in my hand just as Sebastian said, "I also want to give a toast to Anne."

Turning to face me, he said, "You never give up, even when others think you should. Thank you for bringing all of us together in one place so that we could get to know each other." He raised his glass high. "To Anne."

"To Anne!" everyone chorused.

As I took a sip of my champagne, I toasted a silent cheer to Mary. Because without her unending love for Harrison, we wouldn't all be here together. Mary and Harrison were going to meet if I had anything to do with it. Sebastian was right—I never give up.

Anne's getting married and nothing can stand in the way. Except maybe trying to combine two cultures into one wedding and coercing family who have been avoiding each other for decades to celebrate together.

CLICK HERE to continue Anne's journey in *Family Blossom*: Skyline Mansion Book 4.

Join Nola's newsletter to be the first to learn about new releases and receive a FREE copy of *Something Gained*.

https://www.subscribepage.com/nolalibarrnewsletter

WHAT'S NEXT

**Family Blossom
Skyline Mansion Book 4**

For Anne, family is everything—but at what cost?

Anne is the happiest she's ever been, and her wedding is just around the corner. This is meant to be the biggest moment of her life—a chance to celebrate the love she has found with not only Sebastian but also her new-found family.

But Anne is the wealthiest woman in town and her upcoming nuptials provide an opportunity for her enemies to undo her newfound happiness. As the big day draws closer, the complications keep mounting, and Anne is torn four different ways: planning the wedding of her dreams, bridging the gap within her family, fighting off slanderous attacks, and supporting her husband-to-be when his own long-kept family secrets are exposed.

Being true to herself could very well mean losing the family she's only just found.

Family Blossom is the fourth and final book in the Skyline Mansion family saga series. Join Anne as she learns to navigate societal and cultural expectations and what it means to have and be loved by an extended family.

CLICK HERE to continue reading Family Blossom
or read on for a sneak peak

Family Blossom
Skyline Mansion Book 4

"So, we have flowers, draped cloth, a beach, and a sunset in the background." Victoria turned to show me a page out of the magazine she was holding. "This is the dream destination wedding! What do you think?"

I shifted on my bed, knocking a pile of magazines on the floor as I leaned in for a look. I scrunched up my nose at the images. "Um, flowers yes, but I was thinking that we'd stay in Portland and have the wedding in the garden out back. You know, with some twinkly lights for outdoor lighting. Nice and simple."

"What fun is that?" Victoria exclaimed, staring at me as if I'd grown horns.

"But it's all that's needed."

Her eyebrows shot to her forehead. "You have all the money you could ever imagine to throw a big wedding, and that's all you want? Wait—don't answer that! I already know what you are going to say."

"Victoria . . ."

"I'm just saying it might be fun to throw a big party that's for you and not others for a change."

Victoria was throwing out ideas at me while we flipped through the pages of Wedding Boutique, ogling beautiful pictures of dream weddings. We'd been best friends since high school, and, as Victoria knew wedding planning was the last thing I wanted to do, she'd planned a sleepover party around it. We'd had fun doing our nails and watching romantic movies, but now she was making me look at wedding magazines.

I loved the weddings that looked simple; nothing too over the top. But the only thing I had learned from the bundles of magazines Victoria had bought for us was the more I looked, the more confused I was. I had absolutely no idea what I wanted or where to start finding out. Dreaming about my wedding was not something I did growing up. But now, here in front of me, were images of happy couples with beautiful color coordinated decorations. Ugh! I could never pull this off.

Victoria's phone buzzed, and she shoved a new magazine into my hands before turning to pick it up. I looked down at the cover to see this one focused on winter weddings. My musing was cut short when Victoria announced, "Oh, it's Paul. He just texted me to say he's leaving campus and wants to see me." She looked at me with pleading eyes. "Do you mind?"

I laughed at the absurdity of the question. "Of course, I don't mind."

Relief hit her features. "I'll help you with more ideas tomorrow, okay?"

"Sounds good. Go. Have a fun night with Paul."

Her face split into a smile. "You're the best, Anne." She jumped off the bed and gave me a hug before grabbing her purse and running out of the house.

I hadn't seen Victoria this happy in a long time, and it made me happy to think that if Paul proposed, she would also become my cousin. I looked back down at the magazines and realized all my excitement had left with Victoria. Pushing the pile aside, I called Sebastian.

"Hi, my love," he said after only one ring.

"Hi! I keep looking at this glittery ring wondering if this is all a fairy tale."

"Nope. It's all real." There was a muffled sound, as if he'd placed his hand over the phone, and then I heard him call out to his secretary for a file.

"You sound busy," I said as he came back on.

"I'm just buried in paperwork."

"The thing that you were telling me about yesterday?"

"Yes, 'the thing' as you so call it, amongst other projects," he said, laughing.

"Hey! I don't need to remember all that lawyer jargon."

"It's just you and your words." He continued chuckling, and I heard papers rustling in the background.

"Did Jack make a final decision?" I asked.

"He did. He's going to take a more active role on the board, hence why I'm buried. It's something he's never done before because Anthony was always around. But now that he knows the extent of how much Geraldine had her hands in company matters, he wants to see if there's any other fishy things going on. So, he's hired me to be the head lawyer of the Wilkens's fortune."

I frowned. "Wouldn't I have to be in agreement with that? I own the largest stake in the company."

"Would you disagree?" he asked, sounding a bit worried.

"No! Of course not!" I said, laughing. "I just wanted to play with you a bit."

"Very funny. Ha ha."

"I trust you with all my heart," I said while flinging myself back on the bed. A deep sigh escaped me, and Sebastian chuckled.

"I love you too, Anne. Why don't we go have a nice dinner tonight, just the two of us?"

"That sounds fantastic!"

"It's a date. I'll see you at home about six o'clock."

We hung up, and with new vigor, I picked up the magazine closest to me and vowed to have some sort of color scheme picked out by the time I got to the last page.

CLICK HERE to continue reading Family Blossom

MORE FROM NOLA LI BARR

Skyline Mansion Series

Forbidden Blossom
Hidden Blossom
Secret Blossom
Family Blossom

Companion Stories to the Skyline Mansion Series

Summer of New Love
Summer of Second Chances

ABOUT THE AUTHOR

Nola Li Barr writes family sagas that span women's fiction and young adult with a touch of sweet romance. When she's not writing she can be found reading, making photo books, and navigating the path of motherhood. Connect with her at:

nolalibarr.com
@nolalibarr across social media

Receive a FREE copy of *Something Gained* when you join Nola's newsletter. Be the first to know about new releases and giveaways.

https://www.subscribepage.com/nolalibarrnewsletter